# Carrying the Dead

# Carrying the Dead

## Juliet Rose

Above the Rain

2023

Above the Rain Collective
abovetheraincollective@gmail.com
North Georgia, USA

Contributing Editor: J.A. Sexton

Publisher's note:

ISBN: 978-1-7377970-5-0

julietrose.author@gmail.com
authorjulietrose.com

Cover graphics and interior formatting by J.A. Sexton
Above the Rain logo artwork by Bee Freitag
Original untouched cover photo by Justin Sexton

To my brother, Scott. Oh, the trouble we got
into in Mexico and beyond...

# PROLOGUE

*T*he thing about that day, it was beautiful. Sunny, clear. The leaves were changing and Hannah was mesmerized by the vibrant colors around her as she drove. It was the first day in six months she'd felt the inkling of joy come back into her soul. A glance in the rearview mirror revealed a blush to her cheeks she hadn't seen since... since losing the baby. It'd been unplanned, the pregnancy. She and Parker weren't expecting to be expecting. Sure, they'd been a couple for a few years and did almost everything together, but they didn't even live together. They certainly hadn't talked about anything more than the next concert or vacation they were going to take. They were having a good time. While the word love came easy, it was never followed by anything else.

So, when the second line appeared on the pregnancy test, all hell broke loose. They fought about it for weeks. They broke up. Hannah didn't want to be a mother but also didn't want to get an abortion. Adoption seemed the best choice, however, Parker refused to sign off on it. No child of his was going to be raised by strangers. Knowing how he liked to get fucked up in his free time, Hannah couldn't sign off on him raising the kid alone, either. But she knew she didn't want to be a mother.

A late night of cramping a few months into the pregnancy, followed by passing blood and tissue into the toilet the next morning, ended all that. A trip to the emergency room confirmed a miscarriage, and an invasive procedure to remove any remnants completed the chapter on the child that never was. Parker wanted to get back together, Hannah wanted to be left alone. She grieved for a child she'd never even wanted. In truth, maybe she was grieving for the part of her who'd come and gone. Either way, she hated Parker for it.

But that was six months ago and she'd moved on. Parker had a new girlfriend but still called Hannah drunk about once a week. She was the love of his life, he'd claim. She didn't care. Now, though, she was ready to seize the future. Not let anything, or anyone, determine who she was or what she'd do. It was October and for the first time in a long time, she didn't mind thinking about the days to come. She could put it all behind her and discover a new journey in her life. Nothing could take that away from her.

A song she loved came on the radio and she cranked it up as the cool breeze blew through her rolled-down window, causing strands of her golden-brown hair to fly around her. She tried to tuck her hair behind her ears but it whipped across her face. As she neared her street, she let her hand drift just outside the car, catching the wind between her fingers as she brought the car to a stop. Oncoming traffic was thick and she glanced into her rearview mirror to make sure no one would rear-end her as she waited. The car behind her slowed and the woman inside sighed impatiently.

Hannah waited for a break in the traffic coming toward her in the other lane, so as soon as she saw even a sliver to slip through, she could hit the gas, feeling proud of herself for being so aware and brave. She saw her chance and bobbed her head to the beat of the music. She yanked the wheel to the left, pressing the gas to the floor to glide between a pickup truck and a blue SUV. However, she didn't glide.

See, about ten cars back behind Hannah, a couple of guys on motorcycles were waiting. They'd been out riding all day, raising a hand at other motorcyclists who passed. They felt invincible, part of a special club. After waiting for Hannah to turn, they decided they could cut around instead, seeing as their bikes were small enough to fit through. Nothing could stop them. As they neared Hannah's waiting car, one cut around the right of her, the other cut to the left.

To the left. Just as Hannah saw her opening and gunned her engine, turning her wheel hard to the left. To the left, as her car and the motorcycle collided. No, not just collided. As the motorcyclist saw what was happening, he tried to turn to avoid the collision, instead causing his bike to careen sideways and slide. Right under Hannah's wheels. The force of the wheels and the bike hitting each other created a slingshot, and the motorcyclist was catapulted across the asphalt into oncoming traffic.

The sound was horrific. Like a bomb of nails exploding. Cars, not able to avoid the accident, slammed into each other, strewing bits of rubber and metal everywhere. When it was all said and done, there were multiple injuries. Hannah was without a scratch. What remained of the motorcyclist was hard to say. Scraps of his colorful leather suit and parts of his body were scattered all over the highway.

Hannah climbed out of her car and stared blankly at the scene. People were getting out of their vehicles, stunned. The music was still blaring from her car as she walked toward the middle of the highway. With the sun glinting off of the crumpled metal and the strips of bright leather fabric, it almost seemed festive. Like a street carnival.

Her mind went back to the morning she saw the bloody pulp of tissue in the toilet. Now, seeing the bits of bloody pulp on the road caused a break in her mind.

She began to scream.

# CHAPTER ONE

A ll that was left of her nails were the nubs on the skin where her teeth couldn't reach. Hannah perched on the edge of the bed, waiting for the door to open. She wasn't even sure she wanted to leave. At least here she felt controlled, secure. Outside, who was to say? Her eye caught the shadow of the certified nursing assistant at the door window. He smiled as he opened the door.

"Hey, Hannah, you about ready to fly the coop?"

She'd miss him most of all. "Not really, but Bob... uh, Dr. Gallager says it's time. I think he's wrong."

"He's not. You're just a little scared. It's hard to face the world sometimes."

"Ain't that the truth? I'll miss you, Buzzy."

Buzzy laughed and sat down next to her on the bed. Buzzy. He'd told her he was named after his grandfather George, but they'd started calling him Buzzy after a buzzcut when he was two. Now his light auburn hair was to his shoulders and tied in a knot. He sighed, placing his hand on her shoulder.

"You know where I work."

Hannah chuckled. "That I do. Can I write to you sometime?"

"Of course. You know, Hannah, I've worked here for about six years and I honestly can say I'm not sure you needed to be here in the first place. You just went through some shit, you know?"

"No, I did. I felt like my brain was cracking down the middle. After the accident, every cell in my body was shaking. I don't feel much better but at least now I have 'tools', as Dr. G. says, to cope."

Buzzy nodded, watching her closely. "Fair enough. I'd like to hear from you now and then, find out how you're doing. Give yourself a break, Hannah. Take it in small increments."

"I'll try. What's your full name, so I can write you? Not sure if I just put Buzzy on the envelope, it will find its way to you."

"It probably would, how many Buzzys do you know? However, my full name is George Bartholomew Finley. The third."

"Yikes. Hard to imagine a baby with that name."

Buzzy laughed, his head tipping back. "Right? I guess that's why they gave me a nickname."

Hannah eyed him. He didn't really seem like a Buzzy, either. Names are funny like that. It was a weird place to have made a friend, but here they were. "Okay, George. Should I write to you here or do you have an address? Email?"

Buzzy grinned at her, his hazel eyes twinkling. "I'll write them down for you. Email is fastest but I like a real letter to read. So, what's next?"

"I have no damn clue. I guess I'll go home and figure it out from there. My mother says I should take a trip. Honestly, I just need to walk out the door and see what happens. She's picking me up."

"Your mom? That's good. Alright, Dr. Bob is coming in to see you in a few minutes. I hope to hear from you, Hannah. I'll miss seeing you around here, but it's time to go."

He stood up, then headed to the door. He paused, watching her for a moment before raising his hand and ducked through the opening. Hannah flopped back on the bed and let out a deep breath. She didn't want to leave, but he was right. It was time. She'd been here six weeks. Six weeks of therapy, support groups, medication. Six weeks since the accident. It still seemed like yesterday.

The blood. The screaming.

She wasn't found at fault. Legally. It was determined since the motorcyclist had illegally passed her on the left as she was turning, he was at fault. Hard to blame a dead guy. She was numb briefly. Like a few hours. She didn't even remember talking to the police, but they had her statement on record. The road was closed for hours as they cleaned up the accident. The bits and pieces. There was still blood splattered everywhere.

The police let her leave once they were done talking to her, so she walked up the street to her house. When she got in, it was so quiet she felt like every movement, every sound, was amplified through a microphone. She thought about calling Parker, but that ship had sailed. So, she got obliterated on wine and vodka. She passed out in a recliner and when she woke in the middle of the night, *he* was standing there.

He was in his colorful, leather motorcycle jacket and pants, his helmet covering his face. At first, she thought it was just a trick of light and the alcohol but as she sat up and blinked, he was still there. Standing feet from her, his hands opening and closing in his leather gloves. She was too shocked to scream, her voice lost in the tightness of her chest. She closed her eyes and reopened them. He came closer, leaning toward her to where she thought she could see his eyes behind the tinted glass.

She scrambled onto the floor and stood up, running past him. She bolted out the door, barefoot, to the neighbor's house. Afraid to look behind her, she pounded on their door, screaming for help. A sleepy woman in a robe opened the door, confused. Hannah begged to use their phone, crying and reeking of booze. The woman let her in and showed her to the phone. Hannah shakily dialed her mother and blurted out what she'd seen.

It had been chalked up to being drunk. Hannah knew better. She'd *seen* him. He'd been inches from her face before she ran. She stayed with her parents for a couple of days. On the second day, she grabbed the newspaper from the driveway, and there he was. In print, this time. His picture and his name, Logan Slip. Eighteen years old, smiling at her from the black and white photo. Short, dark hair and light eyes turned down at the edges, giving him a sweet, innocent appearance. Not the scattered body parts on the road she remembered.

Her mother found her sobbing at the end of the driveway, clutching the newspaper in her hands. After hours of screaming and wailing, Hannah fell silent and asked her mother to drive her to the hospital before she killed herself. She was admitted and told the young intern on duty she wanted to end it.

She asked to be put in the psych ward, from there she went to an inpatient treatment program at her parents' insistence. They were scared for her and encouraged her to seek help. That was six weeks ago. Now, she had to leave.

A soft knock at the door broke her out of her thoughts and she sat up. Dr. Bob G. was standing at the door. He was older, his graying hair and beard somehow neat but unkempt at the same time. He came in and pulled a chair up near her. She liked Dr. Bob. Like an Uncle who wasn't trying to be funny. Just nice.

"Good morning, Hannah. How are you feeling about leaving today?"

"Not great, Dr. Bob, to be honest. But here I am, at the end of the road." Hannah's attempt at being funny just sounded bitter.

"Don't look at it as the end of the road. Just another fork. This is merely a resting place. You are ready for the next leg of your journey."

"Am I, though?"

Dr. G. nodded. "You are. You went through trauma and you will still need to face that as you go, but I believe you can do that on the outside. You have Dr. Toomey's number. She is well-versed in grief and trauma. Set up a time within the next week to meet with her. She's expecting your call, I've already gone over your information with her. Do you want Buzzy to walk you out?"

Hannah shrugged. "Yeah, okay."

After Dr. Bob left, she gathered the few items she'd had during her stay and went to the door. Buzzy met her and they walked out in silence. Her mother was waiting in the car and waved. Hannah turned to Buzzy.

"I don't know if I can do this, George."

Buzzy met her eyes. "You can. Why are you calling me, George?"

"Because Buzzy is the you *here*. In order to walk out the door, I need to find a way to let the me *here* go, to figure out the me outside. I know it's stupid. I do want to stay in touch."

"George it is then," Buzzy said and hugged her tightly. "Won't be the same without you here, Hannah."

Hannah stared back at the building, then peered up at him. "Who knows? Maybe I'll be back soon."

"Nah, you got this. Write to me, okay?"

"I will. Bye, Buzzy..."

On that note, she headed toward her mother's car and climbed in. Her mother chatted about nothingness on the drive home. Hannah asked to go back to her own house. When they pulled up, she was surprised to see Parker standing there, leaning against his car. She shook her head, then glared at her mother.

"How does he know I'm coming back today?"

"Oh, honey, he'd called and I thought it might be good for you two to see each other. You were together for so long, I thought you might want to talk things out with him."

"You thought wrong," Hannah replied, her voice heavy with resentment. "Fuck."

She got out of the car and snatched her bag from the backseat. Her mother gave her an apologetic look as she drove away. Hannah walked up to Parker. He stubbed out the cigarette he'd been smoking and gave her an awkward hug.

"Hey, Hans," he said quietly.

"Hi, Parker. What are you doing here?"

"I was worried about you."

"Oh. Well, don't. I'm fine," Hannah lied.

Parker watched her, nodding like he didn't believe her. "Okay. Look, I know we are in a weird place, but that doesn't mean I don't care about you. We have a history, you know? We've been a big part of each other's lives."

Hannah listened and glanced at Parker. They did have history. At one point, he'd been the love of her life. She was giddy just thinking about him. Not now. Now, he was like looking at pictures of a great vacation she once took. Memories that made her smile, but she wasn't there anymore. Now, it was just photos to reminisce over. She still loved him, but love without passion.

"Thanks, Parker. I appreciate you coming to check on me. We do have history and I'm glad for that. I hope, once I get my shit together, we can still find a way to be friends."

Parker seemed a little disappointed but grinned and took her hand. "We always were good at that part. I want you to know, Hannah, I'll always love you. I don't think we ever got it right, but you mean a lot to me. We had a lot of good times."

Hannah could agree with that. She squeezed Parker's hand. "That we did. I want you in my life, Parker, just in a different way."

Parker bobbed his head, his dark brown eyes glinting. He understood. They were at a fork in the road, each taking a different path. He bent in and kissed her on the cheek. Hannah instinctively put her hand in his black hair and met his eyes. Breakups were never easy. She let her hand drop and stepped away. That was it. Parker got in his car and drove away as Hannah walked to her door.

As she pushed the door open, she half expected to see him standing there. Logan Slip. Her heart began to race as she gazed around the stale living room, searching for what she anticipated would be waiting for her.

She was alone.

# CHAPTER TWO

T
he sound of a baby crying woke Hannah with a start. She sat up in her bed and peered around the darkened room. It was silent. She fell back in the bed, her heart racing, and steadied her breathing. The nightmares had increased as she neared the anniversary of losing the pregnancy. But this seemed real. Like the sound was outside of herself. Once her heart settled, she knew she wasn't going back to sleep anytime soon and slipped on her robe. Another late night of coffee drinking and mindless television surfing lie ahead of her. She padded to the kitchen and clicked the coffee pot on. It was always loaded and ready to go due to her many late nights.

She checked her phone and sighed. Parker stopped calling a few months back, he and his current girlfriend had set a wedding date. It amazed Hannah how quickly he'd moved on. A year ago they were fighting about the impending baby, not knowing just weeks later it would become a non-issue. Then he pestered her for months to get back together. They should never have been together in the first place. They were glorified friends with benefits. Good friends and the happy times together were just that. Good. But still, did he have to jump headlong into a serious relationship so soon after?

She'd pushed him away, she knew that. It was the right thing to do. If anything, the pregnancy showed them both they weren't lifelong material. As soon as they were faced with something other than partying and hanging out, they turned against each other. She still loved him and always would, but in the way someone loves a cousin or long-time friend. He'd always hold a part of her heart, but she didn't want him as a partner. That chapter was closed.

She typed out a short message on the phone. "Hey, George, you up?"

The coffee maker dinged it was finished, so she poured a cup and headed for the living room. The light was still on from when she went to bed. She hated to admit she was afraid of the dark now and left a light on in case she needed to get up in the night. She clicked on the tv and sat down on the couch. Her phone lit up with a message.

"Yeah, working the night shift. Why are you up?" Buzzy texted back.

"Nightmare. Well sort of. Heard a baby crying."

"Oh, damn. You alright?"

"More or less. Drinking coffee and watching tv. Anything exciting there?"

"Nope, all's quiet. You need to talk?"

"Nah, texting is fine. Just didn't want to be sitting here all alone, thinking."

"Well, you know you can always call me, too, if you need to. I'm around."

She and Buzzy, aka George, had emailed after she checked out, then began calling and texting once they saw their friendship grow outside the walls of the mental hospital. They'd met a couple of times for coffee, however, mostly chatted through screens. Sometimes she felt weird that he'd seen her huddled on the floor screaming in the hospital, however, he never made her feel like she was a patient. Just a friend. Dr. Bob had advised against the friendship in the kindest way possible, but Hannah assured him they would've become friends no matter where they'd met. It was easy to be around Buzzy. Natural.

"I'm okay. Up for the rest of the night, likely, dealing with the *day* coming up."

"When you lost the baby?"

"The pregnancy, yeah. Just need to move past it. Put it behind me. I don't even know why it's causing all these feelings in me. I didn't even want it."

It was a few minutes before Buzzy responded. "You still going to therapy?"

"Geez, Buzzy, you sound like Dr. Bob now. Going a little." It was a lie, but one she could live with. She went for a couple of months after getting out of the hospital but felt like they were going round and round on the pregnancy and Parker issue.

"Sorry. It's my day job, you know? Hard to walk away from that. I just want to make sure you're alright. I know it's a tough time."

"Yeah, can you just be my friend, though? Not a mental healthcare worker?"

"Fair enough. You want to get coffee later today?" he offered.

"Maybe. I may call out of work, anyway. Dealing with customers is not something I want to do on less than three hours of sleep."

"Try to get some more sleep. You need to take care of yourself. Not just your body."

Hannah cut him off. "If you say mental health, I'm going to scream."

"Also your mental health," he finished texting.

"What time for coffee, Dr.?"

"Haha. How about ten? I need to run home and shower and take care of a few errands."

"Sure. At the Deep Pour?"

"You know it. Hannah, call me if you need to before then. I'm up all night."

"Thanks, George. Think I'm going to watch this terrible small-town girl in the big city movie streaming on tv, now. Who even makes this shit?"

"Well, to be fair, you *are* about to watch it."

"Right? What is wrong with me? Alright, I'll see you at ten." Hannah hoped that would come sooner than later.

"See ya then," Buzzy signed off.

Hannah turned up the volume on the tv and stretched out on the couch. The movie was terrible and Hannah began to feel her eyes get heavy. Maybe she could go back to sleep, after all. The voices on the tv seemed to drift farther and farther away and soon became incomprehensible. The weight of sleep overtook her and she let go to sink into the depths.

Images of Parker flashed through her mind. Him laughing and holding her. He was so beautiful, she was enamored when they first met. He was confident and funny. His dark brown eyes twinkled with mischief. Oh, how she'd been drawn to him. Loved him. A pang of longing passed through her as she fell into a deep sleep.

She dreamt she was walking along the highway. It was empty even though it was the middle of the day. The sun was warm and she was humming a song she didn't recognize. An ice cream truck came rumbling down the road, matching the tune she was humming. All of a sudden, she was a child again, clutching a dollar in her hand. Excitement bubbled up in her as she ran toward the ice cream truck. As she neared the window, the truck stopped and a man in a mask came to the opening. The mask appeared to be old and made from wood. It was half a smiling clown and half a skull, but Hannah wasn't afraid.

She handed the man her dollar and pointed at the picture of a pushup pop on the sign. He nodded, then disappeared into the truck. Hannah waited patiently for what seemed like forever and glanced around at the highway. It was still empty but a stop sign had appeared on the side of the road where it shouldn't be. Hannah cocked her head and stared at it. Where had it come from, and why was it there? The man reappeared at the window and was handing her the pushup pop. She took it and stepped away as the truck continued its slow trek down the highway. The music had changed and seemed like some sort of crazy circus music.

Hannah peeled the top off the pushup pop and licked the orange coolness. She looked around and saw she was now standing in her childhood bedroom. She went out and ran down the stairs to find her mother, but the house was empty. She walked from room to room but couldn't find her way out. The rooms stretched into hallways and the hallways became stairs. At the top of one of the stairs, she came to a door and pushed it open. Inside was a young boy, holding a baby. He smiled at her and waved her over.

"Isn't she pretty?" he asked and tipped the baby gently toward her.

"Yes, she is. Who are you?"

"You don't remember me?"

Hannah peered closer but she didn't recognize the boy. Or the baby. The boy had dark eyes like Parker's, but he wasn't Parker. "I'm sorry, I don't know you."

"That's okay, it's been a long time." The boy shrugged and smiled back at the baby, who grinned in response.

"I don't understand. Who are you?"

The boy didn't answer and kept staring at the baby. Hannah began to slowly back out of the room. The boy met her with a firm glare. "Don't go."

"Why?"

"Because we have to stay together."

"Here? Where's my mother?"

"Keeping secrets."

Hannah became very uncomfortable with the tone of the conversation and shook her head. "No, I need to go. I have to get back."

"Don't you miss me, Hannah?" the boy asked, his voice low and sad.

"I don't even know who you are. This is just a dream, right?"

The boy shook his head, then shrugged. "I wouldn't know. I've been here forever."

The baby began to fuss, so he focused his attention down on her. "Shhh, Hannah, it's okay. I'm here. Pretty, pretty Hannah."

Hannah stared at the boy and the baby. "No, but I'm Hannah."

The boy nodded. "You are. This is you." He held the baby toward her. The baby writhed from being held up and began to bawl.

Hannah stepped away, afraid of the boy and the baby. The ice cream she had been holding was starting to melt down her arm, so she went to wipe it on her shirt. When she glanced down, the melted ice cream had turned to blood and was dripping all over her. She dropped the pop, putting her hands up toward the boy and the screaming baby.

He met her eyes.

"You can't run from me, Hannah."

But run, she did. She fled the room and tripped down the stairs, trying to find a way out. She ran by a room where her mother was decorating a birthday cake with the number five on it. Hannah wanted to run to her, however, the hallway kept dragging her along. It pushed her toward a large door that opened just as she reached it.

In an instant, she was outside. It was dark and she was stumbling through the woods. She could still hear the baby crying in the distance and felt the wetness of the blood dripping down her arms. Branches scratched at her arms and legs as she pushed her way through.

She could see her house in the distance and moved toward it as her robe snagged on a branch. Her robe. She glanced down and she was in her robe and slippers. She wasn't a child anymore. Blood ran from gouges in her arms and she was holding the tv remote in her hand. Hannah began to sob as she realized she was no longer dreaming and was somehow in the woods behind her house. She was awake, this was real.

And yet the baby continued its low, painful wail.

# CHAPTER THREE

*H*annah was already at the coffee shop when Buzzy arrived. She'd been there for hours. By the time she'd gotten back to her house, bleeding and terrified, she was wide awake. She showered and tried to drown out the sound of the baby crying. It eventually faded off as the sun came up. Part of her said to scour the woods in case there was a baby out there... but she knew there wasn't. She was simply losing her mind. Again. She checked the wounds on her arms and could see they were either from the branches or self-inflicted. Considering she picked skin out from under her nails, the latter was likely.

Buzzy raised a hand at her as he went to order a coffee. She waved back and considered what she'd tell him. She'd worn a hoodie to hide the marks on her arms, however, she needed to talk to someone. He'd always been a good listener. Well, in the six months she'd known him. She half considered putting herself back in the hospital but her job's insurance was crap and her parents had already shelled out enough on her last stay. She'd have to go it alone. Buzzy came over to her sipping his coffee, then sighed with pleasure.

"Damn that's good. Better than the watery shit at work," he said as he slipped into the chair across from her. "You been here long?"

"Probably too long. I have the jitters from too much coffee and not enough sleep."

"Did you ever get back to sleep?"

Hannah nodded and felt tears welling up in her eyes. She couldn't lose it here. "I did but had nightmares."

Buzzy stared at her and squinted his eyes, reading her face. "Do you want to tell me about it?"

Hannah shook her head. "You aren't my therapist, remember?"

His warm hand covered hers as he nodded, concerned. "Yeah, but I am your friend. I can at least offer a listening ear, you know?"

Hannah met his eyes and smiled, her lips wobbling at the corners. "I heard the baby crying again. Well, first, I had a dream where I was a kid and walking along the highway where the accident was. It was empty, though. Then an ice cream truck came and I bought a pushup pop."

"Not so bad so far. I'm guessing it took a turn?"

"It did. Next thing, I was in my childhood home. It became a maze and I came to a door and opened it. There was this little boy, maybe five or six years old, holding a baby. He told me the baby was me."

"Weird. Did you recognize him?"

"No, but he seemed familiar, as well. He was comforting the baby. I got scared and ran. I saw my mom and she was decorating a cake with the number five on it. I tried to get to her but the house pushed me out. Then I was standing in the woods, hearing a baby cry."

Buzzy watched her, waiting on her to finish. "So, it ended with you standing in the woods, hearing the baby crying. Strange, but doesn't seem too terrifying."

Hannah leaned forward to him, her eyes darting around the coffee shop. "George, I was *actually* standing in the woods. Like me now, not as a kid. I woke up bleeding in my robe in the middle of the woods."

She shoved her sleeves up to show him her arms. The long scratches were clotted but dark red and angry looking. Buzzy tried to hide his alarm but was unsuccessful. He reached out and ran his fingers along her arm. Then he sat back in his chair and stared at her.

"Whoa, Hannah. That's not good. Sleepwalking can be dangerous. What if you'd wandered out in front of traffic?" His voice was tight with worry.

"That's not all. I heard the baby crying. Like when I was awake and until the sun came up. I almost checked the woods to see if it was a real baby someone abandoned, but I knew it wasn't. George, I'm losing it. I'm afraid if I try to sleep, I'll wake up and not know where I am, or worse."

"That's a valid concern, Hannah. You need to get back into therapy. Are you on any meds?"

Hannah shook her head. They'd tried a few cocktails when she was in the hospital, but other than valium, nothing helped. She didn't want to live her life on that, either. "I still have the valium prescription. Not taking it, though. I felt like I was doing pretty good until about a week ago. I guess with everything coming up, my brain is dragging things to the surface."

Buzzy took a sip of his coffee and peered out the window, his hazel eyes catching the sun. When he glanced back at her, she could see he was trying to be a friend and not a hospital worker. He chewed his lower lip and tapped his foot on the floor.

"Can you stay with your parents, at least for a couple of weeks? Until the anniversary of losing the baby passes. Get into therapy? Hannah, I'm trying to come at this as your friend, however, I'm worried about you. I remember the state you were in when you came to the hospital and don't want you to suffer like that again."

"Thanks, George. You're right. I shouldn't be alone right now. I'll see if I can camp out over at my parents' house. I'll set up therapy, too. Sorry to burden you with this."

"Never a burden. I care about you, Hannah. What you went through last year would break anyone down. This isn't a reflection of you, of your mental ability. You suffered trauma. Once you recognize that and allow yourself to be vulnerable, you'll find a different level of healing."

Hannah didn't know how to reply to that and considered cracking a joke. She fiddled with the coffee cup handle instead. Buzzy cleared his throat.

"Let's go back to the boy in the dream. You said he seemed familiar. Like, how he looked or something else?"

"I guess how he looked. He had dark brown hair and dark brown eyes."

"Eyes like yours?"

Hannah thought about it. She also had brown eyes but hers were lighter than the boy's. His were more like Parker's. So dark they almost appeared black. Her eyes were like the watery coffee at the hospital. The thought made her chuckle. "No, more like my ex-boyfriend Parker's."

"Hmm, could he have been a representation of Parker? Especially with holding the baby?" Buzzy offered.

"Maybe. I hadn't thought about that. But he said the baby was me."

"Yeah, the mind does weird things when dreaming. I heard once that everyone in our dreams is just an element of ourselves because our mind creates them."

"Really? It didn't feel like it, though. I felt like he was trying to tell me something."

Buzzy considered this, then took a gulp of his coffee. "There is also the belief that dreams are messages from the spiritual realm."

"Are you spiritual or religious?"

"I dabble," Buzzy replied, laughing. "Seriously though, I'm open to the idea. I sincerely doubt this is all there is, but I have an aversion to man-made churches."

"Me too. I don't think I'm spiritual either, though. I suppose I've never really thought about it. This world is enough as it is, you know?"

"I think the idea of spirituality is that it can lift the burdens of this world. I find myself most in tune with that in nature. Like when I go hiking or camping, I feel connected to a part of something I don't elsewhere. I can't really explain it, but there I feel like I'm surrounded by something greater than me."

Hannah watched him, as his eyes glazed over talking about it. She'd never had that experience. The closest she'd to come to anything divine was taking mushrooms at a concert with Parker. Even then, she felt she was more inside of herself than out. Buzzy came back to himself and grinned.

"Not trying to get all out there on you, Hannah. Just my thoughts. I once read that some people believe mental illness is a form of connection to something otherworldly. I'm not sure how I feel about that, but I do feel like if we brought more spirituality into mental health, it might offer another option for those struggling. I don't know. Just rambling here. I guess what I'm saying is, if we weren't simply trying to cope, we might find paths of treatment that offer solutions and acceptance."

Simply trying to cope. That's exactly how Hannah felt. Even in the hospital, she felt like she was coping with what was happening. None of it was real and they were teaching her to come to grips with that. But it *felt* real. She'd seen Logan Slip in her living room. She'd heard the baby crying. Nothing they said or did, changed the fact that she *knew* that was real. They would say that was the problem, she wasn't accepting it was a mental break.

"Hannah?"

Her eyes flitted up to meet Buzzy's. He was watching her and he reached out to squeeze her hand. She smiled, shaking her head.

"Sorry, I was just thinking."

"About?" Buzzy asked.

"What if I'm not losing my mind and this is actually happening?" Even saying the words aloud scared her.

"Okay, so let's say it is. How are you going to deal with it differently?"

"Oh. I don't know. If it's real and Logan Slip is visiting me and the baby is really crying, then I'll end up losing my mind anyway."

"Does it help to talk about it?"

Hannah considered this. It hadn't. It was comforting to have someone to turn to, however, talking hadn't changed anything. If anything, things were getting worse lately. "No. But meds didn't help, either."

"I won't pretend to be a doctor, or expert, but working in the hospital I've seen a lot. To be honest, not much helps. Some people just need a breather, or meds, or to talk. But there are a lot of people who cycle in and out and never get better. I think we may be approaching what they're going through all wrong."

"That's not comforting, George."

Buzzy chuckled, then shrugged. "Here as a friend, remember? As a friend, I don't know what to offer other than my thoughts. You lost a baby, you accidentally killed Logan Slip. No amount of trying to make it better will take that away. Somewhere in your brain is a disconnection, trying to connect. Part of you is running from yourself, I think. Just my humble opinion, not based on any science or medicine."

Hannah could see the imagery. Her running from herself. It was the one thing that made sense. She was her own enemy and the only one who could help her. She sighed and rested her chin on her hands on the table. She was exhausted and just wanted it to stop. "I need to sleep."

"You're always welcome over to my place to sleep if you think it'll make a difference. I have a spare room with a futon you can sleep on. Not glamorous, but maybe not being alone would help?"

"Okay."

"Okay? That's all it took to get you to accept help?"

"I'm too tired to fight it. I can't stand the thought of going back to my place alone. If I don't sleep, I may start hallucinating and I don't need that added to what I'm already seeing."

Buzzy took his last sip of coffee, then stood up. "You want to follow me?"

# CHAPTER FOUR

H annah dragged herself out of the chair and bobbed her head wearily. Buzzy's car was parked near hers, so she followed him out of the parking lot. Her head was swimming with lack of sleep and she tried to focus on the back of his car. Somewhere winding through town, she lost his car at a red light. She peered around, then texted him to send his address, so she could find her way. The light seemed to be excessively long and she glanced around at the storefronts.

That's when she saw him. He was standing in the reflection of a large windowpane across from her. Logan Slip. He was in his motorcycle outfit, the glass of his helmet covering his face. But she knew it was him. She gazed around, attempting to see where he was, where the reflection was being cast from. She couldn't find him, but he continued to stare at her from the window glass. Hannah's heart began to race as he raised his hand and pointed at her. Horns blared behind her as she saw the light had shifted to green and she was stalling traffic. She slammed her foot on the gas pedal, jerking forward into the intersection just as a car whose driver was waiting to turn, decided to go while she was holding up traffic. Hannah hit the brakes right before smashing into the side of their car. He flipped her off and yelled as she burst into tears.

By the time she made it to Buzzy's, she was a wreck and pounded on his door. He opened the door, his eyes wide, peering down at her.

"Hannah! What happened?"

"I almost got in a car accident coming here. It was my fault. Shouldn't even be let behind the wheel of a car," she blurted out.

Buzzy led her inside and showed her to the living room couch. "Are you alright?"

"I'm a train wreck. I'm alright. I hit my brakes right before t-boning the other car. I saw him, George."

"Who?"

"Logan Slip. I was at the light and saw him standing there."

"Probably just another motorcyclist. They all dress the same," Buzzy reasoned.

"No, it was him... because I could only see him in the reflection of the glass window. He didn't exist on the street. He pointed directly at me."

Hannah could see the wheels turning in Buzzy's mind. He was deciding on whether or not she'd seen Logan. She clearly believed she had. He sat down on the couch next to her but didn't speak. What could he really say? At least he was there with her. Hannah gazed around the room, decorated with various masks from other cultures. She remembered the strange mask from her dream.

"You collect masks? Have you ever seen one that was half clown face, half skull? Like split down the middle?"

Buzzy thought about it, then shook his head. "I haven't seen one like that, but I have a book of masks you can look through if you want. Why?"

"Oh, in my dream the ice cream man was wearing one. It seemed ancient, made out of wood. Very rustic."

"Okay, hmmm. I can find that book and we can see if it's in there, or anything like it. First, though, I think we both need sleep. I'm off tonight, so why don't we get some rest? When we get up, I can make us food and we can see if we can dig anything up. The bathroom is the first door on the right. The spare room is across from that on the left. My room is at the end of the hall if you need anything. Are you going to be okay?"

"Yeah. Thanks, George. Hopefully, I won't wake you up, screaming with any visitors in tow."

"If you do, I'll manage. Get some rest."

Hannah made her way to the spare room and collapsed on the futon. It was lumpy and uncomfortable, but she found herself slipping into a dreamless sleep as soon as her head hit the pillow. When she woke up, she could tell it was early evening and heard Buzzy moving around the kitchen. She went to the bathroom and used her finger to rub toothpaste across her teeth. Going to sleep with coffee breath made her mouth taste like something died in there. She brushed her hair with Buzzy's brush and peered at herself in the mirror. Her hair and eyes were almost the same color. Dark golden brown. She was the spitting image of her mother at that age. Round face, large expressive eyes, snub nose. Or as her father said... a button nose. People always assumed she was younger than she was because she was cute. Not striking or stunning. Adorable. Parker said she'd never age because she always looked fourteen. At twenty-five, she still got carded to get into bars.

Buzzy was standing at the stove, barefoot in a t-shirt and scrub bottoms. She wondered how old he was and wondered if it was rude to ask. He turned and smiled at her.

"Did you sleep?"

"Yes, thankfully. No dreams or strange visitors. What time is it?" She felt like her nights and days were upside down.

"Seven-twenty. Are you hungry?"

"I am! What are you making?"

"Grilled cheese and tomato soup. I'm no chef but can whip together something edible."

Hannah laughed. She was no chef, either. Tomato soup and sandwiches sounded great. "If you don't mind my asking, how old are you?"

"Thirty."

"Oh, I'm twenty-five, will be twenty-six in a couple of months."

"I know."

Of course, he did. Everything about her was in her records at the hospital. He probably knew as much about her as she did. She felt exposed and vulnerable. Reading her thoughts, Buzzy turned around and leaned against the counter. His face was thoughtful.

"Let's level the playing field. You know my real name and how I got my nickname. So, here's the rest. I'm from a large family. The middle child of three boys and one older sister. She's

38

the oldest. Kept us in line. As much as she could anyhow. We were terrible. We got into so much trouble. My parents separated when I was in high school. I was in marching band, pretty nerdy. Wanted to become a rockstar until I realized the clarinet wasn't going to get me too far."

Hannah busted out laughing at this as Buzzy grinned. He handed her a bowl of soup and motioned to the small kitchen table. She sat down and blew on the soup. He joined her with a plate of sandwiches and a cup of soup.

"Out of high school, I went to technical school to get my CNA and over the years have been working on my nursing degree. Slowly. I work so much, I hardly have time for anything other than sleep. Was in a serious relationship for six years, but as we both became adults, we drifted apart. I've been single for three. No kids, no pets. Wouldn't be fair to have something need me and I can't be there."

"Six years is a long time, though. Parker and I were together for three. Mostly just having a good time... until life had other plans."

"You miss him?"

"Sometimes I do. He made me laugh. Parker has this personality that draws people to him. He's easy to be around. As long as it doesn't get too serious. Neither of us handled the pregnancy well. We fought and blamed each other. It sucked. He wanted to get back together after I miscarried. I hated him for everything."

"Did you hate *him*, though? Or did you hate the situation you were both forced into?" Buzzy asked, his eyes reading her soul.

"Good question. I don't know. I hated that he wasn't just there for me. Supporting me, telling me it was going to work out. I needed him to be there for me."

"Were you there for him? Supporting him, telling him it was going to work out?"

"Ugh, George. Why do you have to turn things on me like that? Stop being so logical."

Buzzy laughed. "Sorry, but I'm sure it was tough on both of you. It's pretty difficult to be there for someone when you are struggling, too. Maybe cut him a little slack."

Hannah eyed Buzzy with impatience, but he wasn't wrong. She'd wanted Parker to push aside his own feelings and fears to address hers and that wasn't fair. "Fine."

Buzzy's eyes softened as he met her eyes. "I know it's hard. Dealing with something like that and not having a support system must've been really tough. I'm sorry. Then losing the baby..."

"...and feeling guilty for having never wanted it," Hannah finished.

"How far along were you?"

"Twelve weeks. We heard the heartbeat. Well, I did. I was always so mad at Parker, I didn't tell him about the appointments. Hearing the heartbeat made it seem real and I started to think about what I was going to do."

"Did you ever consider not keeping the baby?"

"I did, but I was too afraid to pursue it. Stick my head in the sand and hope it all works out," Hannah confessed.

Buzzy nodded, eyeing her. "You know, it's okay to forgive yourself."

Hannah laughed nervously and got up to wash her bowl. She kept her back to him while she took more time than needed to clean and rinse it. She rested it on the drying rack and turned around. Buzzy was focused on his food and she gazed in his direction for some time. Feeling like he was being watched, he cocked his head toward her.

"You get enough to eat?"

"I did. George, is this weird for you? Us talking about this?"

"No, why would it be?"

"I don't know. I mean, you saw me flailing on the floor and clawing at myself in the hospital. I remember you having to hold me to prevent me from hurting myself. You sitting on the floor with your arms wrapped around me as I kicked and screamed. Doesn't it make this strange?"

Buzzy rotated to face her completely and met her eyes. "If I dragged you from a burning car, would it be strange to become friends? Would you feel ashamed for needing my help in that situation?"

"No, but you didn't drag me from a burning car," Hannah replied, not seeing the correlation.

"Didn't I, though? Were you not in trouble and needing someone's help to get out? Someone to be there for you? To protect you."

"I guess..."

"We need to stop thinking of mental suffering as somehow different from physical suffering. You needed help, I was there. We are friends. Simple as that. I like you, Hannah. We relate to each other."

Hannah smiled bashfully. Buzzy always seemed to put things in a way to allow balance. He never made her feel like she needed to justify where she was coming from. He'd come into her life at just the right time. "I like you too, George."

"Now that's settled, you want to look through that book of masks and see what we can find?"

# CHAPTER FIVE

*T*hey went page by page through the book Buzzy pulled out, however, nothing quite matched. Some masks seemed familiar but not quite right. Not like in Hannah's dream. After they went through that book, Buzzy dragged out a stack of anthropology books and sat down on the floor with them spread out.

"These aren't just masks, but we may be able to find some in the pictures," he explained.

Hannah picked up a large book and set it in her lap. "Why do you have all of these?"

"I wanted to go to school for anthropology. It was a lengthy degree and I was afraid I wouldn't be able to get a job using the degree. It's still something I'm passionate about."

Hannah nodded and began flipping through the pages. The pictures were fascinating, showing ceremonies and daily life of people who seemed so far removed from her modern life. The idea that somewhere in the world, other people were living off the land and basically unaware of people like her, made Hannah feel a little uneasy. Like she didn't completely exist. As she paused at each picture, Buzzy gave a quick explanation of the culture and what was occurring in the photo. Many had masks in them, however, none like the one in her dream.

After scouring through about ten books, Buzzy offered to make them coffee and disappeared into the kitchen. Hannah glanced around his space and shuddered at the masks on the wall. They were beautifully made but most appeared angry, maybe even a little demonic. She could only imagine what their original intent was for. Buzzy came back in and handed her a cup of steaming coffee.

"It's instant. Hope you don't mind. I'm rarely here for too long and keep instant around for a quick cup on the way out the door," he explained with a shrug.

"Thanks, it's fine. I'm no connoisseur. So, why do you have so many masks? Where do you get them?"

"I try to travel a couple of times a year. Go places and study the history, the culture. I may not be able to do it for a living but it's still important to me."

Hannah gazed around, trying to imagine the places the masks came from. "They're a little scary."

Buzzy chuckled and cocked his head. "I can see that. Without understanding the stories behind them, it's easy to find them intimidating. Most of them are positive, though. Sun, protection, even fertility."

"Keep those ones away from me," Hannah joked, her voice tinged with bitterness.

Buzzy smiled as he picked up a book and flipped through the pages. He stopped at one page and peered closer. He glanced at Hannah, his finger pointing to the photo. "Is this it?"

Hannah slid over and looked closer at the photo. It was a far-off photo and slightly blurry, but she could see it. A man had his head turned toward the sky, however, she could make out the mask. Half a skull and half what appeared like a clown or some form of painted face.

"Yeah, not exactly, but that's basically what it was," she agreed, tracing the mask with her finger.

"Appears like it's an Aztec duality mask," Buzzy murmured, reading the text below the picture.

"What does that mean?"

"Each half represents the duality of life. Living, dying."

Hannah felt the hair stand up on her arms. "What does that really mean? Like a harbinger of death?"

"Don't read into it that much. Most ancient cultures embraced death as part of the journey. There's no omen in this, likely. Often it has to do with understanding parts of yourself. Accepting both sides of who we are. The conflict within us and our relationships with others."

Hannah sighed. "Now, I'm even more confused."

Buzzy smiled and met her eyes. "Like I said, don't read too much into it. If there is a message in your dreams, it's probably to look inside of you and see if there is a part of yourself you're ignoring. Neglecting."

Hannah sipped on the coffee and turned the idea over in her mind. In the dream she was a child, then a baby. The boy knew her, but she didn't know him. Then the blood. Outside of school parties to celebrate cultural holidays, often incorrectly, she'd never been exposed to other cultures or beliefs. She was out of her realm, attempting to understand the symbolism.

"I'm in over my head, I think. I don't understand how any of this pertains to me. What any of it means."

"It's hard to jump in head first without truly understanding the basis of the culture. When we try to understand the history or symbolism of other cultures, we often try to make it fit into our own culture or comfort level. This just creates confusion, or worse, disrespect of the original culture," Buzzy replied.

"So, how do I get there?" Hannah tried to quell her frustration, but she felt like she was going in circles.

"Maybe you don't. Or maybe you allow it to unfold without forcing it. I believe that's why it's important to immerse yourself in the culture. Visit the countries, speak to the residents."

"Wait, so I need to go to... where is that mask from?" Hannah blurted out.

"The mask is from Mexico. Ideally, yes." Buzzy's voice had changed, becoming lower and more insistent.

Hannah felt like she was being admonished or spoken to as if she was a child. "That's ridiculous! I can't just up and leave my job to jaunt off to Mexico because I had a dream with a mask in it, George!"

"No one is saying you have to. What I *am* saying is that if you truly want to understand the message from a culture, you have to understand the culture... you can't do that from the comfort of your home. If it's not important to you, then yes, read a book about it and you'll gain some general knowledge. However, you won't understand the culture, or what it's trying to communicate, without immersing yourself in it."

Hannah glared at Buzzy and saw he was dead serious. His face was kind but unrelenting. She blew out her breath and relaxed her shoulders. She'd come to him with this and couldn't get upset at him for being honest. She wanted an easy answer, not a journey. Now it seemed like she was being dragged down a rabbit hole.

"Sorry, George. I see what you mean. I think this is spiraling out of control. I want to understand why I keep seeing Logan Slip and what my dream meant, but I guess I was being more conversational, than trying to take a trip into unknown lands."

Buzzy smiled but kept his gaze steady. It was almost unnerving. "Mexico is hardly unknown lands. Planes go there and everything."

Hannah chuckled, recognizing her overreaction. "True. I'd be terrified to go to another country alone, though. I can barely order food at a Mexican restaurant. I'd never be able to make my way around the country. Have you been there?"

"I have. I go every couple years, at least. I have a family of sorts there, who I've become very close to."

"Do you speak Spanish?"

"I do. I took a couple of years in high school and took refreshers for work. Honestly, when I go there I fall easily into speaking it."

"Oh. I pretty much flunked out of Latin in high school. The teacher passed me simply because I really tried and eked out enough to almost pass the final. I remember nothing," Hannah responded, then blushed. "I suppose that's what I get for taking a dead language."

Buzzy laughed and took their empty cups. "If you go there, to Mexico I mean, you'd be amazed how fast you'd pick the language up. Not to mention, most people there have some grasp of English."

"Still, there is no way in hell I'm going to a foreign country alone."

Buzzy paused at the kitchen door, watching her. "What if you didn't go alone?"

"Oh, so do you have someone who would be willing to be my guide?"

Buzzy glanced away and for the first time ever, she saw him blush. He looked back at her and put his hands in the air. "Yeah. Me."

They stared at each other for what seemed like minutes and Hannah felt her scalp get hot. Was he seriously offering to go with her to Mexico to find out what her dream meant? She resisted the urge to pinch herself to see if she was having another weird dream. She shook her head.

"George. You can't be serious. I know we're friends, but we've only known each other for six months, some of which I was in a *mental* hospital. I'm having hallucinations, hearing things, and am not sure I'm even sane. While I appreciate your wanting to help, I think us running off to Mexico to chase down the meaning of a mask is a bit of a stretch. Not to mention, we both have jobs, I have no money, and outside of today I've never even seen you outside of the coffee shop or... the *hospital*!"

Buzzy flinched as her voice raised and he shrugged. "Like I said, I go to Mexico every couple years. I'm due for a visit. Hannah, I'm offering as a friend, nothing more. I won't bring it up again. Do you want to watch a movie or something? You are welcome to use the spare room tonight, as well."

Hannah stared at him, feeling embarrassed for her reaction. She nodded and moved to the couch. "Sure, let's watch a movie. I may head home after."

She didn't head home. She must've fallen asleep during the movie and woke up on the couch with a blanket over her. Buzzy had gone to his room. She sat up and stretched. It was almost four in the morning, so she decided to wait to drive home until the sun was up. She went to the kitchen to heat up a cup of coffee, trying to be as quiet as possible. She heated water on the stove and pulled it off right before it began to whistle. She found the instant coffee and eyeballed some into the cup. She stirred it with her finger, not wanting to search for spoons, and was just about to take a sip when she heard someone clear their throat behind her.

Expecting to see Buzzy when she spun around, she was shocked when she saw Logan Slip sitting at the kitchen table, his feet propped up on the other chair. His helmet glass was up and a trickle of blood ran from his empty eye socket. He grinned at her and pointed his finger in a small wave.

"Sure, I'd love a cup."

Hannah screamed and dropped the cup of coffee she was holding in her hands. It shattered on the floor, splashing her legs with hot liquid. She instinctively bent down to protect her skin and crouched against the counter, afraid to look up.

Buzzy ran into the kitchen and grabbed her, lifting her over the broken mug and hot coffee. He set her down away from the mess and grasped her chin with his hand, turning her face up to his as he searched her eyes. "Hannah, are you alright? What happened? I heard you scream."

Hannah, still afraid to look around, locked her eyes on Buzzy's and whispered, "Is he still there?"

"Who?"

Hannah pulled her eyes away and let them dart to where she'd seen Logan Slip sitting. The chair was empty. She glanced back at Buzzy. "Logan Slip. He was here. Sitting right there."

Her hand shook as she pointed. Buzzy followed her finger and frowned. "Hannah..."

She knew. Logan Slip hadn't been there. Or if he had, only she could see him. He was stalking her. No. He was haunting her. She shook like she was freezing and stumbled into the living room. Buzzy must think she was mad. She wrapped the blanket he'd placed on her earlier around her and sat down. Maybe she *was* mad. Buzzy came to the door and watched her. This wouldn't end until she understood why it was happening. Until she immersed herself. She peered up and met Buzzy's eyes.

"You'll go with me?" she asked.

"Go where?" Buzzy replied, confused.

"To Mexico?"

# CHAPTER SIX

"Y ou can't go! That's crazy!" Hannah's mother threw her hands in the air as she practically yelled the words. They were sitting in Hannah's parents' kitchen and her mother appeared like she'd been slapped in the face, red splotches dotting each cheek.

"Mom, please don't say it's crazy. It makes it sound like you're saying I'm not in my right mind. Also, I won't be going alone."

Her mother spat out what sounded like a cross between a laugh and choking. "Hannah, you can't be serious. You've hardly ever left Virginia. Now, you are planning to go to a whole other country? Can't you just take a trip to another state?"

"I could, sure. But I *need* to go to Mexico."

"Need? No one *needs* to go to Mexico. Ken, tell her she's being ridiculous."

Ken, Hannah's father, was standing at the counter reading the paper and looked up. He usually stayed out of their conversations and was more of the type of person to pass through a room, than to sit in a deep discussion. He glanced between them, then sighed. "It might be good for Hannah to go experience something. She's had a tough year, Lynn. I think she can handle it."

Hannah smiled with relief at her father. He was quiet but weighed in when he felt it was necessary. She couldn't say they were close necessarily, however, he was there when she needed him. On the other hand, Hannah's mother was glaring at him, not having been backed up.

"Ken. She is going with some strange man."

"Mom, George is hardly some strange man. We met when I was in the hospital and he's been honestly my only friend since I got out."

"What about Parker? Does he know you are going to another country with this man?" her mother asked, knowing full well Parker was out of the picture.

Hannah laughed, shaking her head. "That's an odd card to pull. Parker has moved on with his life, I've moved on with mine. He's marrying the girl he is with now."

"Ugh, that's just stupid. He was with you for years. You two should've gotten married, started a family. I always liked Parker. He was something special, Hannah."

"Wow, Mom. We were *never* getting married. Parker and I had a good time. We were two kids who liked to party and go to concerts. Nothing more. We should've just stayed friends in reality and skipped the whole relationship business. I think you liked Parker more than I did. I love him, but as someone I shared part of my life with. That's all."

Her mother shook her head, the wheels in her mind turning, attempting to find a suitable argument. She stared at

Hannah's father, who was wisely keeping his eyes on the paper. "Why Mexico?"

"Well... I had this dream, nightmare sort of, and I think maybe some clarity might come from taking this trip. If nothing else, I need to step away from everything that's happened and clear my mind." Hannah went on to tell her parents about the dream. When she got to the point about the boy and the baby, her mother frowned and glanced at her father. Hannah knew it sounded off the rails to them but she wanted full transparency. She knew if she didn't take steps to figure out what was happening, she'd end up back at the hospital. The room fell silent as she finished and said how she found herself bleeding in the woods.

Her father cleared his throat, setting the paper on the table. "Han, do you think maybe talking to a therapist might be a good idea, first?"

"Dad, I have. For months. They referred me to a psychiatrist. It's not helping and they are pushing heavy meds. Let me just take this trip. When I get back, if things don't get better, I'll try the meds."

"So, this George. Do you feel safe around him? You will be far from home and if he tries something..."

"He won't, Dad. I trust him. We're just friends and he goes to Mexico often. I feel safer going there *with* him. He'll be my guide."

Her parents stared at each other, a message passing between them. They were just worried was all. Their only child, taking a trip to another country with someone they didn't know. Hannah took a deep breath, knowing they needed more.

"I can invite him over for dinner before we go if that will help. You can meet him and grill him then."

Hannah's mother bobbed her head. "Yes, do that. Hannah, you have to understand we are just worried for you. This came out of nowhere."

"I know."

They let the conversation drop and Hannah gathered her bag to leave. "I'll let you know when. We fly out Tuesday, so it will be before then. We'll be gone for two and a half weeks."

"What about work?" her father asked.

"I'm taking a leave of absence. I let them know I was coming up on the anniversary of losing the pregnancy and HR approved it. I'm good to go."

Hannah's father looked like he wanted to say something, then pursed his lips and went back to reading his paper. Hannah waited and seeing her parents had given up the fight, for now, headed out the door. She texted Buzzy about the dinner requirement. He texted back a thumbs up. It would be awkward, but she couldn't do this without him. By the time she got home, it was getting dark. She hated being there alone anymore. Sometimes she stayed in Buzzy's spare room, but she needed to pack and get organized for leaving. She threw a premade meal in the microwave and clicked on the radio for noise. Buzzy was working the night shift, so she didn't want to bug him.

After she ate, she took out the list of items he recommended packing and dug through her closet for her suitcase. It was hardly used, she and Parker had only gone on overnights for shows. They never took romantic getaways and they both grew up in Virginia. Family visits were typically day trips. Life had been within a few hundred miles of home. Mexico seemed a world away.

Once the case was packed, she could barely keep her eyes open and lay on the remaining clothes on the bed. She dragged a blanket over her and dozed off. It was early morning when she was woken up by the sound of a motorcycle revving its engine. The sun was just bringing color to the sky and she sat up, rubbing her eyes. She'd slept almost eight hours. The motorcycle continued revving outside. It wasn't uncommon, as a makeshift shrine had been made on the highway by other motorcyclists after the death of Logan Slip. Sometimes they would rev when driving by it.

This sounded different, though. It sounded like it was right outside of her house. She went to the window and peered out. The street was empty. The sound paused and she figured they must've gone on. She got dressed, then headed down and turned coffee on. She only had a few days left of work before she was off for three weeks. It was the longest she'd taken off since she'd started working at eighteen. By the time she needed to leave for work, she'd polished off almost a pot of coffee, feeling jittery from it.

She made it to the end of her street and stared at the vanishing shrine on the side of the road. When the accident first happened, it was littered with flowers, balloons, teddy bears, motorcycle paraphernalia, and pictures of Logan. Now, it was some tattered fake flowers, a crooked wooden cross, and a picture so faded she could only make out his teeth and one eye. It was sad, really. People moved on. She thought about his parents and pain flashed in her chest. They hadn't moved on. In attempts to keep him alive, they'd started a charity in his name, using a photo of him smiling as the logo. Sometimes she'd see the fliers around town for fundraising events. She wasn't even sure what they raised money for.

On her way to work, she was lost in thought, thinking about how different things would've ended up had she not miscarried. Logan Slip would be alive. Maybe, or at least not dead by her actions. She'd be a mother now. Maybe she and Parker would have committed and married. Her mind played a reel of a happy little family sitting in a sunny living room. Her, Parker, the baby. As she let her mind fantasize about this, she heard the rev of a motorcycle engine again and snapped back to reality. She couldn't see where it was coming from and glanced in her mirrors. There was no motorcycle.

She gripped the steering wheel and focused on the road. Her mind went back to the image of the sunny living room. An image she hadn't seen before appeared. In the corner, the little boy from her dream was playing with legos. He was holding up what he made to the family. The family was somehow different. Familiar... but not Parker or her. Her mind tried to focus. Just as the image started to form, Hannah was startled by a movement in her rearview mirror.

A motorcycle.

Hannah felt her hands get clammy and looked for a place to pull over. There wasn't one and she began to panic. She put her foot on the brake and tried to keep it together. All of a sudden, the motorcycle veered around her on the left and revved its engine as it flew by her. The motorcyclist cut close in front of her and flipped her off as he sped away.

Hannah felt the panic overtake her and found the first parking lot she could to divert into. She turned off the car and leaned her head against the steering wheel, sobbing. It was likely just some kid on his motorcycle who was pissed because she'd hit her brakes. She couldn't freak out every time she saw a motorcycle. She cleaned herself up in the mirror and reapplied her makeup. Her nose was red and her cheeks blotchy. She'd wait in the car at work until she looked normal. She didn't want anyone asking what was wrong. One little tap and she'd fall over the edge.

Work was a blur and before she knew it she was driving home. Buzzy was working right up until they needed to leave, so she was on her own until then. He agreed to an early dinner the following night at her parents'. That would be weird. Buzzy was from a part of her life her parents weren't connected to. He knew things about her no one did. Now, they would sit around a table and have to make general conversation.

The good thing about Buzzy was he could adapt to any situation. He picked her up at her home and they rode over together in his car. He'd switched out of his normal t-shirt and scrub bottoms into slacks and a button-down shirt. His golden-red hair was combed and drawn neatly into a tie at the base of his neck. He didn't seem nervous at all, but Hannah was. Her mother could be intense at times. They went right in and met her parents on the back porch.

Her mother smiled genuinely at Buzzy as she extended her hand. "Nice to meet you, George. I'm Lynn, Hannah's mother. Would you like something to drink? We have beer, tea, and some soft drinks."

Buzzy glanced at Hannah with his brows raised, smirking as he mouthed, "George?"

Hannah blushed as she shrugged. He winked and turned back to her mother. "Tea would be great."

"Perfect. Hannah, why don't you help me grab drinks? George, this is my husband and Hannah's father, Ken." She waved her hand toward Hannah's father who was sitting in an armchair, his legs crossed in front of him.

Ken stood up and eyeballed Buzzy. He grasped Buzzy's extended hand, keeping his mouth in a straight line, with an expression Hannah hadn't seen before. He cleared his throat and spoke low, his voice showing no emotion. Hannah started to follow her mother out of the room when she heard her father's words cut through the air.

"So, George, is it? What exactly are your intentions with my daughter?"

# CHAPTER SEVEN

H annah froze by the door, mortified. Her father wasn't
that kind of father. They'd welcomed Parker in without
batting an eye. Her father was present but not overly
protective when it came to guys. Hannah felt her ears get hot and
turned to face them. Her father was close to Buzzy, his eyes set
hard. Buzzy didn't seem taken aback by the question, but
Hannah was. This had come totally out of left field. She went to
step toward them when her mother grabbed her arm. Hannah
yanked her arm away and bolted toward her father and Buzzy.

"Dad! What the hell?"

Buzzy raised his hand to show her he had it handled and
smiled at Hannah's father. "My only intention has always been to
be Hannah's friend. While I appreciate you looking out for your
daughter, I can promise you she doesn't need you worrying
about her. Hannah is a force to be reckoned with."

Ken stared at Buzzy, his mouth slightly open as if he was
about to speak. He snapped his mouth shut and turned to
Hannah. "Of that, I have no doubt. However, you and my
daughter are leaving for another country and this is the first time

we've met you, George. How can we be sure you don't have any malintent?"

Buzzy considered this, then shrugged. "I guess you can't."

That wasn't the answer Hannah's parents were expecting and they stood in stone silence. Hannah, realizing things were spiraling down fast, cleared her throat and placed her hand on Buzzy's arm.

"Mom, Dad, I wouldn't be going with George if I thought there was any risk. We've already *had* this conversation, as well. This is weird. Can we just have dinner and you two trust my judgment?"

The four of them stood awkwardly while Hannah's words hung in the air. Finally, her mother sighed and broke the silence. "Ken, can you help me grab the drinks? We can move to the dining room since dinner is about ready. Hannah, why don't you show George around?"

Hannah's parents left the porch and Buzzy turned to face Hannah, his brows raised. "Wow, you didn't tell me your parents were out for blood."

"I didn't know. That isn't how my father usually is and my mother tends to be more passive-aggressive than anything. I don't get it. They were so welcoming to Parker and practically pushed us together. I told them we are just friends but their reaction was bizarre. I'm sorry. You might require a stiff drink after that. So, do you want a tour of the house?"

Buzzy chuckled. "No worries. Your parents don't scare me. I think I'll skip the tour. Also, I don't drink."

"Like at all?" Hannah asked, surprised.

"Nope." Buzzy tapped his skull with his pointer finger. "Like to keep a clear mind."

Hannah watched him and thought back. He'd never smoked or drank around her. "Oh. That's cool. Honestly, I've probably done too much of all of it. Drinking, drugs. Parker and I tried just about everything. Are you completely sober? Like, have you ever drank or done any drugs?"

"You know, in high school, I definitely experimented. Some in my early twenties. Haven't drank at all since then. I do have my demons when it comes to drug use in the past. Some I'm not proud of. I also have used hallucinogens, psychedelics, spiritually... meditatively."

Hannah didn't even know what he meant. She'd taken acid and mushrooms, resulting in hallucinations... but not spiritually. Or maybe it was spiritual. She couldn't say as she didn't consider herself a spiritual person. "What's the difference? I mean, I've taken hallucinogens but while I saw trippy stuff, I can't say it was spiritual."

"Were you alone?"

"No, it was with Parker and friends."

"I can't speak for anyone else, however, when I'm trying to get to a place of connection, of spirituality, I usually take it as part of a ceremony alone or with a small group of like-minded people. My intent is to go within, to expand my knowledge."

Hannah laughed. "Yeah, that's not why we did it. Our goal was to see how much we could blow our minds."

Buzzy winked with a slight smile. "I've done that, too."

Hannah's mother appeared at the door, waving her hand toward the dining room. "Dinner's ready."

They followed her to where dinner was laid out on the table. Ken seemed more relaxed and made small talk while they ate. He asked Buzzy about his job and his family. Buzzy graciously answered the questions without getting flustered. As they finished dinner, he glanced at the time and gave Hannah a furtive glance. She realized he needed to leave soon to get to work on time.

"Hey, we need to head out. George is working night shifts and he needs to drop me at home, first."

"Why don't you just stay here, honey? Dad can drive you back in the morning," her mother offered.

"I have work in the morning, can you get me home with time to change?" Hannah asked.

"Sure, you know Dad is up at the crack of dawn."

"Okay, yeah, that sounds nice. I'll walk George out and be back in a few minutes."

Buzzy stood up and extended his hand to Ken. "It was nice to meet you both. Perhaps we can do this again once we get back from our trip."

Ken took his hand and shook it without speaking, the trip still being a sore point. Lynn chimed in, "Yes! You'll have to tell us all about your travels."

Hannah led the way to the door. Once they were outside, she took a deep breath. "Sorry about my parents. They'll come around. It's been a weird year. I think they just can't wrap their brains around the fact that we can be friends only. If you were female, they wouldn't be acting so irrational."

"Don't stress it. My feelings aren't hurt. Tomorrow is your last day at work before the trip?"

"It is. I wish I could just skip it but I'm pushing it as it is. I'm packed already, though."

"You have your passport?" Buzzy asked, fishing his keys out of his pocket.

"No, but I have an appointment after work to get it."

"Cutting it close, Hannah."

"I know, I know. This is all new to me. I promise I'll be good to go by Tuesday. They said they could expedite it."

"Alright, I'd better head on. Hopefully a quiet night. Text me if you want to chat." Buzzy leaned in and gave Hannah a hug. Regardless of her parents' fears, she didn't feel anything more than friendship for him. After Parker, she figured it would be a long time before she could be in another relationship. She still felt pretty hollow inside.

She watched Buzzy drive away and turned to face her childhood home. For a second, she thought she saw a curtain move in one of the upstairs bedrooms. Her mother's craft room. Were her parents spying on her? She sighed and headed in. Both of her parents were sitting in the living room watching television and no one was out of breath from running down the stairs. Hannah frowned.

"Were either of you just upstairs?"

Lynn shook her head. "No, we have been in here since you went out with George. Why?"

Hannah shrugged. "Nothing. I thought I saw someone at the window of your craft room. Well, really just the curtain moved."

"Oh. Hmmm, maybe I left the window cracked. I was airing it out yesterday."

Hannah sat down in an armchair and rested her head back. "So, do you have questions about George?"

"He seems nice," her father replied, a switch from his earlier on-the-hunt persona.

"He is. That's it? You don't have twenty questions?"

"No. We still aren't thrilled you are going to Mexico with him, but he does seem to care about you and have your best interest at heart," her mother responded.

Hannah let her guard down. She shifted her focus to the tv and wondered what had come over them. First, they were ready to pounce, now they were hardly interested. Either way, she was glad the evening was over. Her mother brought her cocoa and they chatted about nothingness until Hannah felt her eyes get heavy. Her father was already asleep in a recliner and her mother covered him with a blanket. Hannah watched her parents and felt a pang in her heart. She didn't know what that kind of love was. Her mother turned off the light and cut down the volume on the tv.

"I'm heading to bed. He'll come when he wakes up in a bit. Are you staying down here?" Hannah's mother said as she made her way to the hall.

"No, I'll follow you up. I'm pretty tired."

They climbed the stairs and Hannah headed to her childhood bedroom. It'd been cleared of any teenager remnants and made into a guest room, but it was still her old bed and dresser. She slid under the covers and closed her eyes. It'd been a good childhood. Loving parents, stable home. But there was always something off. Holidays, vacations, get-togethers always seemed to be lacking. Missing something.

Her parents showered her with love and things, however, they always seemed a step away. Like a thin veil separated them from her. She didn't know if it was all in her head. There was nothing specific she could put her finger on. Just that she never felt as if they were totally present. Like they were afraid she'd disappear if they got too close.

Later, she heard her father ascend the stairs and go to her parents' room. She could hear them talking softly and swore she heard her mother crying. She sat up and strained to listen but it fell silent in their room. Not before she distinctly heard her name pass between them. Feeling like she did as a teenager when she knew a teacher had called, she felt her breath get short and her face hot. Why was her mother crying? About her going to Mexico? Hannah was an adult and that seemed like a stretch. Why was this such a trigger?

She laid back down and yawned. It was going to be okay. She'd go to Mexico and come back, they'd see there was nothing to worry about. She closed her eyes and as she dozed off, she had the sensation of something warm curled up at her side. She placed her hand down but nothing was there. Even so, it was comforting and she slipped into a dreamless sleep.

She was the first one up in the morning and got the coffee started. Her father came down, his eyes puffy and tired. He rubbed his head, making his hair stick up, and poured a cup as the coffee maker continued to drip. He looked at her over the rim of his cup.

"You sleep okay, Han?"

"Yeah, heavy. It's weird how being back in my old bed feels like home."

"You're always welcome here, you know that. I think your mother would never let you leave if she could."

Hannah chuckled. That might be true. "I need to grow sometime. Can you get me home in a bit?"

"Sure, let me grab my keys and shoes. Thanks for putting coffee on."

He left to get ready and Hannah looked in the cabinets for a covered coffee cup, so she could bring coffee along for the ride. She checked under the counter where her mother stored all kinds of storage containers and lids, and found an insulated mug. As she was pulling it out, something on the back of the cabinet caught her eye and she peered in. Written in crayon on the back wall of the cabinet was a smiley face and the letters HM on one side of the smiley face and TM on the other. HM. Hannah Moore. Those were her initials. She ran her fingers across them, the aged, bumpy, crayon etching raised under her fingertips. She didn't remember ever writing that back there.

And who the hell was TM?

# CHAPTER EIGHT

*H*annah had never been on a plane and wasn't sure what to expect. She followed Buzzy's lead as he expertly maneuvered the airport and security check. He explained he flew a lot but that they would fly into San Antonio, Texas, rent an RV, and travel the rest of the way in that. Hannah wasn't sure why, however, trusted his judgment since her experience was basically none.

Her parents weren't travelers and didn't take vacations. Even though they were well enough off, any time off was usually spent around the house or at most, trips in the area. The only times she'd gone any distance as a child was for school trips and even then she had to beg them up until the deadline.

Maybe that's why once she was out from under their watchful eye, she got a little wild. Nothing major, but she and Parker took their fair share of recreational drugs at concerts and parties. Mostly just weed and molly, occasionally acid and mushrooms. Her parents never would've approved, and Parker was smart enough to give a clean, upstanding, outward appearance around them. They thought he was a sweet, hardworking, young man. Which he was... but he also liked to get bombed out of his mind.

Once Hannah and Buzzy were on the plane and seated, she took a deep breath. It was crowded and a few rows back a baby was crying. Or at least Hannah thought there was. She shifted her eyes back and was relieved to see a woman cradling a baby to her shoulder, trying to get it to settle down. Hannah watched for a moment and felt an unfamiliar pang. Not a longing, however, something in the same family. A tug of some sort. She turned to face forward and sighed. Nothing in her wanted to be a mother. But something in her reminded her she almost was.

Buzzy smiled over at her and glanced past her out the window. "We should be taking off in a minute. Are you nervous?"

"A little," Hannah confessed.

"You got this. Once we're in the air, it will feel almost like we are just sitting there. It's the take-offs and landings which are a little bumpy."

"Good to know. When do most plane crashes happen anyway?" Hannah asked and peered around. Most people seemed irritated but not scared.

Buzzy chuckled. "Uh, at take-offs and landings. I think the largest percentage at landings."

"Oh. So, what you're saying is, I can't relax until we're off the plane."

Buzzy rested his hand on her shoulder for comfort. "Technically... no. But we'll be fine. I do this all the time. Just look at it as an adventure."

"An adventure," Hannah murmured. "Not sure I need more of those."

Buzzy didn't respond but handed her some lozenges. "Natural, good for calming."

"If you say so. At this point, I'll try anything."

The plane began to taxi down the runway and Hannah popped a few lozenges in her mouth. She felt gravity dragging on her sense of being as the plane lifted off the ground. It rose smoothly into the air and settled into a pattern. Buzzy winked at her as he began flipping through a guide of Mayan and Aztec ruins he'd brought for their trip. He suggested those would be the best place to start once they got into Mexico. He'd given his friends a head's up they were coming, as well.

They switched planes in Atlanta and went through the process all over again. When they flew over the Mississippi river Hannah got ill and vomited into a bag in the holder on the back of the seat in front of her. By the time they landed in Texas, she was physically and mentally worn out and was glad they'd booked a hotel by the airport for the night. A shuttle took them to the hotel and Buzzy ordered pizza to the room. Hannah fell back on one of the beds and groaned. Not only was she almost on the other side of the country from her home, she felt out of sorts in her own body.

They watched tv until the pizza came and made small talk. Hannah felt bone-tired and rested back on the bed as she ate a piece of pizza. She started to feel herself drift off when Buzzy came over and shook her awake.

"Hey, I'm going to go for a swim at the pool. Will you be okay?" he asked.

"Oh, sorry. Yeah, George. Go on. I guess I need to close my eyes for a bit."

"Sounds good. You want me to take that pizza you're holding or are you wanting it for comfort?"

Hannah laughed, handing him the pizza. "Funny. I'll eat it later. Wake me up when you get back if you're still not tired and we can hang out."

Buzzy took the pizza and slipped it back into the box. "Will do. There's a spare key on the stand and I'll bring my phone in case you need to reach me."

As soon as he was out the door, Hannah let her eyes close and drifted off to sleep. A door slamming startled her awake a little while later. It was pitch black around her. She peered around to see if Buzzy had come back and fumbled for the lamp switch. Her hand landed on something unfamiliar and she jerked it back. She sat up and rubbed her eyes. She didn't know where she was but she wasn't in the hotel room anymore. As her eyes adjusted, she saw she was outside somewhere. Her clothes were damp and she was laying on the ground. She scrambled to her feet as fear overtook her.

Where the hell was she?

A door, she'd heard a door slam. She turned around to see she was near a large building and walked toward it. As she neared the structure, she saw it was some sort of hospital or nursing home. She followed a man walking around the side and came to the entrance. A nursing home. Embarrassed, she waited a moment, then walked to the front desk and cleared her throat.

The man behind the desk stared at her with surprise. "Visiting hours are over."

"No. I'm lost, I think. I'm staying at a nearby hotel. The Calliope Inn?"

"The Calliope Inn? Are you sure?"

"Yeah?"

The man shook his head, eyeballing her. "Are you on something? Like drugs or something like that?"

Hannah blushed and glanced away even though she had no reason to. "No, sir. I must've been sleepwalking."

"I sincerely doubt that."

Hannah felt shame and anger wash over her. "Look, I don't know what your problem is, I just need to get back to my hotel. Why are you giving me a hard time?"

The man watched her, then shook his head again. "Miss, The Calliope Inn is almost thirty miles from here. So, unless you're confused about where you were staying, or on something, I don't see how you could've gotten that lost."

Hannah froze. Thirty miles away? She couldn't have even walked that in a night. "What time is it?"

"It's one-forty in the morning."

She'd fallen asleep at around seven-thirty. Six hours. She didn't walk there. She didn't have her phone or purse on her. "You haven't seen me before now, right? Or anyone else out of the ordinary?"

"Nope. It's been pretty dead here all night. Until you walked in, nothing unusual occurred. You're the weirdest thing that's happened all night."

Hannah dropped her head and stared down at her feet. She was dressed and had shoes on. That was something, at least. "Can I please use your phone?"

The guy lifted the phone and set it on the desk. "No long distance."

"Okay." Hannah had no idea if Buzzy's cell was considered long-distance and didn't care. She dialed his number and prayed he'd pick up a number he didn't know. It rang three times and he answered. His voice was tired and worried.

"Hello?"

"George! It's me!" Hannah bit back tears.

"Hannah, where the hell are you? I have the police out looking for you. I came back to the hotel room, the door was wide open and you were gone. All your stuff is here. I didn't know if you were attacked or abducted. Where are you?"

She stared around. "I actually don't know. I woke up and…"

She began to cry and handed the guy at the desk the phone. "The address here?"

He took the phone, staring at her in disbelief. "Uh, hi? Yeah, this is Rodney at the Leisure Waters Nursing Home. You're really at the Calliope Inn? Damn. Alright, you have something to take down the address?"

Hannah wandered away from the desk and sat on a vinyl-covered loveseat by the door. Rodney hung up the phone and stood up. "Your friend is on his way. He said to hold tight and for me not to let you out of my sight. There's coffee over there if you'd like."

Hannah followed where his hand was pointing and got up. She didn't want coffee, but holding something might steady her hands. She poured a cup and tried to stir the powdered creamer in. It left a coating of little blobs of white goo on the surface. She sniffed the coffee and decided it would serve as something to hold, however, nothing more. Rodney mostly ignored her but took his word to Buzzy seriously and checked on her now and then.

After about thirty minutes, Buzzy rushed in, his eyes wild and stressed. He saw Hannah sitting in the corner and moved toward her. He knew better than to spook her and stopped a few feet away. "Hannah."

She gazed up at him, her eyes locked on his. "This was a bad idea. It's one thing to wander away from my home, another to wander away from one place I don't know to another."

Buzzy nodded and came to sit next to her. He put his arm around her shoulder. "I shouldn't have left you alone. Your brain is just stressed out. What I don't get, is how did you get here?"

"No clue. I went to sleep in the hotel and woke up out there in the grass. Maybe I hitchhiked?"

"Maybe... but why here?"

Hannah laughed, her voice cold. "Million-dollar question. I think it's random. I don't think I picked it. Does the hotel have cameras?"

"The police asked that, too, but they admitted they haven't maintained them. So, no. They are checking street cameras now as well. I need to talk to the guy at the front here. He's who I spoke to on the phone?"

Hannah nodded and pointed toward Rodney, even though he was the only other person around. Buzzy hugged her, then got up to talk to Rodney. Hannah followed, not knowing what else to do.

"Hey, thanks for the help. The police may come by to talk to you, though now that Hannah's been found it's not as dire. Did you see anything unusual?"

Rodney shrugged. "Like I told her, not until she walked in. Our linen delivery came and I went out to bring in the bags after they left. I smoked a cigarette and brought the bags in. A minute after I came back in, she appeared like a ghost standing in front of me."

Buzzy considered this and his eyes lit up. "What's the name of the delivery company?"

"For the linens? Bright White."

"You have their number handy?"

Rodney dug around on his desk and handed Buzzy a post-it note. Buzzy typed the number in his phone and took a step back to make a call. Hannah threw the coffee in the trash, standing awkwardly until he was finished. He hung up and pulled her aside.

"They delivered to the hotel tonight. My guess is somehow you got onto their truck, then got off here. Not sure why, but it adds up how you ended up so far away. They made about six stops between the two and grabbed fast food. Accounts for the missing time. Not sure why they didn't notice you in the truck unless you were at the back behind the bags. Do you remember anything? Any dreams?"

Hannah shook her head. It was like she dozed off on the hotel bed and woke up a minute later here. No dreams, nothing. Buzzy could see she was on the verge of losing it and waved to Rodney.

"Thanks again, man. We're heading out."

He guided Hannah to a small red car in the parking lot. She frowned at him. He laughed and shook the keys. "Hotel night manager. I think she could see how freaked out I was and offered her car. I promised to bring her back some fries and a sandwich. I filled the tank, too."

Hannah was embarrassed so many people had been brought in on her weird adventure. Now, she wished they'd never come. She climbed in and rested her head against the window glass. Buzzy fired up the car and jerked out of the parking lot. They went through a drive-thru for food and made it back to the hotel in silence. Hannah felt like she was holding a blinking neon sign that flashed *crazy*, blink, *crazy*, blink, *crazy*, blink, *crazy*."

Buzzy ran in to give the manager her keys with the promised food, then they walked to the hotel room. Once inside, Buzzy placed a chair under the door handle and put whatever he could find on the chair seat to make noise if it was moved. Hannah watched, her ears hot, and held a pillow to her chest. Buzzy turned to face her and smiled with genuine concern.

"I'm sorry, Buzzy. For dragging you into this."

"What? No George?"

"George is what I call you when I'm not batshit. I might as well call you Buzzy since you are having to take care of me like at the hospital."

"Hannah, you aren't batshit. You're traumatized. And I'm here for you as a friend. That's what you are to me, Hannah. My friend, who I care very much about and want to be with."

Hannah stared at Buzzy, grateful for his consistent, nonjudgemental presence, then nodded. "Same here, George."

# CHAPTER NINE

T hey rented a small RV, in case they needed somewhere to
crash out while traveling through Mexico. The built-in
couch turned into a bed and there was a crawl space with
a mattress above the driver and passenger seats. It smelled like
stale beer and smoke but appeared somewhat clean. Buzzy
checked the tires and engine before signing the rental agreement
from what looked to be a hundred-year-old woman, clearly
smoking weed as she barked out instructions. Hannah tried not
to laugh and stood back while Buzzy finalized the paperwork,
then loaded their bags. He checked the locks on the doors as he
explained to Hannah they might go through some rough areas.
She wondered if he was checking the locks because of her
wandering away in her sleep. Either way, they worked fine and he
was satisfied.

Once they got to the border, they were stuck in a long
line, waiting to cross into Mexico. Some vehicles were being
directed to pull off to the side while the border patrol went
through them. Hannah held her breath when they approached,
not sure why she was nervous. Buzzy rolled down his window

and smiled at the agent, who didn't smile back. They went back and forth on what Buzzy and Hannah were going to Mexico for. Buzzy didn't bat an eye and gestured toward Hannah.

"I'm taking my friend on a tour of the ruins and sites."

The agent eyed Hannah, who gave a small wave at him, before peering back at Buzzy with his long hair and beaded necklace. "You aren't trying to bring anything illegal back, are you, son?"

Buzzy shook his head. "No, sir. Maybe a couple of knick-knacks for the family. We just want to check tourist areas. My friend has never been."

"How long do you intend to be in Mexico?"

"Just a couple of weeks. We both have to be back to work after that."

The agent glanced at Hannah, then sighed. He stepped back, waving them through. They passed by what looked like a tollbooth and Hannah observed as agents pretty much tore apart a car coming into the US from Mexico. She shuddered and stared forward. Maybe coming to Mexico hadn't been the best idea. She turned and watched as the border disappeared in the background. Buzzy fiddled with the radio, which crackled but nothing else. He looked at Hannah.

"Next time we stop, I can hook up a little player I brought, so we can listen to music. You okay?"

Hannah nodded. "Yeah. That was intense back there. I'm surprised they didn't make us pull over."

Buzzy chuckled and clicked off the radio. "When I'm by myself, they usually do. I guess with you on board with me, I look a little less sketchy."

Hannah stared at him and considered that. She'd first known Buzzy at the hospital where he'd had his shit way more together than she did, so she never considered he might put off a sketchy vibe. He did have long hair and smelled like incense most times, but she saw him as someone who guided her out of the hole she'd been in. She cocked her head.

"Are you?"

"Am I what?" Buzzy replied, furrowing his brows.

"Sketchy? Like, do you ever do anything illegal, now? Drugs or anything else?"

Buzzy's eyes got wide and he busted out laughing. "Drugs? No, they do random drug testing at work. Nothing which can be tested for, anyway. Only done psychedelics in ceremonies, stuff like that."

"Oh. Like I said before, I did a lot of drugs with Parker but they never tested where I worked. I haven't since... well, I guess since I found out I was pregnant. Then with losing the baby and everything else, it hasn't crossed my mind. You said you experimented in your twenties?"

Buzzy stared out the front window and didn't respond. His jaw clenched and he set his mouth in a grim line. Hannah was embarrassed she'd asked and looked away. She rolled down her window as the warm, dry air hit her face. They were on a long stretch of road and she wasn't sure where they were going first. Silence filled the space between them and she tried to redirect the energy.

"Sorry, that was none of my business."

Buzzy turned his head slightly toward her and smiled painfully. "It's not that. There is something I didn't tell you when I was filling you in on my past. Something I just wanted to put behind me."

Hannah didn't know if she was supposed to respond, or just listen. She brushed the hair out of her face and twisted it behind her neck. Buzzy didn't go on at first. She could tell his mind was playing over a memory, trying to decide how to go forward. He cleared his throat and met her eyes.

"We aren't so different, you know, Hannah? When you came into the hospital, I saw a similar desperation in you I'd felt in myself at one point in my life. I think that's why I was drawn to you, beyond you being a patient and needing my help."

"I'm not sure I get what you mean. I understand us being friends and honestly you're my best friend now, George. Or my only friend anymore."

Buzzy snickered, bobbing his head. "Believe it or not, I get that. There was a time in my life when I had no one. My parents stood by me and tried to help but I was in a deep hole. It destroyed any relationships I had and almost cost me my life."

"What happened?" Hannah asked, genuinely curious as to what could've done that to Buzzy.

"When I was twenty-three, I was spelunking, cave exploring. We were using equipment and one of my carabiners wasn't fastened correctly, causing my rope to give and fell about thirty feet to the cave floor. I couldn't move and wrenched my neck really badly. They had to take me out on a makeshift gurney. I was in rehab for months and they prescribed Oxycontin for pain. Do you know what that is?"

Hannah shrugged. "Oxy? I've heard of it, yeah. Some kids we partied with used it to get high."

Buzzy chewed his lip, then sighed. "It's good for that. Not so much for pain. At first, it helped but it kept wearing off as my tolerance got higher. By the time my pain was under control, I was hooked."

"On Oxy?"

"Yep. I couldn't stop and when I couldn't get insurance to approve the prescription, I started buying it on the street. When I couldn't afford that I considered heroin."

"You did heroin?"

"No, I considered it. Coming back to random drug testing, I knew I'd lose everything I worked for if I did heroin. I went to my parents and told them everything. They emptied their savings to get me into rehab."

"Did it work?"

"Yes and no. It broke the initial cycle, but as soon as I was out, I wanted to use Oxy again. I was scared. Oxy messes with your brain. It attaches so deeply, you never don't want it. I started researching, but so much of what they use to break the addiction could create a new addiction and prevent me from working in the medical field. That's when I began studying psychedelics in the treatment of opioid addiction."

Hannah listened in awe. "Does it work?"

"Jury's out still on a grand scale but there are studies on it. It did for me."

"Wow, how did you even know to research it?"

"Honestly? I think I was just reading about different drugs and came across Ayahuasca in one of the articles. It was fascinating and it seemed if Oxy had rewired my brain, maybe psychedelics could undo that, or rewire it to a healthy state."

"So, you took Ayahuasca? How did you get that?"

"I came here. To Mexico. I researched and found Miguel. He is trained to administer it in a ceremony, so I reached out to him. He was very adamant that it was not recreational and can bring up terrible things. I told him about my addiction and he agreed to have me come to observe a ceremony. If after that, I was still wanting to go through the process, I could stay with him to prepare myself to be open to the tea ceremony."

"How did you not lose your healthcare certificate?" Hannah inquired, knowing the risk involved.

"Well, the Oxycontin was prescribed originally, so it wasn't illegal on the books. I took a month's leave of absence to come here and stayed with Miguel and his partner Sebastián. It was therapy of sorts. I stayed until after the ceremony and by the time I came home, I was alright to go back to work."

"Does Ayahuasca not show in a drug test?"

"It'd been almost a month since I'd gone through the ceremony before I was tested, so it didn't show. Not sure it ever does. To be safe, I made sure there was a long period between."

"Do you still do it?"

"Ayahuasca? Only ceremonially to make sure I don't relapse on Oxy. No more than once every couple years. I save my vacation and come here, stay with Sebastián and Miquel, do the ceremony, then travel the remaining time," Buzzy explained.

"I don't even know what to say. It sounds like something out of a movie. Do you ever think about Oxycontin?"

"I'd be a liar if I said I didn't. But it's different now. Like a constant niggling in the back of my brain, instead of screaming banshee, if that makes sense."

"I guess. I don't really know. I never touched anything like that. I did ecstasy but not enough to feel I needed it. Only at parties and concerts. You said it ruined your relationships?"

"Sort of. The whole process did. I told you I was in a long-term relationship? She stood by me during my Oxy days, mostly because of the pain and prescription aspect of it. Once I did Ayahuasca, I changed. Everything about me. I began to see the world differently, developed a different level of empathy and understanding. I suppose we just grew apart because of it. She was very by the book and felt that even considering psychedelics was illegal and too out there. Before long, I felt like when I talked to her about the world, she was just irritated by me." Buzzy laughed bitterly. "I became too radical."

Radical? That's not how Hannah would describe Buzzy at all. He was gentle and thoughtful. He considered more than his point of view and held more patience than anyone she'd ever met. He was the epitome of balance. She tried to imagine him addicted to Oxy but it seemed far-fetched. He didn't even drink alcohol. The image of him trying to score heroin was a stark contrast to the man sitting next to her. She watched him for a minute, then spoke softly.

"George, no matter the journey to get where you are now, you have something to offer. I can't imagine not having you in my life. I'm glad you beat your addiction."

Buzzy smiled, his eyes holding a sadness she'd not seen before. "I didn't beat it. I learned to live with it in my head, but not my body. I closed a door in the house I still live in."

# CHAPTER TEN

The first night, they parked the RV in a small parking area off the road on the edge of the ocean. It was devoid of any people, so they made their way out to the beach and looked around. Unlike American beaches, there were no shops or buildings of any kind. Just the beach and the ocean. They spread a blanket out and sat watching the waves roll in. Hannah hadn't felt this at peace in over a year, if ever. Buzzy built a small fire with wood he collected from the beach and they ate canned food they'd purchased at a store in a town they'd passed through. Suddenly, home felt a world away and Hannah attempted to ignore the panic rising in her chest. She focused on the flames of the fire and steadied her breathing. Buzzy noticing, got her attention.

"Hey, you doing alright?"

"I just realized how far from home I am and it made me feel like I was drifting out into space. Disconnected. Stupid, I know."

"Nah, not stupid. This is far from home. Still on the same planet, though. I felt that way the first time I came. Being raised in America doesn't teach you about being part of a whole planet," Buzzy agreed.

"No, it doesn't. I'm fine, though. At least I'm not alone. You came here by yourself the first time?"

"I did. Probably not the smartest decision. I was fine, but I didn't speak fluent Spanish and didn't know my way around. I was pretty lost."

"Do you speak fluent Spanish now?"

"A fair amount between school and being here. Miguel and Sebastián have become like family to me, so we talk on the phone at least once a week. I can't wait for you to meet them."

Hannah was nervous about meeting anyone new, especially people who spoke a different language and had a different culture than her. She'd been so sheltered from everything growing up. They lived in the same house, on the same street, in the same town her whole life. Even choosing a language in high school was just to check off a requirement. Wanting to change subjects, she thought back to what Buzzy said about spelunking.

"So, how did you get into cave exploring?"

"Oh, I guess we always did it when I was growing up. My father showed us at a young age and took us regionally all the time and to somewhere new at least once a year," Buzzy answered.

"That's wild. My parents are so boring. My mother made me wear sunscreen even if I was playing in the backyard. If I spent the night at someone's house, she'd call to check up on me." Hannah laughed, thinking back on her very protected, unexciting childhood.

"Yikes. My father was always pushing us to the edge. To challenge ourselves. It's probably why I got hurt."

"What do you mean?"

"That day, we were seeing who could move the fastest. We were always competing with each other, my older brother and I. We were speeding through, not paying enough attention. I could see he was going to beat me and got sloppy with my equipment. I knew it, too, but took the risk anyway. I was young and dumb." At this, Buzzy blushed with embarrassment.

"Young and dumb seem to go together often. Do you still do it?"

"Spelunking? Nah, not in a long time. I'll go in where it doesn't require equipment but I'll admit, I'm spooked to try with equipment again." Buzzy stared out at the ocean, then shrugged. "Look where it got me."

Hannah didn't know how to reply and considered where it got him. "Well, you are here with me, so it can't be all bad. If you ever wanted to go, I'd try it."

Buzzy turned to look at her and raised his brows. "Really? I may hold you to that."

"Hold me to it. I need to get out of my bubble."

Buzzy chuckled. "I think you are doing that now. There are some walk-in caves we can check out here in Mexico if you want."

"I'd like that. George, I want you to know how much I appreciate you coming on this journey with me. I would've never had the guts to do it alone. I can't say I'm glad I was hospitalized, however, I'm glad I met you through it. You're so open and honest about everything."

"Yeah? I'm glad to have met you, too, even if it was the way it was. You know, Hannah, we all have to go down that hole and find ourselves. Or at least a lot of us. I'd like to think I went from exploring physical caves to the caves of my mind through all this. The brain has a lot of dark space we don't know about."

"Isn't that the truth? I had this one view on life before all this, now I have a completely different one. But I'm still lost in those caves, searching for a way out." Hannah was surprised by her own words and laughed nervously.

Buzzy reached out, touching her hand. "That's why we're here, okay?"

Hannah was shocked to feel tears pricking at her eyes and stared down to hide them until she composed herself. She nodded, digging her fingers in the sand. "Thanks, George."

They fell silent as the sky became dark. Buzzy fed the fire and Hannah rested back on the blanket, closing her eyes. Buzzy knew to keep an eye on her if she fell asleep, as wandering away in nowhere Mexico was dangerous. She didn't know when she'd fallen asleep but was awoken by someone yelling loudly in her face. She opened her eyes to the barrel of a gun and caught her breath before she screamed. Buzzy was up and talking fast in Spanish to what appeared to be Mexican police soldiers. Hannah tried to understand what was going on, but they were talking too fast for her to make out any words. Buzzy was pointing at the RV as he moved toward Hannah. He put his hand down to her, which she gratefully took and stood up. The soldiers were waving their guns, pointing for them to leave.

Buzzy grabbed their blanket and squeezed Hannah's hand. They moved toward the RV with the soldiers following closely behind, their guns still on them. Hannah stumbled in the sand and Buzzy pulled her up next to him tightly, guiding them forward. Once inside the RV, Buzzy fired up the engine and drove out of the area.

As they got back on the main road, he eyed Hannah carefully. "I'm sorry, Hannah. I must've dozed off and they came upon us. I'm usually better about being on guard. Are you alright?"

"No. What the hell was that all about?" Hannah wrung her hands together, breathing in slowly to quell her heart palpitations.

"No one is allowed on the beach," he answered flatly.

"Why?" Hannah stared at him in shock.

"Uh, I didn't get that far. They just kept yelling we were trespassing and we couldn't be there. I didn't ask questions."

"That scared me to death. Do they always put guns in civilians' faces?"

"If they want to. Sorry. I should've stayed awake. I was trying to let you rest and lay back to watch the stars. I fell asleep, which was stupid," Buzzy explained, his voice full of regret.

"No, you have the right to rest. Couldn't they have just told us without all the drama?" Hannah replied with exasperation.

"Things are different here. I won't let it happen again."

They drove for a while until they found a campground and pulled in. Buzzy paid the woman at the cantina and they eased into a spot. Hannah took the upper bed and Buzzy converted the couch into the other bed. He peered up as he lay back and smiled at her.

"Sorry again. I know better. We'll stick to clearly marked areas. Get some rest and I'll show you some cool spots in the morning."

Hannah yawned and drew a blanket over her. "You won't get me arrested, will you?"

Buzzy snickered, shaking his head. "I certainly hope not."

They slept until almost noon. By the time Hannah woke up and shook away the cobwebs, Buzzy had coffee made and handed her a cup. She sipped it gratefully, gazing out the window.

"Where are we?"

"Near Tampico," Buzzy replied.

"Oh. That doesn't mean much to me, I guess. Where are we going?"

"We're heading down to the Yucatan Peninsula."

"Again, not sure why I'm asking. I have no idea where any of that is." Hannah shrugged and sighed, trusting Buzzy on their trip.

Buzzy pulled out a map and showed her where they were, where they were going. He traced his finger along the route from where they entered Mexico to where they'd end up.

Hannah peered at the unfamiliar expanse. "How long will that take?"

"Well, straight driving time is about twenty-one hours. But we are going to see things along the way. It's all part of the journey. We'll get there in about three or four days. Then we will stay with Miguel and Sebastián for a few days before we head back. We'll do things all along the way. I have a lot to show you."

"Lead the way. Where do you think we might find more information about that mask from my dream?"

"Not sure exactly, but I thought we'd look at places as we went. I've seen a lot of masks here and I think if we keep our eyes peeled, we may be able to track it down. If nothing else, Miguel is an expert on the culture and could help."

After coffee, Hannah headed for the campground bathrooms and paused to watch a group of children playing. They were taking turns swinging a child in a hammock around and around, singing a song, and laughing. After a few turns, a different child would get in and it would start all over again. Hannah went on to the bathroom, thinking about how easily children could entertain themselves, no matter where they were. They used whatever was around them.

She used the bathroom and washed in the concrete shower. It didn't have a door or curtains and while she felt self-conscious, she stank too much to give it a second thought. Besides, she didn't know when they'd be near showers again. She toweled off and threw on fresh clothes. Another woman came in, smiling shyly, and went toward the shower. Wanting to give the woman privacy, Hannah headed back out. As she came around the side of the building, she again saw the children playing their game.

This time a small, dark-haired boy was watching them from around a tree, his eyes intent on them. As Hannah moved past them, she saw the boy was not observing the children anymore, though. He was watching her as she passed by them, his eyes focused and alert. She stopped and stared for a moment, about to practice her Spanish *hello* on him.

Just as she opened her mouth, the word caught in her throat in almost a scream. Hannah felt like the world around her slipped into an alternate reality and she clutched the clothing in her hands as if it would hold her in place.

The boy wasn't one of the local children.

He was the boy from her dream.

# CHAPTER ELEVEN

H annah didn't remember how she got back to the camper but when Buzzy found her, she was sitting on the fold-out steps, rocking back and forth with her arms wound tightly around her. He didn't say anything and sat down next to her. She stared at her feet, deciding if she'd seen what she thought she'd seen. She took a deep breath and glanced at Buzzy. His eyes were concerned but he remained quiet.

Hannah cleared her throat. "Do you think worlds can cross? Like spiritual and non-spiritual realms?"

Buzzy eyed her, considering where she was going with that, then nodded. "Of course. We're taught to believe what we see here is so concrete, however, other cultures embrace the fluidity between the worlds. Why do you ask?"

Hannah laughed and thought about how crazy what she was about to say would sound. "I saw the boy from my dream. Like, I saw him just yards away from me."

"Oh? Here?" If Buzzy was surprised, he didn't let on.

"Yeah, when I went to take a shower. I came back out and watched the kids playing. I noticed this young boy standing off to the side and went to say hello to him when I recognized him."

"Did he speak to you?" Buzzy asked, his voice gentle and soothing.

"I have no idea. My brain must've done that thing where it spaces out segments of time. The next thing I remember, I was back here."

Buzzy gazed off in the direction of the shower. "Do you want to walk back over there? See if we see him again?"

Hannah didn't, however, knew she needed to start facing whatever was going on and stop running. She glanced over to the area where she'd seen the boy and while she saw the other children playing, she didn't see the boy. She nodded and stood up. Buzzy got up and held her. Normally, she'd push off any type of physical affection that wasn't connected to a romantic relationship, but his arms felt nice around her and she allowed them to comfort her. He gave her a squeeze, then let go.

"It's just a walk. We can head down along the beach, too. The cantina is open, so why don't we grab some food to go and make it an adventure?" Buzzy offered.

Hannah laughed. Everything with Buzzy so far had been an adventure. "Sure, George."

They ordered food at the cantina as Hannah took time to appreciate their surroundings. The cantina was in the center of the campground and palm trees swayed all around them. Each camp area had a picnic table, grill, and firepit, yet the cantina was still the place of action. The food was basic–tamales, taquitos, burritos, and general American fare thrown in to appease the tourists. Buzzy ordered a selection of local food and paid.

Hannah was interested to see they accepted American money, as well, and the girl behind the counter spoke clear English. She was telling Buzzy something and making eyes at him, which made Hannah smile. His reddish-blond hair and hazel eyes seemed to draw a lot of attention.

Once the food was ready, Buzzy collected the bags and handed Hannah two bottles of soda. They headed toward the shower area which had a boardwalk to the beach. Hannah scanned for the boy but only saw a group of local children playing what looked like tag. While the boy had dark hair and eyes like them, his skin was lighter. She would've noticed him immediately. She paused, then walked around the tree she'd seen him standing behind. Something on the ground caught her eye. It was a small stone with letters on it. She picked it up and held it in her hand, trying to make out the word. Segura. She didn't know what it meant and walked over to Buzzy.

"Hey, George. Do you know what this means?" she asked, holding out the rock toward him.

He took the stone and peered at it. "Hmmm... segura. I think it's the Spanish feminine of the word *safe*. Not sure why it would be written on a stone."

"Maybe part of a child's game or something? I don't know. I found this over by the tree where I saw the boy. Do you think it's connected?"

Buzzy eyed her. "Question is, do you?"

Hannah considered it, her mind saying no but something deep in her telling it was. She nodded. "Maybe. Either way, I like the word. I haven't felt safe in a long time."

"Do you now?"

Hannah shrugged. "Well, waking up to have men pointing guns at us, not so much. But for some reason, being here with you I do... at least more than I have. If that makes sense."

"It does. Regardless of the pitfalls of this trip, I believe you are on a journey you're supposed to be on, Hannah. I also promise I'll keep an eye on you. I know this is all new to you and I messed up back on the beach, but I won't let it happen again. I'll keep you safe."

Hannah pushed down the independent part of her that wanted to argue with him, to tell him she could take care of herself. She could and he knew that, but it was also nice to have someone on her team. With Parker, they were just kids, figuring out their adult world. Parker was fun, they had great times together, however, neither of them even knew what it meant to be on the other's team. They played alongside each other, each with their own goals in mind. She grinned at Buzzy.

"Team George."

He laughed, shaking his head. "I have no idea what you mean, but it's team *us*."

"Team *us*. Team Amigo."

"See, you know some Spanish," Buzzy teased.

"Only what I learned from cartoons," Hannah replied, only half joking.

They wandered down to the beach, which took Hannah's breath away. The water was so blue and gently lapped against the sand. She was amazed she could see down to the bottom and ran her hand through the warm water. It was like a picture on a postcard. *Wish you were here.* She was here. On a beach in Mexico. With a guy she met in a mental ward. It was almost too surreal. She turned to see Buzzy standing with his eyes closed, his face turned up to the sun. In his tank top and board shorts, he looked like he should be in a movie about surfing. He opened his eyes and grinned at her.

"You hungry?"

"Seriously? Yes!"

They sat on the soft, fine sand and pulled food out of the bags. Whatever Buzzy ordered smelled amazing and Hannah popped the sodas open, twisting them in the sand to create bottle holders. Buzzy handed her a tamale in a wrapper and she took a bite. It was like nothing she'd ever had. Delicate and spicy. Her family had made tacos and eaten at Mexican restaurants, but it was nothing like this. As they ate, a large white and gray bird flew across the water in front of them, its wings outstretched as its stomach grazed the top of the water. It was huge and seemed too big to fly.

"Albatross," Buzzy said.

"It is? Wow, I've never seen one before."

"Surprising to see one now. They are endangered or threatened, at least. So beautiful," Buzzy murmured.

Hannah agreed as she watched the bird disappear out of view. They ate the rest of the meal in silence, mesmerized by the view in front of them. Hannah yawned as the food caused heaviness in her. Adventure or not, she was exhausted and needed to sleep. She stood up, brushing the sand off her, and peered down at Buzzy.

"I'm going to go grab a nap back at the RV. I feel like I'm still trying to catch back up."

"Sure thing. I'm going for a hike but will be quiet when I come back. I wanted to show you something at dusk."

"Sounds good. I'll see you in a couple of hours."

Buzzy stood up and stretched, collecting their trash. Hannah put her hand out and took it from him. "I got it. You go, have a nice hike."

He smiled and nodded. As he walked away from her on the beach, she had no doubt he was sent to her to help her get through all of the trauma she'd been through. She headed back up to the camp, stopping at a trash can to throw away the wrappers. She placed the bottles in a recycle bin and glanced back at Buzzy, making his way down the beach. He was just a blip in the distance, yet she still felt close to him. The stone in her pocket weighed against her leg and she smiled. Segura. Safe.

A few hours later, Hannah woke up from the deepest sleep she'd had in a long time. She felt disoriented and sat up, glancing around the camper. It was still light out but the sun was starting to set in the sky. She could hear activities ramping up at the cantina as music and laughter filled the air. She brushed the tangled mess her hair had become and weaved it into two braids. Checking her reflection in the tiny, plastic mirror above the sink, she noticed she'd gotten some sun. Still, she looked fourteen. The braids didn't help. Shrugging it off, she put on lip gloss, a fresh blouse, and skirt. Mexico was a whole different kind of hot.

She wandered toward the cantina and saw Buzzy dancing with the girl from earlier, who'd taken their order. He was laughing and the girl had her eyes set on him. Hannah, not wanting to interrupt, made her way to the counter and ordered a drink. She watched Buzzy dancing and smiled to herself. He had no inhibitions, no worries about the outside world. He was present in the world and with himself. He caught her eyes and waved, then focused back on the girl in front of him. Hannah took her drink and meandered outside of the cantina, watching the children running around. They'd sometimes pick up small pebbles and throw them in the air. When they did, something would swoop down, then disappear. The sun dropped and the sky was turning gray, so Hannah wasn't sure what creature she was looking at.

"That's what I wanted to show you," Buzzy's voice said from behind her.

Hannah turned to face him. "What is that?"

"Bats. The kids throw pebbles and the bats think it's bugs, so they swoop down."

"Oh, that doesn't seem very nice. To trick them like that?"

"Nah. But you know kids, they don't think like that. Besides, bats are smarter than us. They know pretty quickly," Buzzy replied, tapping the side of his head. "Maybe they are playing the game."

A shudder went through Hannah. Everything she knew about bats was negative, so she wasn't sure if she should be standing there. "Will they hurt us?"

"The bats? No, they're just living their life. Bats are pretty docile. I think movies have made them out to be vicious, but they're really very sweet."

Hannah watched the flutter of wings as they dove down and wasn't so sure. Did they bite? Buzzy, noticing her discomfort, came closer and pointed at one of the trees.

"They are hanging out there. They don't want to harm anyone. They only bite if they feel unsafe. Like mice with wings."

Hannah peered at the tree and the creatures flying in and out. They didn't seem harmful. She liked the thought of mice with wings. "Have you ever held one?"

"I have. I've been around them a lot, cave exploring and here. They are super beneficial to us. They also aren't blind like a lot of people believe. They just see things differently, the way they need to, to survive. Some people here believe they have a special purpose. There's a folklore that says they carry the souls of the dead into the afterlife."

Hannah watched the bats with a new form of appreciation. Not only were they not there to harm, they could be there to help. So much of what she believed growing up was shifting, opening her mind to different possibilities. Everything around her had a purpose and wasn't merely background scenery. Nothing existed just for humans, but everything affected the world they lived in. On a physical level, but perhaps even on a spiritual level as the folklore expressed.

Hannah saw a bat swoop down near her, this time catching some sort of insect to eat. She could see it closer, its small black eyes catching a reflection in the rising moonlight. *They see things differently to survive.* That she could relate to. As if seeming to sense her presence, the bat flew by her head. Hannah quenched her fear and watched it, wondering how it saw the world. She tried to imagine the world through bat eyes, flying through the dark. Maybe to a bat, the dark *was* the light.

As the sun finished its trek into the night, the bats began to vanish into the dark. Hannah strained to see where they went but could no longer make their forms out against the night sky. She knew they were still out there, as their time was just beginning. They'd be out long after the world went to sleep, doing their work.

Carrying the dead.

# CHAPTER TWELVE

*T*he dream started out like the day before on the beach. Hannah was walking along the shoreline. It was sunny and warm, she liked the way the water trickled between her toes as the low waves came in. She could see Buzzy ahead of her. He didn't seem to notice she was there. He began to move at a faster pace, focused on a set direction. Hannah watched him creating distance between them and tried to increase her speed. Her eye caught the movement of a boat out on the ocean, anchored not too far offshore. She paused and stared at the boat. An old man was standing facing her, his skin worn and leathered from years in the sun. She lifted her hand in a wave and he stared back, shaking his head. Not in condemnation, she thought... a warning. He turned and disappeared into the hull of the boat. She spun around to see where Buzzy went and saw his form heading off the beach into the tree line.

"George!" she called out, however, her voice faded into the air. She tried to run to catch up with him but her feet continued their slow pace. By the time she got to where she'd observed him leaving the beach, there were only footprints to follow. They vanished at the tree line and she considered not stepping into the lush forest. A movement caught her eye and she followed a small, overgrown path toward it. By the time she got to where she'd seen it, she was alone and the beach no longer existed.

Hannah glanced at her surroundings as fear gripped her stomach. How would she ever get back? How would she ever get home? Plants behind her had covered the path and there was nowhere to go but forward. She continued wandering the thin path until she came to the opening of a cave. She was afraid to go in. What might be in there, ready to seize her? She sat on a rock outside the wide mouth and began to cry. She couldn't do this alone. Why did Buzzy leave her behind? Now, she was lost. A light flickered in the depths of the cave. Hannah wiped her face and stood up, moving closer to the opening. There it was again. Just a flash, as if someone lit a lighter. She walked into the opening, letting her eyes adjust. Bats flew out as she entered, screeching back at her.

The cave was magnificent. From the light coming in from outside, she could see drawings on the wall. Ancient people, she thought. As she moved closer, she saw the scribbling more clearly. While they looked old, they couldn't be. There were buildings and cars scratched on the stone walls. Then it caught her eye. A motorcycle on its side. And a body. Or bodies. The motorcyclist, the boy, and a baby. She gasped and drew back. Her mind tried to understand how these could be in the cave. She glanced back at the stone wall and her eyes grew wide.

Above the scene was a larger figure. A monster with a large, gaping mouth, jagged teeth, and long, sharp fingernails. It hovered over the bodies, laughing. Hannah peered closer. The monster had a round face and long golden-brown hair. It was wearing her clothes.

She was the monster.

*She was* the monster.

Hannah went to run out of the cave but the opening was gone. She was down in the depths and began to scream. Running down a pathway, she found herself deeper and deeper within the heavy contoured walls. She hit dead ends every turn she made and knew she'd never see daylight again. She crouched against the wall, hyperventilating when a flash of light caught her eye. She stood and moved toward it. It took her toward a room in the cave.

There she saw Buzzy with his back to her. He was talking to someone, his hands raised in expression. He tipped his head back, laughing. Not Buzzy's laugh. Not gentle and kind. Mean. Vengeful. He shifted slightly and Hannah was able to see who he was speaking to. The motorcyclist. She caught her breath and took a step back. All of a sudden, Buzzy turned toward her, his eyes cold and hard. The motorcyclist raised his arm and pointed at her, his arm no longer flesh and blood. Only bone. Buzzy nodded and moved toward Hannah as she tried to run. She tripped over a rock and fell back hard on the ground. As she scrambled away, Buzzy bore down on her. He reached out to grab her, his fingers turning to bone.

Hannah sat up in the bed, smacking her head painfully against the low roof of the camper from the space above the driving cab where she was sleeping. She could hear herself moaning in terror and Buzzy was standing beside her, his face at the level of the mattress. He reached out and she jerked away, pushing herself to the far back of the wall. His eyes were concerned and he dropped his hand.

"Hannah, it's just a nightmare. You're okay." His voice was soothing.

Not like the Buzzy she'd just been trying to get away from. Hannah shook her head as she felt tears stream down her cheek. For all she knew, she could still be in that other world, still dreaming. The man on the boat tried to warn her.

About Buzzy?

"Why did you bring me here?" Her words were scared and shaky.

Buzzy tipped his head in confusion. "To Mexico?"

She nodded and waited. He shook his head but didn't speak at first. Finally, he sighed, then took a step back.

"You asked me to, Hannah. Don't you remember?"

As the dream faded and reality began to creep in, she remembered. She *had* asked him to. The dream about the ice cream truck and the boy. The boy. She remembered the drawings on the cave wall and began to sob. After all, *she* was the monster. She'd killed the motorcyclist and her baby because she didn't want it. The boy was dead in the drawing, too. She didn't know the boy and certainly hadn't killed him. Why was Buzzy conspiring with the motorcyclist and chasing her?

Buzzy could see she was hurting, however, made no move to touch her, knowing she needed to process the dream. He went to heat water, his back to her. She watched him from her perch and the fear began to subside. Nightmare Buzzy wasn't real Buzzy. But still. What if he had ulterior motives? He made them each a cup of tea and brought her one. He handed it up to her and she shook her head.

"No, let me come down. Can I sit with you?" Hannah asked, feeling embarrassed about her reaction earlier.

"Of course," Buzzy replied, setting the tea on the table. The couch had been converted to his bed and he sat on the edge. "Do you want me to put the bed up to sit on the couch?"

"No, it's fine. We can sit on the bed." Hannah climbed down and stood awkwardly for a moment. "I'm sorry, George."

"Do you want to tell me about the dream?" Buzzy asked.

Hannah shook her head, then sat on the bed. Buzzy handed her the tea and she clasped it in her hands. They sat sipping in silence when she finally felt ready to tell him.

"I was walking along the beach and saw you up ahead. There was this old man on a boat and he was trying to warn me about something. When I looked back, you were gone and I went to find you. I ended up at a cave. There were these drawings on the wall. Modern drawings. Bad things." Hannah shuddered at the memory.

"Bad how?"

"Bodies. The motorcyclist, a baby, and the boy. There was this monster hovering over them. *I* was the monster."

"Oh." Buzzy shifted to sit cross-legged on the bed, facing Hannah. "Perhaps you're processing everything that occurred?"

"Maybe. It gets worse, though. I got lost in the cave and came to this room-like space. You were there with your back to me. When you moved, I saw you were with the motorcyclist. You weren't you, though. More like an evil twin version of you. The motorcyclist was transforming into a skeleton and pointed at me.

He wasn't like Logan Slip, either. He was sinister, soulless. You came after me, like to hurt me, I think." Hannah eyed Buzzy, who visibly flinched at this.

"I would never hurt you," Buzzy said, his voice just above a whisper.

Hannah knew that. She thought she did anyway. As the power of the dream eased, she could see the Buzzy she knew. It was hard to disconnect from the imagery of him standing over her with hatred in his eyes, however, sitting there the two were not one and the same. They appeared the same but that's where the similarity ended. She smiled, her face feeling wobbly.

"I know. It was terrifying, but I know, George. You're my best friend. I don't know what the dream meant, but I know you aren't that person."

Buzzy watched her, his eyes sad. "I hate you even having that image of me now. I promise you I only brought you to Mexico to help you find answers. I want you to know you are safe with me. I think the world of you, Hannah."

Safe. Segura. She was safe with Buzzy. She didn't know what the dream meant if anything. Maybe it was just fear taking a hold of her mind. She nodded and breathed out heavily. Now that the nightmare faded, she felt sleep weighing on her again. She glanced up at her bed and anxiety crept in. She couldn't go back up there.

"Thank you, George. For being here for me. For putting up with my craziness. You said once that perhaps we're everyone in our dreams. Maybe it's all me losing my mind."

"You aren't losing your mind. Your mind is just processing. I do believe in messages in dreams, though. They just aren't what we first perceive. Sometimes it represents something else. Do you journal your dreams?"

"I haven't. I probably should. They haven't always been like this. So vivid. Just since..." she trailed off.

"Being here might make them more so. You're opening up to new paths, new ideas."

Hannah thought about that. It was true. She was seeking answers, which could be stimulating different parts of her brain. She yawned and set her teacup down. "Hey, do you mind if I lie here, instead of up there? I'm scared to be alone."

Buzzy frowned and looked at his small bed. "With me?"

"Yeah." Hannah laughed. "I won't put moves on you or anything. I just can't go back up there."

Buzzy smiled, setting his cup down. "It's a tight squeeze, but sure."

They lay down and he wasn't kidding. If they both were on their back, they were edge to edge. Hannah rolled on her side, facing Buzzy. He pulled a sheet over them. Hannah felt the draw of sleep coming over her and watched him for a moment. He was clearly unsure what to do with himself, in order to give her space.

"I don't mind if our bodies touch, George. We're friends, it's alright."

Buzzy visibly relaxed and his body settled into the mattress. Hannah rested her forehead against his shoulder, sighing. He placed his hand on the back of her head and chuckled. Hannah fell into a dreamless sleep, warmed by the safety of their proximity.

When she woke up, Buzzy was reading in one of the dining chairs. He didn't notice her awake, so she watched him.

He had his hair loose and tucked behind his ears. He was intent on the book he was reading, his brow furrowed. The sunlight danced across his face, catching the copper in his eyes. He rubbed his nose, deep in thought and Hannah smiled to herself. He was one of a kind. He turned the page, tapping the table with his finger.

"Whatcha reading?" she asked and propped herself up on her elbow.

Buzzy met her eyes and grinned. "Hey. I'm glad you got some more sleep. Reading this book on the ruins in Mexico."

"What exactly are ruins?"

"Yeah, like really old structures built by ancient cultures. There is a lot of lore around their purpose and history. Very mystical. I thought we could visit some sites to see if we could track down some information that might help. If nothing else, they are fascinating to see. Dark sometimes, but like nothing else."

"Dark how?"

Buzzy tipped his head, thinking. "Well, like some of the history of human sacrifice is pretty disturbing."

Hannah wrinkled her nose. Human sacrifice? She wasn't sure she wanted to dig into that type of stuff. Buzzy peered at her, concerned.

"We don't have to go, Hannah. I mean, I hadn't thought about that. It might be triggering."

"No. We should go. I'm already having nightmares and scary visions. Maybe it will help."

Buzzy sat back in his chair, eyeing her. "I need to tell you something."

Hannah sat up in bed, running her fingers through her hair to detangle it. "Okay?"

"Last night, I had a dream, too. I didn't tell you because I didn't want to freak you out."

"Is it bad?"

"Yes and no. In the dream, you were in danger. I tried to save you, but I couldn't. I was being told I could only protect you if you went through a trial."

"A trial. Like a court trial?" Hannah asked, confused.

Buzzy shook his head. "Not exactly. More like a trial of the soul."

Hannah stared at him. What did that even mean? A trial of the soul. Like judgment day? "I don't understand."

"I don't totally, either, but in the dream I was told you'd need to go through an intense spiritual journey, which wouldn't be easy. That you might not come out of it."

"What do you mean, not come out of it? How?"

Buzzy shifted to take her hand, holding it tightly in his own. "No matter what, Hannah, I'll be there with you. The whole way. We'll do this together."

"Not come out of it how, George?"

"Mentally."

# CHAPTER THIRTEEN

They packed up and headed out of the campground. It didn't escape Hannah's notice, the pretty girl from the cantina was sad to see Buzzy leave and handed him a note. Hannah would've teased him about it, but her head was elsewhere. What he told her about his dream scared her, mostly because she was already wondering if she was losing her mind. Slipping to a deep, dark place she couldn't come back from. Seeing Logan Slip, the boy, the baby. It all made her wonder what was real and what was her fading more and more from reality. Buzzy was quiet, lost in thought. While that wasn't unusual, the reason was. His face was grim as he finished making sure the campsite was clear. Hannah sat on the picnic table and stared out at the ocean. What next?

"Hey, you ready?" Buzzy asked low and soft.

Hannah sighed, then climbed off the table. Ready for what? The end of life as she knew it? Sensing her mood, Buzzy came over and wrapped his arms around her. No matter what, he was with her, by her side. He wouldn't let her just disappear into insanity. In her whole life, she'd never had a friend like him. A calm, steady force. She'd called other girls best friends in school, even though all they shared was about their crushes and favorite music. Parker had been a friend but only in the good times. She was an only child and her parents, while loving, were supportive to an extent. There were often things she felt she couldn't share with them.

Even when she snapped after killing Logan Slip and losing the baby, her parents were the first to support hospitalization but couldn't talk to her about what was going on in her head. They seemed almost afraid. She caught the furtive glances between them, unspoken messages about her, passing back and forth. They hugged her and told her everything would be okay, not convincingly. She was on a boat and they were on the shore.

She drew back and peered at Buzzy, mouthing the words, "thank you". He nodded and took her hand, leading her to the RV. In the distance, she saw the cantina girl frown, disappearing back behind the counter. Hannah wanted to let her know she had nothing to worry about, that Hannah and Buzzy were just friends. Regardless, they likely wouldn't be back that way anyhow. They were just passing through. There would be plenty of cantina girls in Buzzy's future. Hannah slid into the passenger seat, then looked at Buzzy.

"Where to?"

He glanced at the map and ran his finger along a road. He met her eyes and smiled. "Miguel and Sebastián are still at least a day's drive away, so I thought we could visit some ruins on the way? Ancient sites. We can start with El Tajin which is about three hours from here."

Hannah shuddered. Something about visiting the ruins made her uneasy. She nodded, unsure, then picked up the book Buzzy brought about the ruins. She flipped to the page about El Tajin and began reading. Pre-hispanic, mesoamerican city. Pyramid. It read like a textbook and she wasn't getting anything from it. She closed the book and rested her head back against the seat. Buzzy was humming to himself, focused on the road. Hannah watched him for a moment, wondering what was going on in his head. Did he regret coming with her? She could see the note the girl handed him poking out of his pocket and touched his arm.

"That girl. She seemed nice."

Buzzy glanced at her, grinning. "Marisol? She was."

"Have you read the note?"

"Not yet."

"Oh. Do you think you'll see her again?" Hannah asked.

"Not likely. Remember, I come to Mexico regularly. She's not the first pretty girl I've met here. But I don't live here."

"Have you ever thought about staying? Moving to Mexico?"

"I have, but honestly I'm drawn to a lot of cultures. Not just this one. Eventually, I'd like to travel more. Study different cultures and their connections to us," Buzzy explained.

Hannah considered this. It would be fun to travel, but did it pay? "What would you do for money?"

"Million-dollar question, isn't it? It's why I haven't done it yet. I've been saving money and living in an RV is a hell of a lot cheaper than a house or apartment, but still requires some funding. Still figuring that out."

They fell silent and Hannah closed her eyes. What would she do if she had money to do whatever she wanted? Travel sounded nice. Where would she go? While fear about being in unfamiliar places had always been part of her, she'd faced that head-on by coming to Mexico. She'd like to travel around the United States for sure.

She was daydreaming about all of the places she'd visit if she hit the lottery when they pulled into the parking area for El Tajin. Pictures didn't do it justice. Stone formations dotted the landscape, rising out of the ground in intricate patterns. How people with only rudimentary tools built this blew her mind. They got out and stretched, the sun already beating down on them. Vendors were set up in the lot, selling snacks and drinks to the tourists.

"You want anything?" Buzzy asked.

"Sure. Maybe a drink and a snack. What do they have?"

"A variety of things. I'll get a selection and we can eat before we go in."

After a few minutes, Buzzy came back with bags of local food, chips, and soda. They pulled out a blanket and sat on the ground to eat. Hannah opened the chips and took a bite, then laughed.

"Is everything here spicy?"

Buzzy grinned. "Define spicy."

"Haha. I swear everything we have eaten has a kick. It's not a bad thing, I just need to get used to it."

Buzzy pulled out an orange he'd bought from the vendor. It was cut in half and he opened it, handing Hannah half. It was covered in some sort of red powder. She peered at it, seeing Buzzy eating his half. She licked the power, then sucked in her breath.

"What *is* that?"

"Hot chili powder," Buzzy replied, chuckling.

"For fuck's sake. They put chili powder on oranges?"

"Try it, it's really good, Hannah. It's not really spicy, so much as flavorful."

"Whatever you say, George." Hannah took a bite and grimaced. The flavors were not familiar and her brain recoiled. She tried another bite and shook her head. "No."

Buzzy laughed and took the orange she was sticking out to him. "In time it becomes more familiar. You aren't used to the combination. Just be open-minded. Be willing to try things. It's good for the brain."

Hannah watched him scarf down her half of the orange and sighed. "Good for the brain. My brain has reached its limits, I think."

"The brain has no limits. Only our comfort level holds us in place. After all, did you ever think you'd come to Mexico?"

"No. That's true. Somehow that was easier than eating that orange."

Buzzy tipped his head back, roaring with laughter. "You are a strange one, Hannah."

"You are the one eating oranges with chili powder."

"A whole culture does. You'll get there."

They finished eating, then gathered their things to put in the camper and began walking the grassy paths through the structures. Buzzy explained different techniques and history as they went. It was fascinating, however, Hannah didn't see anything which made her think of her dream. She was in awe of the buildings and how every little element of the earth seemed to be taken into consideration when they were constructed. Where the sun rose and went down, the topography, the weather. She shook her head in amazement at the minute decorative details.

"I don't get it. How did humans with so little at their disposal go from building this to humans with everything at their disposal building shit structures that collapse in heavy winds?"

"Right?" Buzzy agreed. "My guess is *why* we build things. They were building things to last, to show their appreciation for their world. It was part of their culture. Most people build things nowadays for money. Quick and dirty."

By the time they were done wandering through the city of ruins, Hannah thought the term ruins didn't do them justice. She'd seen more ruins from shoddy work and disregard in their modern-day world than here. Here was beautiful. Strong and intricate. Every detail was thought out. The people who'd lived here were long gone, but their work stood as a testament to what humans *could* do if they put their minds to it. She was glad to have Buzzy as a guide because there weren't many signs. She wouldn't have known what she was looking at without him. Some of the structures seemed too lavish for their purpose.

"How did they do this? Like, how did they move such heavy stones and cut things so cleanly without modern tools?" she asked, staring at the pyramid with all of its tiny windows.

"There are a lot of theories. Some believe they just did it, no matter how long it took or how hard it was. Some believe they had tools given to them, had help."

"From who?" Hannah was confused.

Buzzy eyed her. "Aliens."

Hannah busted out laughing, thinking he was joking. He raised his brows, cocking his head. Hannah stopped in her tracks. "Seriously?"

"It's a theory. Not too far-fetched if you think about it."

"Is that what you believe?"

Buzzy shrugged. "I try to stay away from hard and fast beliefs. Do I think it's possible? Sure. Do I think it's possible we underestimate how ancient cultures lived, convincing ourselves they were less intelligent or civilized than us? Absolutely. These weren't cavemen, grunting and pointing. These were highly advanced civilizations."

Hannah felt shame creeping up, making her ears hot. In her mind they were just above cavemen, grunting and pointing. She hadn't thought of them as structured, intelligent societies, working with what they had. Buzzy wasn't reprimanding her, however, she knew she was guilty of those beliefs. They wandered back to the camper and climbed in. Buzzy picked up the map, checking the time.

"We still have time to visit another site today. Cempoala. Another village. You up for it?"

Hannah nodded. "For sure. This is all so fascinating."

"I'm glad I get to show this to you. I think I've bored everyone to tears with my stories about my travels. Afterward, we can find a place to camp for the night. I'll make you dinner," Buzzy promised and started the engine.

Cempoala was different from El Tajin, with large stone circles outside of a flat-topped pyramid. The site was built near the river and elevated on grassy mounds. Hannah was fascinated by the stone circle and walked around it, feeling somehow connected. Buzzy explained the purpose of the circles, the smaller being for fire and the larger being a fighting ring. She asked about a small, flat, stone structure nearby and he explained that it was for human sacrifice. Hannah stared wide-eyed, trying to imagine a people who regularly sacrificed other humans. It terrified her, yet she couldn't help but feel drawn to it.

A terrible fascination.

By the time they'd seen the site, both were tired and ready to call it day. They drove for a bit but couldn't find a campground, so Buzzy pulled off the main road to a side road and parked the camper. As promised, he made a nice dinner and they rested in bed, talking about the day. Since the night of her nightmare, they'd been sharing his small couch bed, chatting until they fell asleep. Hannah felt safer close to Buzzy and he didn't push the issue.

She'd noticed him reading the note from Marisol earlier. He'd smiled and tucked it in his bag. She respected his privacy and didn't ask, but still, she wondered what the note said. A profession of love? A promise to stay true? It was none of her business, however, since she and Parker had split, she'd felt a loneliness that only comes after being intimate with another person. The little secrets shared. The gentle kisses and deep understanding. The connection without words. Buzzy was her best friend but they still lacked the intimacy only a romantic partner can give.

They drifted off late in the evening and Hannah let her head rest again on Buzzy's shoulder. She needed to not feel alone.

He rested his head against hers as he read from one of the many books he'd brought along on the journey. Hannah drifted off, listening to his breathing and the rhythmic turning of pages.

Hours later she was startled awake by a strange sound. Not sure if she was having a nightmare, she froze, her ears straining to recognize the sound. To determine if her mind was creating it. No, it was coming from outside. The sound of grating metal brought her to her senses and she heard something attempting to pry the camper door open.

They were being attacked!

# CHAPTER FOURTEEN

*B*uzzy was out of the bed and to the door before Hannah had a chance to even yell. Whoever was trying to get in had managed to get a crowbar between the frame and the door, prying it open. Buzzy attempted to hold the door closed and turned to Hannah.

"The keys! They're in my bag, hanging on the back of the driver's seat. Get them and drive!"

Hannah jumped off the bed, scrambling to the front of the RV. She dug through his bag and fished the keys out of the bag. She glanced back, seeing a hand grab Buzzy and yank him out the door. She couldn't leave now. She shoved the keys back in the bag and ran to the back of the camper, peering out the door. There were three men surrounding Buzzy, one wielding the crowbar. Buzzy was barefoot with his hands raised, trying to reason with the men. They were shouting at him, but Hannah couldn't understand what they were saying.

One of the men spied her and a creepy grin broke out on his face. He nudged the guy beside him and they both stared at Hannah with an expression that made her blood run cold. She wrapped her arms around herself protectively, as if she could ward off their thoughts. Buzzy glanced back at her with fear in his eyes and tipped his head.

They were in serious trouble.

One of the men took a swing at Buzzy and Hannah saw him transform into someone she'd never seen before. He moved deftly and grasped the man's hand in his own, twisting it until the man crumpled to the ground in agony. The man with the crowbar swung it at Buzzy's head, hitting him across the forehead. Buzzy stumbled back, disoriented from the blow, and shook his head. Two of the men went toward him, while the other darted toward Hannah. She backed up into the camper, searching for something to protect herself with. She grabbed a can of bug spray and as soon as the man came in the door, she doused him in the eyes with it. He screamed and clutched at his eyes, flailing out of the camper. It wasn't pepper spray, but it slowed him down. She grabbed the machete they stored near the front of the camper and ran out, holding it in front of her.

Buzzy looked like he was in a movie, fighting off the men as they approached, in what appeared to be some sort of martial arts. He managed to control the situation, but being outnumbered, he was starting to lose steam. Hannah ran up, yelling and waving the machete. Buzzy in one single movement, grabbed the machete from her and tucked her behind him. The men paused, unsure of what to do as Buzzy and Hannah backed toward the door. Hannah hit the opening first and bolted in, grabbing the keys out of the bag. As soon as she saw Buzzy was inside, she gunned the engine and pressed the gas pedal to the floor, causing the tires to spin. She eased up and they lurched forward, almost causing Buzzy to fall back out of the door. He closed the door and held it firmly in place as they skidded out onto the road. As soon as it was clear the men weren't following, he made his way to the front and collapsed in the passenger seat.

Hannah had no idea which way she was going but kept driving anyway. As soon as they made it to a town, she pulled off at a gas station and turned the vehicle off. Buzzy was holding his head in his hands, not looking up. She crouched beside him and moved his hands to get a better view. The crowbar had done some damage. He had a large gash across his head and a goose egg the size of a baseball. His left eye had ruptured blood vessels, the skin around it turning purple. Hannah gasped and stood up. Not wanting to leave him, she knew she needed to at least get some ice.

The station attendant peered up at her in shock when she ran in, not used to seeing many people this late.

"Ice?" she asked frantically.

He stared at her confused, then realized what she needed and pointed to the back of the store. She ran back and found a cooler of ice. She grabbed a bag, her eyes darting around for any type of medical supplies. There were none.

"Hospital?" she asked.

He shook his head, they weren't near one. She paid for the ice and ran back to the RV. Buzzy had moved to lie on the bed. She noticed a bowl on the floor near him. He'd vomited and appeared like he might again. She placed the bag of ice on the goose egg and he winced. He waved her away, leaning back over to vomit again. She drew out the map, searching for where they were and the closest hospital. There was one about fifteen miles down the road. She started the camper up and began to drive into the night.

As they drove into Alvarado, she looked for signs for a hospital. The town was quiet and when she finally found the hospital, she wasn't sure it was open. She parked and went to the only door which seemed open and found a sleepy doctor wandering around. He stared at her as if she'd just fallen out of the sky.

"Can you help me?" She didn't know if he spoke English but he followed her when she waved for him to come with her. She led him to the RV and inside where Buzzy was lying on the couch bed.

The doctor went over to him and inspected the wound on his head. Buzzy said something in Spanish to the doctor, who sighed, nodding. He used his pen light to check Buzzy's eyes and helped him sit up. They conversed in Spanish, leaving Hannah with no idea what was happening. The doctor left, holding his finger up to say he'd be back. After he left, Hannah sat beside Buzzy and put her arm around his waist to steady him.

"What did the doctor say?"

"He thinks they fractured my skull. Concussion at a minimum. The x-ray department is closed for the night. I can either stay and wait until morning or assume I have a skull fracture. Either way, there isn't much difference knowing or not. He's going to wrap it and give me some meds. I need to pay him."

"Do they take insurance?"

Buzzy chuckled, touching his head tenderly. "No clue. It doesn't matter, it's cheap. I'll just pay him in cash."

The doctor came back and handed Buzzy a packet of pills. He stitched the wound, then put ointment on it. He wrapped Buzzy's head with gauze and checked his eyes again. Buzzy motioned to Hannah to get his bag. She handed it to him and he drew out money to pay the doctor. The doctor spoke softly to Buzzy like he was speaking to his son, and patted him on the shoulder. Then he left.

Hannah raised her brows. "What did he just say?"

"That we shouldn't be out here alone. He's not wrong. Some places in Mexico are very tourist friendly. Some are more dangerous. We need to stick to areas that are friendly to outsiders. Those men were a gang. The doctor said they are seeing more gangs like that in the rural areas. Preying on unsuspecting tourists and even the locals. They saw the RV and were probably trying to rob us."

"Rob us? They almost killed us, George!"

"The price of the deal. Rob us, kill us. Whatever it takes."

Hannah shuddered. The look the men gave her let her know that wasn't all they would've done to her. The doctor was right, they shouldn't be out there alone. Even with Buzzy's knowledge, they stuck out like a sore thumb. "So, now what?"

"He told me we are welcome to park here for the rest of the night. He'd prefer if we do, because of my head. He wants me to come in in the morning and have it x-rayed. We can stay, but I don't think I'll have it x-rayed."

"Why not?"

"Honestly, it's going to tell me what I already know. Get some rest and we'll head out in daylight. I need to fix the door, so we'll need to find a hardware store. They busted the lock and it doesn't close all the way. I need to stay up to make sure I'm okay."

"I'll stay up with you."

"No, I want you to rest. You'll need to drive in the morning. Can I ask you a favor, though?" Buzzy asked.

"Sure, anything."

"Can I lay with you and hold you? I'm pretty shaken up and it would help settle my nerves."

Hannah nodded. She was shaken up, too, and felt like crawling out of her skin. Buzzy eased back on the bed and opened his arm to her. She climbed in and rested with her back to his chest. He wound his arm around her tightly. What if something happened to him? She'd be all alone in a foreign country, knowing barely any Spanish. She felt her body get cold and shivered.

"I'm sorry," Buzzy whispered.

Hannah squeezed his arm. It wasn't his fault, but she understood. "I'm sorry, too."

Buzzy sighed and held her tighter.

When she woke up in the morning, Buzzy had dozed off. His face was almost unrecognizable, misshapen, and bruised. She sat up and shook him lightly. He stirred, groaning, then moved his head.

"Still alive," he mumbled.

"Do you want me to let you sleep more? I can start driving. I just don't know where I'm going."

"No, let's have tea. I'll show you on the map and I can doze in the passenger seat. Are you ready for this?"

"Absolutely not."

Buzzy laughed, sitting up. He hugged Hannah and brushed the hair out of her face. "Funny. We can do this. I think it's best if we find a campground to stay at for at least a few days. We can go to sites from there in the area but come back at night to be safe. I'll let Miguel know we'll be delayed."

"Are we going to run out of time?"

"We may. We need to make sure we are heading back north in time to catch the plane back."

"Do you have to be back at work at that time?" Hannah asked, knowing they were cutting it close as it was.

"No, I took a leave of absence. You?" Buzzy replied.

"I don't think they expect me back. I was doing a shit job before I left and told them I needed some time to work things out. I may not go back. If nothing else, I can be here longer if we can change the tickets."

Buzzy watched her. "We can change the tickets. So, do you want to stay longer?"

"I do. I want you to have time to heal and not push this. I'll let my parents know since they'll freak out if I don't come home on time. Let's find a campground and figure things out from there."

After breakfast and coffee, they got back on the road, heading south along the coast. Hannah made sure Buzzy rested and she checked on him regularly. As he was dozing, she thought about seeing him fight the men off. How he knew what they were going to do and reacted. Buzzy, who carried spiders out of the RV because he didn't want to hurt them. Once he was awake, she thought to ask him.

"Hey, what kind of fighting was that? How you fought those men?"

"Oh. So my dad also wanted us to learn mixed martial arts as kids. I've taken it since I was four. It was a mixture of different styles."

"It was impressive. It looked choreographed."

Buzzy chuckled. "The key is to stay calm and try to see what the other person is going to do before they do it. Read their thoughts. Even so, three against one is tough to beat. Had you not come out swinging the machete, not sure I'd be here now."

"I'm glad we had it. Were you expecting trouble?"

Buzzy eyed her, then bobbed his head. "Always expect trouble. But here's the thing. We had a machete but not a first aid kit. I don't think I was as on top of things as you make it seem."

Hannah laughed. That was true. They didn't have so much as a bandaid. The doctor left them with a decent amount of bandages and other things, but they should probably get a variety of first aid supplies. She shook her head. How sheltered had she been growing up? Her parents were always one step behind her, making sure she didn't get hurt. Almost ridiculously so. She turned to Buzzy.

"Can you teach me to fight? I may not always have a machete handy."

"Sure. Since we'll be here for a bit, why don't we relax at the campground for a few days and I'll show you some things? Some simple ways to protect yourself."

Hannah grinned at Buzzy, admiring his tenacity. "You sure, with your head like that?"

"As long as you don't throw me down, or kick me in the head, I think I'll be fine. Could be fun."

They found a well-lit campground along the gulf in Paraiso and paid for a few nights. It would give Buzzy a chance to start healing and take the pressure off fitting everything into a set time. They cooked a nice dinner and sat out to watch the sunset. It almost felt like a vacation. Like the last campground, there was a cantina in the center with music, food, and drinks.

The thing Hannah found herself most relieved by, however, there was no pretty cantina girl making eyes at Buzzy.

# CHAPTER FIFTEEN

*T*hey stood facing each other in the sand. Buzzy told Hannah to close her eyes and feel her environment. With her eyes closed, her hearing tuned in and she noticed sounds she hadn't heard before. She steadied her breathing as she saw Buzzy do, attempting to connect within herself. He explained how fighting was less about brute strength or force and more about understanding the other person's intentions.

"I'm not going to hit you, but am going to make strikes toward you. I want you to use your instincts and try to block me where you think I'm striking. There is no wrong answer here, it's about you using your gut and not just reacting," he told her. "Are you ready?"

Hannah felt silly with her eyes closed but bobbed her head. Buzzy cleared his throat, counting down from three. Hannah used her arms and hands to try and block where she thought he was coming but hit air most of the time. Frustrated, she took a step back, opening her eyes. "I suck at this."

"Everyone does at first. We're so out of touch with instinct. We're always looking at things solely from a reactionary level. If even that. Some people would get punched in the face, seeing it coming straight on because they don't believe it could happen to them. Our senses are dulled by the world around us. We're overstimulated by noise, visuals, smells. It makes it hard to shut it all down and pay attention to what is actually happening around us."

"Okay, so how do I tune that out, connect?"

"Let's try meditating. Have you ever done that?"

"Not really. I've tried, but my mind wanders to other things."

Buzzy led her to a flat part of the beach. "Sit down, I'll guide you at first."

Hannah plopped down and crossed her legs. She didn't know what to do with her hands. People seemed to always be holding them in some form when meditating. That felt unnatural, so she held them awkwardly at her sides. Buzzy chuckled and took her hand.

"Don't overthink it. Foremost, is to be comfortable. Experience your environment. You can either use a focal point or close your eyes. Whatever feels most natural."

Hannah closed her eyes and focused on the warmth of Buzzy's hand. She took a deep breath and let it out slowly. Her mind started to wander immediately and she shook her head. Buzzy squeezed her hand.

"Focus on the sounds of the waves, the way the sun warms your face. Don't try to not think because then all you'll do is think. Just feel for now."

Hannah relaxed and enjoyed the way the sun heated her cheeks. The waves continued a soothing lapping against the shore. Her hand rested in Buzzy's and he loosened his grip, so he was just cradling her hand in his own. His voice was soft when he spoke.

"Pay attention to your breathing. In. Out. If it helps repeat *breathe in, breathe out* with each breath. Some people hum, some people use a mantra. Keep it simple."

Hannah said the words *breath in, breath out* in her head as she did, eventually moving to *in, out* with each breath. They sat like this for a while, Hannah feeling like her body was becoming part of the sand, sun, and sea. Her shoulders dropped, releasing their heaviness and she felt like she was in the state between being awake and asleep. As it went on, she was able to open her eyes and stay in the zone. Her eyes unfocused, yet connected to the world around her.

After a bit, Buzzy squeezed her hand and she slipped out of the state, meeting his eyes. "Wow."

"You want to try again, learning to block me?" he asked.

"Yeah, let's do it," Hannah replied, standing up.

They faced each other again and she closed her eyes. Her feet felt heavy like she was part of the earth beneath her. Buzzy counted down from three and came toward her. This time she sensed him more and blocked about half of his strikes. He stepped back, counting back to three, as she opened her eyes. He was grinning, his eyes twinkling with appreciation. He took a small bow toward her, which she mimicked.

"Hannah! That was amazing."

Hannah blushed as she nodded. It felt amazing. "Thanks, George. It felt different this time. Like I wasn't focusing on where I thought you'd strike. Instead, I sensed it."

"Exactly! Humans are rather predictable. Our brains get in the way, but our senses know the patterns. You want to keep going, or grab something to eat?"

"Let's try again, then get something to eat. I don't want to lose the momentum."

"Eventually you won't. You'll be connected to your senses and your instinct and will be able to draw on them. Let me show you some blocks and moves."

They practiced until Hannah's stomach was grumbling and they headed to the RV. They were watching their money closely now that they were staying longer and cooking for themselves most of the time. Hannah sat at the table and cut vegetables while Buzzy pulled out spices and heated the pan. They stood side by side and cooked, joking and teasing each other. Hannah marveled at how close she and Buzzy had become. She'd been with Parker for years and they'd never come to this place. Buzzy was like the big brother she'd never had.

After lunch, they listened to music and read. Buzzy was still healing, though the goose egg was about half the size it had been. His face was bruised all the way down to his chin, an array of blue, purple, and yellow. Yet when he smiled, he was still the most beautiful to Hannah. Buzzy caught her watching him, then cocked his head.

"What?"

"Oh." Hannah felt her face get hot. "I was looking at the bruises. I'm sorry that happened to you."

Buzzy snickered. "Me too, but it looks worse than it feels. The headaches are still terrible but the rest is more visual."

"Is there anything you can do for the headaches?"

Buzzy nodded. "I suppose. The doctor gave me some painkillers, but I am afraid to take them. With my history and all."

"Yeah, I guess that would be scary. What about natural stuff?"

"Absolutely, but I'm not sure where to get them around here. Miguel and Sebastián are both herbalists. Let me call Miquel and see if he knows where I can get some. Maybe we can take a trip into Paraiso."

Buzzy called and spoke with Miguel in a mixture of Spanish and English. Hannah enjoyed how he laughed and became almost boyish when speaking to Miguel. Buzzy's father sounded like he'd been intense raising his children, so she wondered if Buzzy was allowed to be just a kid. He seemed like a kid speaking with Miguel. When he got off the phone, he had a list of herbs and an address. They drove out of the campground, heading for Paraiso. They found the shop off an alleyway and parked, making sure the back door was secured with a chain.

The shop smelled earthy and a small woman sat behind the counter, grinding a mixture with a mortar and pestle. She smiled as they came in, revealing a missing front tooth. Buzzy greeted her in Spanish, mentioning Miguel's name. She clapped her hands and stood up.

"Si, mi amigo Miguel!"

She took the list and quickly began pulling down jars from the shelf behind her. There were two mixtures, one to be used internally and one externally. She came close to Buzzy and touched the wound on his head, shaking her head. "Animales," she whispered, anger in her eyes. "Pandillas."

Buzzy nodded in agreement, then smiled kindly at her. "Estoy bien."

Her eyes were heavy and sad. "Aun asi, lo siento."

"Gracias." Buzzy touched her hand and met her gaze, assuring her he was okay. The woman patted his hand in understanding.

Even though she didn't understand what they were saying exactly, Hannah understood the old woman was apologizing to Buzzy, comforting him. Hannah felt an overwhelming urge to embrace him and pushed down tears making their way out. She brushed one off of her cheek as she watched the interaction. The old woman treated Buzzy like a son, murmuring to him and telling him about the herbs. Hannah sat in the background, feeling like an intruder. The old woman met her eyes, then glanced at Buzzy.

"¿Ella es tu novia?" she inquired.

Buzzy shook his head, his ears turning red. "No, ella es mi corazón."

The woman looked at Hannah and smiled, warm and kind. "Aun mejor."

Hannah had no clue what they were talking about but smiled back at the old woman stupidly. Buzzy gazed at her for a moment, then dropped his head, the pink of his cheeks coming through the bruising. The old woman touched his hand and winked.

"¿Ella sabe?"

Buzzy shook his head. "No."

The old woman turned, disappearing behind the counter. She came out with a sheet of paper and bags of herbs.

She handed them to Buzzy, going over the instructions on the paper. She handed him a separate bag, grinning.

"Toloache flor, por amor. No consumir, solo usar. En un amuleto," she explained.

Buzzy's eyes darted toward Hannah, then back. He bobbed his head, tucking the bags and paper in his backpack. "Gracias."

The old woman waved at Hannah, then went back to her grinding. They left the shop and Hannah stared at Buzzy.

"What was that all about?"

He shrugged. "She asked who you were."

"Oh, okay. It seemed more intense than that. Did you tell her we're friends?"

"More or less. That I care very much for you."

Hannah eyed him. She cared for him as well. "Aw. I was thinking earlier you were like the big brother I never had. I care for you too, George."

Buzzy paused, his eyes on her face unreadable. He smiled and took her hand. "Thanks, Hannah."

They walked around the town and grabbed dinner from a roadside stand. By the time it was getting dark, they knew it was safer to head back home. They walked back to the RV when Buzzy saw a small gift shop.

"Hey, do you mind if we pop in here? I wanted to bring Miguel and Sebastián something to say thank you."

"Sure, I'll grab something for my parents, too. Lessen the blow of telling them I'm staying here longer."

They headed in and Hannah found a table runner handmade in the region. Buzzy was checking out by the time she got up to the register. The girl behind the counter handed him his bag and made eyes at him. Hannah chuckled, not again. She checked out and they made it to the RV right before dark. Buzzy offered to drive and Hannah was more than happy to let him. Once they got back to the campsite, she made them each a cup of tea and they sat out under the stars. Buzzy went inside for a moment and came back out, holding something in his hands.

"Can I give you something?"

Hannah bobbed her head, confused. He pulled out a necklace and handed it to Hannah. It was clear and contained some sort of herb. She peered at it, then at Buzzy.

"What is it?"

"Hannah, I need you to know how much I care about you. We're friends but you are more to me. I want to protect you, be around you, talk to you."

Hannah chewed her lip. "I feel the same."

Buzzy watched her. "When the woman at the shop asked if you were my girlfriend, I told her no. But that you are my heart. Do you know what that means?"

Hannah didn't, or maybe she did. She loved Buzzy, he was her best friend. But their connection was more than that. Not like boyfriend and girlfriend, either. Like two halves of a whole. Like somewhere across the universe their twin souls had been split into two. It was like Buzzy was part of her.

"George, you are everything to me. I've never had someone in my life like you. Not a friend, not a boyfriend. I can't explain it. We just fit."

Buzzy nodded. "It's like nothing else I've experienced. I loved my ex-girlfriend but always felt like I was looking in a window at her. There was some barrier between us. With you, I feel like myself, like you are a mirror image of me. No barrier."

"Exactly. I feel the same way about Parker and about you. He was my boyfriend, you are my other me."

They stared at each other, blushing. It wasn't romantic, it was a revelation. Hannah glanced at the amulet.

"So, this?"

"That is toloache. Locals use it in love potions sometimes. Can be dangerous if ingested. The old woman gave it to me for you to wear, but it's not like that. I don't want you to fall in love with me. What we have is love. I got one for me, too." He drew out a matching amulet and showed it to her. "I want us both to wear them to represent what we *have* found in each other. Does that make sense?"

Hannah touched his amulet. "Of course it does. The connection between us is more than romantic love, George. It's like we are twins separated at birth."

Buzzy tipped his head. "But more than that, Hannah. I don't think I could ever be without you in this world again. As a companion. I'd feel like part of me was missing."

# CHAPTER SIXTEEN

*H*ow Hannah got out of the RV with the doors locked, and Buzzy not waking up, was a mystery. The bigger mystery though, where the hell was she? She woke up knee-deep in the ocean, nowhere near the campground. As her eyes adjusted to her surroundings, panic set in. It was one thing to wake up in another place in the US, but in a foreign country where the most she knew in the language was basic greetings was a whole new realm of terrifying. She stumbled out of the waves and peered around. What time was it? Even the sky looked different, the stars in different places than when they were sitting outside. She was barefoot in only a t-shirt and shorts.

They'd fallen asleep around eleven. It was still pitch black. Making it... somewhere between midnight and five in the morning. That didn't narrow it down. She could've wandered for hours. She didn't know which way she'd gone on the beach. Footsteps. Maybe her prints were still in the sand if the tide hadn't washed them away. It was mid-tide and appeared like it was coming in. Maybe she could see where she'd come from. It was dark as she scoured, searching for any remaining trace of her journey there. After tirelessly looking, she couldn't make out anything that was for sure a trail. She sat down and started to bawl, the amulet hitting her in her face as she bowed her head. She grasped it, trying to summon Buzzy.

"Find me, George." Her voice trickled into the dark.

Buzzy wouldn't know which direction to search, either. She closed her eyes and pictured her hand in Buzzy's, like when they were meditating. She listened to the waves hitting the shore and focused on her breathing. *In, out.* Once her mind cleared, she stood up, still in a trance, and let her feet carry her in the direction they wanted. As she walked, she pictured Buzzy coming toward her. She kept moving, not allowing fear to control her thoughts. Just instinct. As she made her way down the beach, she could see the sun beginning to crest the horizon in the distance. As the sun rose, locals began to come out to the beach. Hannah kept her eyes down, not wanting to try and make conversation. She glanced ahead every once in a while to make sure she watched where she was going. People nodded but no one approached her.

After about an hour, she began to think she'd gone in the wrong direction. Nothing looked familiar and her feet were beginning to hurt. She glanced back down the beach from where she came and sighed. It all looked the same. She could be wandering farther and farther away from the camp. She thought about heading up off the beach and asking people for help but was afraid she'd get even more lost. At least she knew the campground was on the beach. She was about to turn around when something in the distance caught her eye. A glint of something which looked like gold fabric. She stopped and peered toward it. A flicker of reddish gold. She made her way in that direction, afraid to get her hopes up. As it drew closer, she could make out a shape. A man. With reddish-blond hair. Her heart leaped in her throat and she began to run in the direction of the distant figure.

Buzzy spied her when she was a few hundred yards away, his face twisting from agony to relief. When she approached, he fell to his knees as tears streamed down his cheeks. Hannah ran up and fell to the ground, throwing her arms around him. He held her as tightly as he could.

"Hannah! Hannah, I was so fucking scared. I woke up and you were gone. The doors were still locked and I couldn't find you."

Hannah nodded, sobbing. "I don't know what happened, George. I woke up standing in the ocean and didn't know how I got there. I... I meditated, trusted my instinct, and began walking. I had no idea if it was the right way."

Buzzy leaned back, placing his hand on her face. "It was the right way."

"How did you find me?"

"I stood on the beach and pictured you heading toward me, then went in the direction I saw you coming from."

Hannah stared at Buzzy and clasped his amulet in her hand. "You're like a beacon for me, George. My heart knows how to find your heart."

Buzzy got up and pulled her up with him, holding her close and swaying. "This can't keep happening, Hannah. We need to figure out what is going on with you. I'm afraid you'll leave and someone will harm you."

Hannah rested her head against his chest. He was right. What if one of those gangs had been out there and found her wandering alone? "I know, but I don't know what to do. You can't tie me to you."

Buzzy chuckled. "Would if I could. It only happens when you're asleep, however, I didn't even feel you get up. The back door is still chained, so you must have gone through the cab and locked the door behind you. Maybe we can figure out a way to tether you to me when we sleep."

"Okay. Let's figure something out. Right now, I just want to get back. My feet are killing me."

Buzzy looked at her feet and shook his head. "It's another hour back. I can piggyback carry you."

Hannah laughed, pulling away. "No, that's too far. You already hiked to find me."

"Let me try. If I get tired, I'll let you know."

He motioned his arms for her to get on his back and she begrudgingly agreed, knowing her feet wouldn't hold out another hour of walking. He shifted to carry her and she rested her head on his shoulder as he began the trek back.

"You really are my best friend, George."

He held her tighter and kept his steady pace. "I love you, Hannah."

She let the words sit between them. She and Parker had always told each other they loved each other but it didn't feel like this. This weight. It didn't withstand trauma, either. As soon as their life was impeded on, they'd turned on each other. Buzzy only knew her in tragedy. What would happen if she didn't need to be rescued anymore?

"Hey, George... this isn't some kind of trauma bond, is it? You needing to rescue me? Me needing to be rescued?"

Buzzy paused, considering, then sighed. "Hannah, regardless of the shit you're going through, I like you. I like the way you laugh and say everything with a touch of sarcasm. I like how you were willing to come to another country to get answers and are always inquisitive. I like that you don't shy away from things even though they make you uncomfortable. I like how when you're deep in thought, you crinkle your nose. I like your smile and your brain. I could've met you at a coffee shop and would've wanted to get to know you. I like you. All of this is simply to get you free of whatever is haunting you. Our friendship exists because we do. You don't need to be rescued. You need a friend."

Hannah wrapped her arms around his chest and squeezed. "Thanks, George. Can I tell you the reasons why I like you?"

Buzzy nodded and continued walking.

"When everyone else treated me like I had a disease, you treated me like not only a friend but like family. You make me laugh and challenge my beliefs. You're so open and kind to everyone you meet. You're calm and intelligent, allowing ideas to ruminate before jumping on them. When I asked you to come to Mexico with me, you didn't act like you were doing me a favor. You were excited to come. No matter what I've told you, you never once treated me like I was losing my mind. And you always come for me."

A silence passed between them when Buzzy finally spoke, his voice sincere. "I always will."

Hannah laid her head on his shoulder and closed her eyes. "This is why I love you."

They made it back to camp, exhausted and hungry. Hannah climbed into bed, lying on her side, and drew her knees to her chest as she began to doze off. Buzzy made breakfast and set it on the table, then climbed in next to her. He touched her cheek and smiled when she opened her eyes. She smelled the food and sat up, yawning.

"That smells amazing. Thanks."

They ate and looked at the map. They needed to get back to exploring the ruins, to see if they could track down any information which might explain what was going on with Hannah. Las Choapas was near, so they'd go there, then start branching out. They'd need to head toward the Yucatan Peninsula to Miguel and Sebastián's house to see the rest farther away. So, a few more days at the camp, then they'd need to move on.

Every morning Buzzy worked with Hannah on her martial arts skills. She found in learning those, she felt more in touch with her body and her confidence increased. The mixture the herb woman gave Buzzy was helping with his headaches and reducing the damage done to his face. He began to look more like his old self and Hannah found herself drawn to him in ways she hadn't before. She noticed the curve of his lips, the way his eyes shifted color, depending on his moods or the time of day. The way when he was thinking, he'd rub his finger in the space between his upper lip and nose. Sometimes she'd catch him staring at her in the way she was sure she was staring at him. She didn't know what to make of it, but it was there.

By the time they were ready to head on, they'd traveled to the ruins in the area and Hannah began to notice a pattern in the places she was drawn to. Typically, they had to do with sacrifice and fighting. Both were ideas that made her uneasy, yet she couldn't help but feel like there was something there she needed to pay attention to. They agreed to travel to more sites before going to Miguel and Sebastián's, as they wanted them to weigh in on what they'd discovered along the way. They headed south and found another campground, sans cantina, to stay at. They bought groceries in the nearest town to cook on their own.

To keep Hannah from sleepwalking, they moved to the upper bed and Hannah slept on the inside, making it so she'd have to climb over Buzzy and down to get out. He also held her hand and wrapped a piece of fabric around their wrists. Hannah found this oddly comforting. Being an only child, she didn't have memories of being so close with anyone. It was like building blanket forts and the intimacy of telling each other secrets. She was thinking about this one night as they were dozing off when an image flashed through her mind.

The dark-haired boy was giggling and they were hiding in a closet. Except Hannah was a child, too. The boy leaned toward her, whispering, "Hannah Banana. I have a secret to tell you. Can you keep a secret?"

In that second, the closet door swung open and the image ended. Hannah gasped and sat up, forgetting they were in the upper bed. She hit her head on the ceiling, crying out. Buzzy opened his eyes and pulled her toward him as he rubbed her injured head.

"Oh, damn, that had to hurt. You okay?"

Hannah shook her head and buried her face in his arm. "Ow! No, that was stupid. I had this image in my head of the little boy and me. I was little, as well. He was telling me a secret."

Buzzy shifted and peered at her. "What was the secret?"

"I don't know. The image just ended before he told me."

"Could he be someone you were friends with as a kid?"

Hannah thought about it. No, she remembered the kids she played with. He wasn't one of them. "I don't think so. Sometimes he reminds me of Parker because they both have dark hair and eyes, but it isn't Parker. I thought maybe it was a manifestation of him because of what we went through, but I know for sure it isn't. This boy is just different."

Buzzy watched her, chewing his lip. "Hmmm. So, you've never seen him before... anywhere?"

"No, not that I can remember but he also seems so familiar, and he seems to know me."

"Well, the image came to you for some reason. He *is* someone to you, clearly. Try to meditate on that. Ask for clarity and guidance. Does he remind you of anyone?"

"As I said, he kind of looks like Parker, but he doesn't remind me of him. He just has similar physical attributes."

"Yeah, I guess enough people look alike that it doesn't have to mean anything. Get some rest and in the morning we can do some meditation, see if we can draw anything out."

Hannah nodded and squeezed his hand. "Goodnight, George."

"Goodnight, Hannah."

Hannah couldn't fall asleep easily. Her mind kept replaying the image over and over. She hadn't been totally honest with Buzzy when he asked if the boy reminded her of anyone. When she replayed the image and how she felt in it, she could see the boy did remind her of someone. It wasn't how he looked, rather how he made her feel.

Safe.

He reminded her of George.

# CHAPTER SEVENTEEN

T he opening of the cave loomed from the earth, large and daunting. They'd traveled to San Cristóbal in Chiapas, known for its caves. Buzzy found one which they could hike in and out without equipment. It was called the Cave of Curses, which made Hannah nervous at first until Buzzy explained it was a place to leave curses. The terrain was rough and they needed to descend into the cave on foot which was like a dark mouth, yawning from the ground.

They paused at the entrance of the cave and Buzzy murmured something, his eyes peering into the cool inkiness. Hannah turned to him, raising her brows. He grinned sheepishly, then shrugged. "Asking the cave spirit if we have permission to enter."

"Cave spirit?" Hannah asked and laughed.

"Many people believe each cave has a spirit which protects it. I think it's wise to ask permission to enter," Buzzy explained.

Hannah glanced into the cave and shuddered. Not only was the cave dark and intimidating, now it had a spirit guarding it, also? She sent a silent message, asking permission to enter. A breeze kicked up as they headed into the cave. Buzzy clicked on the headlamp he bought in the last town, then motioned for Hannah to do the same with the one he gave her. He had them each carry spiked hiking poles to dig in the ground and they carefully made their way in. Once inside, the outside world disappeared, except for an increasingly smaller beam of light behind them as a beacon back out.

Buzzy led the way, showing Hannah where to watch her footing. Inside the cave was timeless, their senses diminishing to instinct. Hannah felt like she should be afraid but there was something comforting about being down in the earth. Like being part of a secret only she knew. She watched Buzzy in front of her and wanted to tell him that. At that moment, he turned back toward her and smiled. He already knew. He'd been doing this for years.

He led her to a spot where locals left curses. Hannah wasn't sure if he meant they'd leave curses on other people or leave curses they thought were put on them. Either way, Hannah closed her eyes and imagined releasing the curses of killing Logan Slip and losing her baby.

As she thought about the baby she lost, she was surprised when tears sprang to her eyes. In the spot were notes, talismans, even bones. She only had her imagery but reached down and picked up a couple of pebbles to represent Logan and the baby. Buzzy observed quietly, respecting her journey. When she was done, she wiped a tear away and met his eyes. He smiled and took her hand.

"I'm proud of you, Hannah."

Hannah didn't know if there was anything he should be proud of, but she did feel lighter having acknowledged the trauma in a physical way. She tipped her head. "Thanks for bringing me here. There is something magical about this place."

"A lot of native cultures believe caves to be holy places. I like to think of them as a channel to Earth's heart."

"I like that. I didn't think I'd like being in a cave, that it would be claustrophobic."

"Oh, some are. Sometimes you get down and the spaces get smaller and smaller. Like, the cave presses in on either side of your body."

Hannah shook her head. "Why would anyone do that to themselves?"

Buzzy chuckled. "It can be a challenge, wanting to see how far you can push. Going where few, or no, people have gone."

"I take it you've done that then?"

"Of course. My brother and I were always seeing how far we could go. I'll admit it wasn't pleasant and I got it out of my system. Now, I just want the experience, the beauty."

Hannah sighed. "Good, because I will never do that with you, George."

Buzzy squeezed her hand. "So, you *will* do more of this with me? Go cave exploring?"

Hannah looked around and found she felt at home here. Safe. "I will. It's like it was made for me to find, to explore. Does that make sense?"

"Totally. Ever since I was a kid, caves have been my secret places. It was hard after my fall, but that was my own fault. I wasn't respecting the space, only focused on competing with my brother. I know better now."

They wandered as far in as they could before it became too dangerous and headed back up. Hitting daylight was like the first breath after being underwater. The hike back out to flat land was hard and Hannah's legs were shaking by the time they got there. Inside had been cool, then the hike was hot, so Hannah was relieved when a breeze came across them. They arrived back at the RV and made lunch, sitting outside to eat. Hannah watched Buzzy as he gazed off, deep in thought. His wounds were healing and he was starting to get his normal color back. He appeared like he was putting the attack behind him.

For the first time, her mind went somewhere else. He'd always been Buzzy, George, her friend, and like a brother. At this moment, she recognized he was handsome. His hazel eyes were focused off in the distance and she noticed they were a mixture of light copper with flecks of green. His brows matched his hair, a reddish-blond, and his eyelashes were almost blond. His skin was light-golden and smooth. His mouth curved up just at the edges, giving him an air of mischief. When he smiled it was slightly crooked and he had pointy canine teeth. Almost like a bat. Hannah laughed at the thought, she'd never noticed that before. He glanced at her, waiting to see what had caused her eruption of giggles.

Hannah blushed. "You have vampire teeth."

Buzzy tipped his head and frowned, grinning. "I do?"

"Like a bat. It's kind of cool. They are naturally like that?"

"No, Hannah, I took a file and made them that way."

"Haha, George. I mean, mine have a slight point but yours are definitely sharp."

"Better to suck your blood, my dear," Buzzy joked.

For a second Hannah pictured Buzzy's mouth on her neck and didn't mind the image. She kind of liked it. Afraid he'd be able to read her thoughts, she glanced away, pretending to look at something in the distance. Buzzy finished his food and took his last swig of water.

"You want to head on? We can go to an ancient site before dark, then head back to the campground."

Hannah shifted her gaze to him and for a second their eyes locked. He really was nice to look at. He grinned and she thought she read something in his face. She picked up her plate and stood up. Best to keep moving.

"Sure. I think my legs can take it."

They drove on to Toniná, also called the House of Rocks based on how it was built. The site was massive and took Hannah's breath away. There were different statues around the site and Hannah found herself mesmerized by the intricate stonework. The ancient communities also seemed to like to carve monuments of their captives.

Buzzy told her they had a record of a female ruler of that site, which Hannah thought was cool. They strolled through the mazes of the area and Hannah felt a familiarity creep up in her. Like she'd been there before. She knew she hadn't, however, she couldn't shake the sense of déjà vu. She caught a glimpse of Buzzy ahead, crouched down to look at artwork on a lower wall. She admired the strength in his legs and found her mind wandering again.

Was it just their close proximity over all of this time, or was she finding herself attracted to him? He didn't notice and stood up to move along the path. Hannah watched him for a moment and wondered for a second if she should say something to him. No. What they had was sacred, not some schoolgirl crush. She needed him. She picked up the pace to catch up to him and slid her hand into his.

"Hey. Thank you for being part of my life. I've seen so much since I met you. I never would've done this on my own," she said.

Buzzy grinned at her. "Happy to help. You're good company."

They walked on, comfortable with what they had. Evening came before they had time to finish exploring and they meandered back to the RV. Buzzy drove back to the campground as Hannah dozed off on the passenger side. The physical exertion of the day had worn her out. She woke up at the campground, just as Buzzy was turning the engine off. He was staring at her and she sat up, confused.

"Everything okay?"

"Yeah, it's fine. Can I tell you something?" he asked, shifting to face her.

Hannah cocked her head. "Yeah?"

"I needed you in my life, too. Ever since the accident, getting addicted to Oxy, then losing everything I thought I had in my life, I've been pretty much alone. Just working, exploring. But you are the first person I connected to since all of that. I don't want you to think I see myself as some sort of savior or guide to you. You're showing me as much as I am you."

150

Hannah smiled. "Well, look at you, George. Getting all sentimental on me?"

Buzzy chuckled. "And there it is. Yes, Hannah. I am getting all sentimental on you. This has been a hell of a road trip and I'm glad we are doing this together. I've always been the solitary sort, mostly because of the things I want to do, no one else has. My ex was not interested in cave exploring or other cultures, and my brother would do some things with me but only as a competition. You're the first person I met who wants to do things like I do, for the reasons I do. That's all I'm saying."

Those words meant a lot to Hannah. She also felt solitary even though she and Parker were in a large social circle. They were always doing things and around people, but often she still felt alone. "I was just teasing, George. I agree. Being with you is almost too easy."

"Like we've known each other for many lifetimes," Buzzy agreed. "Oh, hey, I saw this flier at the campground entrance. They are having some dancers come through to the community building. Do you want to go? It's tonight."

"What kind of dancers?"

"Some native, traveling kind. Not sure, it didn't have many details. We can get cleaned up and go."

"Sure, sounds fun. I need to shower though, I'm pretty rank."

Buzzy climbed into the back of the RV and dug through his bag. "It starts in just under an hour. Let's get ready and walk over."

By the time they were ready, it was almost dark and they took the road toward the small community center, pretty much just a covered stage with benches around it. They took seats off to the side and waited. There were a few other campers and a surprising number of locals. After a bit, dancers came onto the stage. The women were in colorful, multi-tiered dresses, and bright red lipstick, with their rich, dark hair twisted up on their heads. They were stunning. The men were more simply dressed in black pants, vests, and white shirts with sombreros. The music began as the women twirled, using their hands to move their skirts. It was a beautiful, whirling carousel. Hannah wasn't sure where to look. The men acted as anchors, clapping to the music and stomping in a synchronized dance pattern. It was magical.

After a few dances, they started to pull people from the audience onto the stage to dance with them. One of the men encouraged Hannah to come up but she shook her head. A female dancer dragged Buzzy on stage and he naturally moved along with her. The woman caught Hannah's eyes and waved her hand for Hannah to come up. Hannah again shook her head, embarrassed she'd make a fool of herself. Buzzy spun around with one of the female dancers as her dress created a kaleidoscope of color. Hannah wished she had the confidence to jump in, feeling like an ugly wallflower. All of a sudden, Buzzy took a quick bow to his partner and came over, grabbing Hannah by the hand.

"Come dance with me," he urged.

She followed, worried all eyes were on her, however, when they got to the stage, she saw most of the audience had joined in. She let her guard down as one of the ladies showed her some of the moves. Hannah was wearing a sundress but nothing like they had, so her movements seemed less lavish. After a song, she felt more confident and began to laugh as she tried the movements. Buzzy grabbed her by the waist and spun her around, then pulled her in close. She couldn't deny the heat from his body was welcoming. She'd never felt more alive as the music and colors surrounded her. She tipped her head back giggling, letting the moment sweep her up.

The dance picked up and she was rotated between the performers, dancing for a moment and moving on to the next. In an instant, the music shifted and the male dancers disappeared. The female dancers moved in unison to the more chaotic music, their arms in the air. The music built to a crescendo and the male dancers hopped back on stage, their shirts now black and wearing a variety of carved masks.

The music shifted to sound almost carnival, sinister, and the dancers began to swirl around. Hannah worked her way to the edge of the stage, not seeing Buzzy, in the attempt to go sit down when someone grasped her hand and brought her into the middle of the dance. She was spinning, getting disoriented by the sheets of colorful fabric and circus-like music. Hands were grabbing her and turning her from person to person.

Hannah could see Buzzy across the stage dancing, but she couldn't get to him. Every time she attempted to make her way over, someone would turn her around in the other direction. She was beginning to feel nauseous and wanted the music to stop. The music and chaos reminded her of something, but what? Then it dawned on her. The accident. The music. The strips of fabric strewn across the highway. Colorful pieces of Logan Slip. Panicked seized her and she tried to call out to Buzzy, however, he couldn't hear her over the loud music.

She tried to run, just as she was thrust back into the dance. She landed in the arms of a male dancer wearing a mask. The mask from her dream. Half skull, half clown. She began to scream, thrashing to get free. She felt herself starting to pass out as she saw Buzzy busting through the line of dancers to grab her before she hit the floor.

# CHAPTER EIGHTEEN

*B*uzzy's face was inches from Hannah's. Everything was blurry and her heart was racing. She was on the stage floor with the dancers around her. Everyone was worried, peering down at her. She tried to force her eyes to focus and drew Buzzy down to her.

"The mask, George," she whispered.

He glanced around and saw the dancer now holding the mask in his hands, his face lined with concern. Buzzy stood up and spoke with the dancer in Spanish. The dancer nodded and Buzzy turned back to Hannah. He scooped her off the floor and carried her off the stage. She tried to protest, to tell him they needed to talk about the mask, but he shook his head, his mouth in a grim line.

"I asked if they'd be around tonight. They're staying at the campground. Let me just get you somewhere safe and I can deal with it. You could've been trampled, Hannah."

She rested her head against his chest, knowing it was pointless to protest. Not that she had it in her. She was shaking and dizzy. Buzzy set her down outside the RV and opened the door, helping her in. He seemed angry and she felt terrible for making a scene.

"George, I'm sorry I created an issue."

He stared at her, then shook his head incredulously. "Hannah, I'm not mad at you. I'm mad at myself for letting that happen. You didn't even want to come on stage and I persuaded you to. It got crazy and when I saw you freaking out, I knew I'd messed up."

"You couldn't have known. I just..." Hannah didn't want to explain that the dancers and music reminded her about killing Logan Slip. "Maybe I was tired, then seeing the mask set me off."

"Yeah, the mask. What are the odds? We've been to multiple sites and related museums and haven't seen it. All of a sudden, out of the blue, a group of dancers comes through to a random campground we're staying at and one of them has the mask? It makes me think."

"About?"

"We're going about this all wrong. We're trying to force answers, instead of letting them come to us. We need to stop seeking and start listening."

Hannah knew what he meant. While she'd enjoyed visiting the ruins and learning about the culture, it hadn't brought her any closer to answers to why she was sleepwalking, having vivid dreams, or seeing daytime visions. The dancers tonight were the first actual connection to any of it.

"So, now what?" she asked.

"First, I'm going to go talk to them about their masks, what they mean, where they got them. Next, I think we need to focus inward. Like with learning to fight, you need to meditate to understand your instinct. Visiting ruins is one thing, trying to connect to the forces there is another."

"Okay. So, meditate there?"

"Sort of. Open ourselves to their messages. Are you going to be alright if I go speak to the dancers? Will you be okay alone?"

Hannah nodded. Right now, she just wanted to bury her head under the covers and disconnect. Buzzy came over and kissed her on the forehead. "I love you. I don't want anything to happen to you. Inside or out."

Inside or out. Mentally or physically. He worried for her sanity, too. She'd just screamed and passed out at a fun show. Flipped out, causing a scene. Hannah met his eyes, wanting to assure him she'd be alright, but she knew better. This was a race against her brain going off the edge. She smiled wobbly.

"George." It was all she could say. There were no words for what was going on.

His eyes were sad and he put his fingers on her chin. "You're the strongest person I know, Hannah. It's just a puzzle and we don't have all the pieces yet. We will find them. I promise."

Hannah knew he was good to his word. He'd do everything in his power to put the puzzle together. "I know."

He headed toward the door. Hannah called out.

"I love you, too, George."

He paused and smiled, lifting his hand. "Rest. I'll be back shortly. Tomorrow I want to take you somewhere I discovered on one of my trips. Not far from here. A break from this journey." He stepped out into the night, leaving Hannah alone with her thoughts.

What if they didn't find an answer and this went on for the rest of her life? She'd eventually be locked up for her own safety. Or she'd end up dead because of what she was doing. Buzzy couldn't babysit her forever. In time, he'd go on with his own life, meet someone, fall in love. They were taking this trip together and loved each other, but it wasn't enough. He'd want a real life eventually. She'd become a burden. She closed her eyes and stifled the pain in her heart. Maybe if they'd become friends in a different way, without all of the issues, they could've been something different. He was blaming himself for something he had nothing to do with.

Buzzy came back a while later and crawled in next to her. She touched his arm to let him know she was still awake.

"Hey, what did you find out?"

"So, this group travels all around Mexico performing. The guy wearing that mask said he got it at Chichen Itza. That's out toward Miguel and Sebastián's town. I'm sure you saw the pictures from there. It's one of the best-known sites in Mexico. Not sure how it would be connected, but we can go there and explore. The dancer said he got the mask from a vendor there. It's obviously a replica."

"Okay, so we go to Chichen Itza, then what?"

"We just go and open our minds. Meditate, see what comes to us. It's a highly spiritual place, so it may open things in you, though. Dark things. Are you ready for that?"

Hannah let her mind consider the possibility. "It's happening anyway. Maybe there I will expect it."

Buzzy rolled over, slipping his arm over Hannah. He rested his head against hers. "I'll do my best to protect you. However, you have to go in as a warrior, a fighter. Not a captive."

Hannah thought about the circle she'd seen where they made the captives fight for their lives. She was going into that circle. If she came out, it would depend on what kind of warrior she was. Unfortunately, Buzzy couldn't help her once she stepped into the circle in her mind. He could accompany her up to the entrance, from there she was on her own.

"George, you've been my guide, my confidant, and my protector. You've taught me to fight both physically and mentally. I want to believe I can do this."

"I want to believe you can, too. Now you are fighting for your future. For..." he trailed off and didn't say anything else.

Hannah rested her hand on his arm, letting it protect her, and dozed off.

The next morning, Buzzy was up and ready to go. He wouldn't say where they were going but was excited about it. They drove down an empty dirt road and pulled off into a grove of trees. From there, they'd be on foot. Buzzy told her to wear her swimsuit, so she'd put it on under her t-shirt and shorts. They wandered through the woods until the sunlight was barely filtered through the density of leaves. Hannah could hear the sound before she saw where they were going and tried to peer ahead. They came out of the trees to a waterfall cascading into a natural pool, surrounded by rocks and plants below. They set their packs down on the rocks and slipped off their shoes. Hannah was in awe.

"How did you know about this place?"

"A few years ago, I was hitchhiking through Mexico and some locals picked me up. It was so hot that day, they asked if I wanted to go for a swim. They brought me here. I didn't want to forget, so I marked it on my map. I don't know if this is someone's land, or what, but no one is ever here."

Hannah stepped into the water, cooler than the air but warmer than she expected. She slipped off her shirt and shorts and dove in. She came up laughing and saw Buzzy watching from the rock, a soft look on his face.

"What are you waiting for, George? Come in!" she yelled at him, breaking the trance.

"You have the best laugh, Hannah. It's nice to see you happy."

Hannah floated on her back. She needed this, not trying to figure things out. A day to play. She splashed Buzzy. "Well, come on in then!"

Buzzy pulled off his shirt and grinned. "You asked for it." He ran and cannonballed off the rock into the water near her, sending a splash over her.

Hannah sputtered, shoving water toward him. "Ugh, you are so rude!" She laughed and swam away.

They swam for hours until hunger took over. Hannah spread their towels on the rock and they took out the sandwiches they'd made. She could see a thin path that wound behind the waterfall. After she ate, she got up and followed the path. It ended behind the waterfall, looking out over the pool. She ran her fingers through the waterfall, liking the feeling of being hidden by something so powerful. Buzzy joined her and they stood, peering out. Hannah sighed.

160

"There are so many beautiful, secret places on earth. I've seen pretty much none of them until now. I want to see them all."

"So, come with me. Let's say goodbye to our old lives and travel."

Hannah eyed Buzzy. "You know it would be fun for a while, but eventually you'll want to settle down, meet someone, have children. I don't think your future spouse would want me tagging along."

Buzzy glanced away, his jaw set firmly. "Hannah, how do you see me? Outside of this journey. When you wake up in the morning and see me, what's your first thought?"

Hannah thought about it. "I see my best friend, the big brother I never had."

Buzzy nodded, then took a step back. "I see. Have you ever looked at me in any other way?"

Hannah was confused. What did he mean? "You're always kind and supportive. Fiercely protective. I don't understand."

Buzzy moved toward her and wound his arm around her waist. "How do you feel when I do this?"

Hannah blushed. "Safe."

Buzzy chewed his lip and stared through the waterfall. Hannah wasn't being totally honest. She felt warm, out of breath, tingly. She rested her hand on his back. He turned back to face her, his eyes considering. He leaned in and kissed her. Whether or not she wanted to, she responded. No, she wanted to. She drew back, breathless, her eyes wide.

"George, I didn't think you saw me like this."

"Like what? Beautiful, smart, sensual? I've always seen you like that."

Hannah frowned. The first time he'd seen her, she was on the floor of the mental hospital, losing her shit. She was pretty sure she'd screamed at him then. It'd been slow to come to, but she knew she felt this way about him, as well. More. More than Parker. This was different. Parker was attraction followed by sex and a relationship. This was friendship followed by an unbreakable bond and then attraction. How would this change things for them? For their journey?

Buzzy let her go, shaking his head. "We've been going about this all wrong. We haven't relied on each other completely. Every step has been a test. Could we be friends? Could we be best friends? Could we depend on each other? Could we be more? We were always more. Why do you say I'm like a big brother?"

Hannah closed her eyes and thought. She didn't know what it was like to have a big brother, but she assumed it would be fun, safe, telling secrets, joking, someone to depend on, someone who had your back no matter what. All the things she felt with Buzzy. "I guess all the things we have. I can be myself with you. Tell you anything and you don't go away."

"So, like a partner?" Buzzy pressed.

Like a partner. Not a sibling, but someone to lean on, rely on, be close to. Feel safe with. While she'd cared about Parker, he gave her none of those things. Only the fun. A light clicked on in her brain. She and Buzzy were already in a relationship. All the important parts of one. She glanced at him, then nodded. "I see what you are getting at, George."

He smiled, his eyes twinkling. "It took you long enough."

Hannah laughed and went to playfully shove him when he grabbed her hand and pulled her into the waterfall with him, letting it cascade over them. They stood as the water washed over them, resting in each other's arms. They moved back behind the waterfall and stared at each other bashfully. Hannah watched Buzzy and felt like she was seeing things for the first time. Why did she see him as Buzzy, but call him George? He was both, but he was her George. She'd been unintentionally creating distance between them when there was none. He'd always been George, she just had to see it.

She stuck her hand out to him. "Hi, George. It's nice to meet you. I'm Hannah."

He took her hand in his and shook it.

"Hi, Hannah, it was nice for you to come. I've been waiting a long time for you."

# CHAPTER NINETEEN

*T*he first night after their revelation to each other, Hannah and George made dinner and talked at their tiny table about what it meant moving forward. Both agreed nothing should change. They could continue taking it slow and focus on the path they'd been on. The difference they both felt was when they held each other, it meant something more. Deeper. Oh, and the kissing. That was new. Wonderful and new, but as far as they let it go. Hannah was feeling fragile and George wanted to respect what they'd formed so far.

They headed for Chichen Itza, knowing the signs were telling them that's where they needed to go. When they got there, Hannah immediately knew. There was something different about this site. She felt a strange sensation pulling at her. They got out and walked toward the pyramid. It was massive and seemed to loom over the area with a spiritual intensity she had yet to experience. George felt it, as well. He grasped her hand, meeting her eyes. This was the place. They didn't see a vendor selling masks, but they didn't have to. Like in the dream, that was just a message to get her there.

Hannah held back initially, feeling something dark in her. She glanced at George and he understood. They found a quiet place to sit and meditate. Hannah closed her eyes but her head was buzzing, unable to settle. George held her hand in his and reminded her to breathe in and out. She repeated this over and over until her brain calmed and let her senses take over. Feeling the breeze, smelling the grass. Her breathing regulated and she was able to open her eyes, focusing on the pyramid. She'd seen it in pictures but this was different, almost living. They meditated for a long time. Once Hannah felt her mind was no longer reacting, she squeezed George's hand. He turned his amber eyes toward her, his gaze reading her thoughts. They got up and walked the grounds, allowing their instinct to lead them. They stopped by a tour where the guide was talking about human sacrifices and the games played there, how the winners severed the heads of the losing teams. Hannah trembled.

The tour moved on and they followed. The tour operator explained that there were ritualistic sacrifices, where the person being sacrificed was still alive when they'd have their chest cut open and their still beating heart pulled from inside them. Hannah was horrified an intelligent society could resort to such barbaric ceremonies. She wanted to leave but knew she needed to stay and listen. They moved through the area where the games were played. It was the first time she'd seen him in Mexico.

Logan Slip.

He was crouched in a doorway of the Temple of the Jaguars. Not decomposing like in her dream. Just him in his motorcycle outfit, observing her. She paused and watched him back. What was he trying to let her know? To blame her? Hold her accountable? She wasn't afraid but still didn't understand. She sent him a silent message. "I'm sorry, Logan. I didn't know."

He didn't move as the tour headed on. Hannah looked back and he was gone. They went on to the Sacred Cenote, a giant sinkhole in the ground filled with water. Where young men and boys as young as three were sacrificed, thrown in to drown to appease the Mayan rain god, the guide said. Hannah's heart hurt hearing this and she felt something in her soul tug at her. A memory. A boy. The dark-haired boy. The group moved on and she turned back for a moment to gaze into the cenote.

This had something to do with the boy. She glanced to the other side of the cenote when she saw him standing there. The dark-haired boy. Watching her from across the abyss, his face serious. He pointed at her, then at himself, then down at the water. Hannah looked at the water. Was the boy sacrificed? She watched him as he did it again. He pointed at her, at himself, then at the water. He pointed at her again, his face sad. Hannah didn't know what happened next but she felt something leading her to the edge, coaxing her over. She was just about to step off the edge when George yanked her back, so hard they both tumbled back against the ground.

"Hannah!" His voice snapped her out of the stupor. "What the hell?"

Hannah stared at him, confused, then back to where the boy was standing. He wasn't there. George was holding her tightly, afraid to let go. Her head cleared and she gasped. She'd been ready to jump in the cenote. To sacrifice herself.

"I don't know what happened, George. I saw the boy again. He was trying to tell me something, then some sort of force was drawing me toward the edge. I couldn't stop it. Like a hand from down there was pulling me in."

George got up and moved her toward him, guiding them both far away from the cenote. He spun her to face him and made her make eye contact, his face intent with his brow furrowed. "Focus on me. You need to break the trance. What was the boy doing?"

"He was pointing at me, then to himself, then to the water. He did it a couple of times. The next thing I knew, I was being lured toward the water. Called. Like I belonged in there."

"Do you think the boy was doing it to you?"

"No. I don't think so. It seemed like he was trying to tell me something. George, I think I knew him. Like when I was little. I don't remember him, but I had that image of him and me playing in the closet and him telling me a secret."

"Have you ever seen pictures of him?"

Hannah thought back. No, she didn't remember ever seeing him before he started appearing to her. First in her dream, then in Mexico. The initials in the cabinet. TM. Could those be his? Why would he have been at their house, drawing in a cabinet? A friend's child? He wasn't one of her cousins. She shook her head.

"I don't know. I never saw him before, yet he seems so familiar. There were initials in the cabinet at my parent's house, clearly written by a child. I asked my dad about them, but he shrugged it off."

George sighed, his face lined with worry. "I can't have you being lured to your death. Stick with me, I won't let you wander off. Let's take a break and go back to the RV. Now, I'm even more scared something is trying to harm you, draw you away from me."

Hannah put her arms around Goerge and let her head rest against him. "Maybe we shouldn't have come here."

"Maybe, but more is coming together here. I think there are two different aspects at play. One trying to guide you to the answer, and one trying to hurt you. Why? I don't know. Come on, let's go back and recenter."

They headed back to the RV and lay on the couch bed, George's arms around Hannah. In the short time they'd been there, she'd seen Logan and the boy. The mask had led her here. That much was clear. Question was, was she being led for answers, or to be sacrificed?

They chose to stay in for the evening and made a light dinner. After they ate, they climbed up to the bed above the driving cab and George wrapped the fabric around both of their wrists before they fell asleep. Hannah felt drugged and slipped into a heavy sleep. George lay protectively by her, his body a shield between the outside world and Hannah. But it wasn't the outside world he needed to worry about.

Hannah dreamed she was riding in a car. Her parents were in the front seat, laughing and talking. She was little, strapped in a car seat, waving a doll back and forth. Her mother turned back saying something to her, smiling. Hannah didn't understand and kept waving the doll with her small, chubby hand. All of a sudden, the doll fell to the floor and she began to cry. A hand rested on her seat and she turned to see a boy. A dark-haired boy about five years old. He was smiling at her, telling her it was okay. He was trying to reach the doll, but it was out of his reach. Hannah kicked her feet and cried, but her parents' attention was focused on something ahead of the car. They weren't aware of her tears.

The boy patted her and unbuckled his seat belt to reach the doll. As he bent down, her mother began to scream. She waved her hands in front of her face as the car veered sharply to the right, flipping multiple times, then landing upright. Hannah stopped crying and stared. Her parents weren't moving. The boy was gone. The front window was shattered, leaving a gaping hole. Her mother began to shift and move, blood gushing from her head. She turned to face Hannah in fear.

Her eyes rested on where the boy had been seated and the unbuckled seat belt. She peered around desperately, then out the front window. She began to cry and tried to get out of the car, shoving with all her might. Hannah's father came to and realized what happened. He was pinned to his seat and could only watch helplessly as his wife pushed her way out and ran to the lifeless body of the dark-haired boy. She crumpled to the ground, clutching his body to her breast, and wailed.

Hannah jerked awake, expecting to hit her head on the ceiling again. But she didn't. She wasn't in the RV. She was lying in the middle of the Ball Game, the field where the games were played to the death. She sat up and looked around. How did she get here? Her feet and hands were raw and bloody. George. How had she gotten past George? She stood up and started to make her way back to the RV. Something told her to go to the cenote instead, and she turned that way. George was standing on the edge, frantically looking down.

"George?" she whispered to not startle him.

He spun and bolted toward her. "Where were you? I was afraid you came back here. That you..."

"That I was down there? I woke up in the Ball Game. I don't know why. I don't think I needed to come back here to the cenote. I needed to pay penance for what I did."

"What you did?"

"I think I killed the dark-haired boy. Not intentionally, though. He was trying to help me."

George took her hand as they walked back across to where the RV was parked. "Can you explain?"

Hannah told him about the dream and what happened. George listened, his head low as they walked. He paused and turned to her.

"Do you think the dream was real? Like that happened? Who would the boy be then?"

"I don't know. It was my parents, me at maybe two, and the boy. My parents were devastated."

"You are an only child?"

Hannah was about to say yes when it caught in her throat. The boy was holding her in the first dream when she was a baby, saying she was his Hannah. Then in this dream, he was comforting her and trying to get her doll. Like a brother would. She shook her head. There was no proof of a brother. No pictures, her parents never spoke of one. T.M. Toby. She remembered as a child having an imaginary friend named Toby.

What if he hadn't been imaginary?

What if she'd been remembering her brother? If it was, why would her parents have hidden him from her? Never acknowledged his existence. Erased him from memory. No, it didn't make sense. They wouldn't do that. Toby was an imaginary friend and she must have concocted all of this. She didn't have a brother. She was hallucinating and creating these images. Yet, he seemed so real, the memories flesh and blood.

Hannah met George's eyes and began to cry with the realization. Was her imaginary friend so real to her, she thought he was her brother? She might have led George on a wild goose chase to a foreign country all because she lost the baby and caused an accident. An accident like in her dream. She'd convinced herself this boy was real to deal with killing Logan Slip. It all added up in a twisted way. George wiped the tears from her eyes and put his hand on her chin.

"You aren't crazy, Hannah. Don't go there. This may not make sense, but I know you. Whatever is going on is real." His words were a balm, but she didn't want to accept them. To fool them both again.

"No, George. You don't understand. When I was a kid. I had this imaginary friend, Toby. I called him my brother and pretended he was always with me. He had dark hair and eyes. I eventually outgrew having an imaginary friend but in some stupid way, I think when I met Parker I felt connected to him because he *looked* like Toby. Dark hair and eyes. Then when I lost the baby and Parker and I split, it must have resurfaced in the back of my mind. After the accident where I killed Logan Slip, I think my mind broke and all of these different aspects came together, causing me to create Toby as this boy I keep seeing. And seeing Logan. You're wrong, George. My brain is fucked up. I'm fucked up. None of this is real. I've created this sick reality. For all I know, you aren't real either!"

George sighed and took her hand, leading her back to the RV. Once inside, he turned to her. He kissed her. "That is real. I am real. You are real. Start there."

Hannah wanted to believe him. He kissed her again, pressing her to him. Hannah leaned against him. If she was losing her mind, at least he was in there with her. But how did she leave the RV without him knowing? She glanced at their bed. George followed her gaze.

"I don't know, Hannah. It's like I was drugged. When I woke up, you were gone and my head was pounding. That could be the forces here trying to intervene. Another reason I know you are not losing your mind. Something is at work here. Something, or someone, doesn't want you to find the answers. What or who? I haven't a clue, but I know this isn't in your head. Plus, there is one other thing."

Hannah met his eyes, confused.

"T.M. Imaginary friends don't leave initials."

# CHAPTER TWENTY

*A*fter a fitful night's sleep, they decided they'd seen enough and the risk was becoming too high to stay there. Hannah lay in bed, thinking about what George said about the initials. She wanted to discount them, to say maybe she'd put them there. However, until she'd discovered them, she had no idea they were there. She couldn't sleep, afraid she'd wake up in another strange place. Whatever was there held some power over her, and somehow now George, too. Over breakfast, he set his cup down and put his hand over hers.

"I think it's time to go to Miguel and Sebastián's. I think what we are facing is bigger than us and they may be able to help. They're in tune with the spiritual world and perform Ayahuasca ceremonies. I think bringing them in on this at this point would be beneficial. I'm out of ideas and we seem to be going down a slippery slope."

Hannah agreed. While she seemed to be finding some answers, she also was getting drawn farther away from clarity and sanity. George said he'd drive and for her to sleep while he was awake to keep an eye on her. She curled up in the passenger seat and pulled a light blanket over her. They'd drive straight through to Miguel and Sebastián's. As they put Chichen Itza behind them, Hannah turned to George.

"Do you think I should try Ayahuasca? Do you think it would help?"

George shrugged, sighing. "At this point, I don't know. I'm scared to go too far into this without guidance. We can tell Miguel everything and see what he thinks. Have you thought to ask your parents about the boy? To see if they can shed any light on who he might be?"

Hannah had, but thought they might think she'd gone completely off of the deep end, asking about her imaginary friend as if he was real. The road stretched ahead, taking them through the countryside. Hannah stared out the window blearily, not wanting to dream if she dozed off. When she saw the body on the side of the road, she was sure it was either a mirage or a discarded bag of clothes. As they drew closer, it was clearly a man's body, dumped in the ditch. She looked to George for reassurance, but he stared straight ahead with his teeth clenched.

"Gangs," he muttered.

"What do you mean? Gangs did that? Why?"

"Who knows? To send a message, kill an informant, mark their territory. It's not uncommon in some places. You usually don't see it out this way so much. So, I'm guessing it is a family member of someone who crossed them."

Hannah watched in the rearview mirror as the body disappeared out of view. How could a country with so much beauty and history have such monsters? She considered the US probably did, too, but she'd been sheltered from it. Her bubble of safety was starting to disintegrate and it scared her. George reached out, resting his hand on her leg.

"Hey, we are okay. We'll get to Miguel and Sebastián's and recoup. We'll be safe there."

"Okay," Hannah whispered, her voice sounding tired and small.

She didn't remember falling asleep, but when she woke up they were driving through a quaint beach town. She gazed at George, who was deep in thought. She nudged him with her foot. "Are you alright?"

He shifted his focus to her and tipped his head. "I will be. I've been questioning every decision I made since we left Virginia. I should've been able to keep you safe, yet time and again, I've dropped the ball. Sheer luck has kept something from happening to you, so I'm deciding if I've done anything to actually help you along the way."

Hannah sat up. "Don't be silly, George. You found me, you fought for me, you helped me sort out what I needed to do. Mostly you stood by me. When I flipped out in front of my parents, they were quick to get me into the mental hospital. Not once did they say what was happening to me could be real. Every time, you approached it as a possibility. That maybe I wasn't losing my mind, and other factors could be at play. If I hadn't had you, I promise I would've locked myself away for good. You're the only strand of hope I have left that something outside of me is happening."

George watched her, assessing her words. He pushed his windblown hair off his face, then smiled. "Are you saying you need me?"

"Need you? Like I need air. I trust you with every ounce of my being at this point. Anyone else would have written me off a long time ago. Would have sent me away."

"Ah, well, where you go, I go. So, if you need to be locked away, they might as well lock me away, too."

"Aw, George, that is the sweetest thing anyone has ever said to me. Fucked up, but sweet."

George laughed and squeezed her leg. "We're almost there. They have the coolest cottage by the ocean."

A few minutes later, they pulled in front of a bright pink and turquoise home with chickens roaming the yard. To the right was a large garden, in it a little old man was picking tomatoes. He waved and grinned. Another hunched old man came to the front door, smiling. Miguel and Sebastián. Hannah wasn't sure which was which, so waited for George to greet them. She climbed out and followed him into the gated yard. He embraced the old man in the garden and turned to Hannah.

"Sebastián, este es mi corazón, Hannah. Hannah, this is mi tío, Sebastián."

Hannah smiled and took his warm hand, weathered, but soft. "Nice to meet you, Sebastián."

He grinned and handed her a tomato. George made his way to Miguel and embraced him. They spoke briefly in Spanish and George introduced him to Hannah. Miguel hugged Hannah, meeting her eyes. His eyes drooped in his face but were kind.

"Nice to meet you, Miguel. George has told me so much about you both."

Miguel smiled at George, meeting his eyes. "George, eh? Do you remember?"

George nodded as his ears turned bright red. Hannah glanced between them, trying to read what was going on. George met her eyes and chuckled. "Uh, so... the last time I took Ayahuasca, I had a vision. An angel told me I'd find my soul and the path to my heart in the one who called me by my given name. My given name being George, even though everyone I ever knew called me Buzzy. Even my parents. You're the only person who ever has called me George as my name."

Hannah felt her cheeks tingle and grinned. She leaned in and whispered, "That's because you are *my* George."

George touched her face, a slight smile playing on his lips. "That I am."

Miguel waved them inside. They followed him into a brightly colored cottage with vibrant art on the wall. It was filled with all sorts of relics and statues, making it seem more like a history museum than a home. The furniture was tucked in between the art, creating cozy nooks. Hannah and George joined Miguel in the sitting room. He had lemonade ready for them and offered each a glass full.

"Abeja, how was your trip? No hiking this time?" Miguel asked, referring to hitchhiking.

George shook his head. "Not this time. We were on a quest. Had to make ground." He turned to Hannah. "Abeja means bee. Buzzy, bee. Abeja. Their little inside joke."

Miguel nodded. "Safer too, to not hitchhike. Abeja is our endearment for our boy, not a joke. Like a nickname. So, did you finish your quest?"

George met Hannah's eyes, then looked back at Miguel. "Unfortunately not, we need your help. Your guidance."

Miguel watched them both as Sebastián came in and set down a large basket of vegetables on the counter. They conversed in Spanish before Miguel turned back to George and Hannah. "Is that so? What sort of help?"

George shifted, taking Hannah's hand. "We can talk more later, but something has been happening to Hannah. We don't know if they are of a spiritual sort, but it is getting dangerous."

Miguel eyed her and put his hand out for her to take. Hannah glanced at George, unsure, then slipped her hand into Miguel's. He considered her with his eyes, his brow furrowed. He cocked his head. "You are having a hard time because you do not know the truth."

Hannah could agree with that. She nodded and cleared her throat. "I'm not sure if this is all in my head."

"Either way, it is in your head because your head is part of your body, which is part of your soul. Two halves of the same whole. You cannot separate them and find the answer," Miguel explained.

Two halves of the same whole. Like the mask. The skull and the clown. Maybe it wasn't a clown, rather a representation of something else, like the soul. Miguel let her hand go and nodded. "It will be okay. You must take a journey to find what you are looking for, but you are taking the wrong journey."

"The wrong journey. Like not Mexico?" Hannah asked, confused.

Miguel chuckled. "Not Mexico, not Earth, not physical. Your journey needs to go inside. You have the answer, you do not have the key."

Hannah was more lost than ever. "Should I have not come here?"

"No, you should have come here, but not for the answer. For the key," Miguel answered.

Hannah looked at George for clarity. He put his hands in the air, showing he had no idea. "Miguel, should Hannah take Ayahuasca?"

Miguel shook his head. "Not yet. Her soul is in chaos, she needs to find her calm to prepare. You work with her and we will see. If her soul continues in chaos, her mind will stay fractured. If she took Ayahuasca while in chaos, she could never come back."

Hannah thought she understood. Her mind was broken and if she took Ayahuasca in that state, it could stay broken. She needed to settle it first. Like a salve for a burn. "So, how do I find my calm?"

Sebastián came to sit and leaned forward, placing his hand over hers. "This is why you are here."

George helped Sebastián cook while Miguel showed Hannah through the house, explaining the history behind the artifacts and art. Everything had a story and in the story, a message. Nothing was just there to be visual. Hannah thought about her parents' house and the generic art they had in there, meant to match the furniture and rugs. Nothing had a story. Being around Miguel, she felt the bubble of safety start to strengthen and she wasn't sure she'd ever want to leave. Once they were out of earshot, she turned to Miguel.

"George told me he met you when he came to try Ayahuasca to treat his addiction?"

Miguel tipped his head. "Yes and no. Abeja found us because his soul was broken and he needed to mend it. But the addiction was not what caused the brokenness. Always being told he was not good enough did."

"I don't understand. Who always told him he wasn't good enough?"

"His father. He did not mean to, but raising his sons to compete with each other, to fight, and strive to be better, made them believe they were not good enough as they were. He saw it as making them stronger, but he was breaking them down. The fall caused Abeja's physical pain, but his emotional pain caused his addiction. He was not needing to break the addiction, he was needing to know he was perfect the way he was. The physical pain was gone and what was hurting him was emotional. Once he came to understand he did not need to prove his worth, his physical pain and addiction were controlled. Not totally gone because we need to always be reminded we matter. But as long as he remembers this, the addiction no longer has a grip."

Hannah absorbed his words like water. She'd never thought about how a parent's, or anyone's, actions could create an external need. Her parents were loving but so overprotective, she was constantly trying to set her own boundaries... even if they were detrimental to her.

George came to the door, watching them. "Dinner's ready. Sebastián worked his magic."

Miguel clapped his hands and headed for the dining room. George paused with Hannah at the door. For the first time, she saw him as the boy trying to prove to his father his worth. She placed her hand on his cheek and met his eyes.

"I love you, George. Just the way you are. You don't owe me anything and haven't failed me in any way. Do you understand that? To me, you are absolutely perfect and I'm glad you exist."

George frowned slightly, his eyes dark. He bent to kiss her, his mouth warm and steady. When they parted, he smiled and twisted a strand of her hair around his finger. His voice was gentle when he spoke.

"I knew I'd find you."

# CHAPTER TWENTY-ONE

*A*fter dinner, Miguel invited them out to his workshop. It was a small but comfortable space where he and Sebastián stored tools, supplies, and created a sanctuary to be alone and focus. They sat on the tufted couch and faced Miguel. Sebastián wanted to read and knew they needed to talk about what was happening, to determine how to help Hannah. He walked them out, then said goodnight. Miguel kissed him at the door and came back.

"So, dear. Tell me what has happened to you."

Hannah met his eyes, unsure of where to start. "What part?"

"Tell me what you think matters to bring you to where you are now."

Hannah began to tell Miguel everything from losing the baby to the accident and the dreams she'd been having, along with the sleepwalking and visions. He didn't pry but scribbled down notes as she went along. At times, she went back and forth, remembering details she'd left out. George held her hand the whole time but let it be her story to tell. When she finally told

Miguel everything she should think of, she paused and watched him, expecting judgment. He didn't speak but rubbed his lip like she'd seen George do. She wondered how much influence Miguel and Sebastián had on George since he'd been coming to Mexico. They, like him, took time to think before they spoke and considered everything.

Miguel set the pad down. "Do you think these things are real, or do you think your mind is playing tricks on you?"

Hannah flushed with embarrassment. He was judging her! "I don't know. I mean, they seem real. They feel real. I... I'm not crazy!"

Miguel leaned forward, his eyes unblinking. "I did not say you were crazy, dear. I asked if *you* thought they were truly happening. The reason I ask is if you feel it is all in your head, it will be hard to address them. Do you see?"

Hannah thought about what he said. He was saying she had to believe herself, otherwise she would undermine any process or progress she made. "I do believe they are real. I don't think I'm losing my mind, though, sometimes it feels that way."

"It feels that way because we are taught to only believe in what we have been told to be true. If you have been told as a small child that the physical and spiritual realms interconnect, you would not be surprised by seeing this young boy or motorcyclist. You would understand they are there to give you a message or to guide you. Instead, you see it as a punishment, yes?"

Hannah nodded. She did see their presence as a condemnation of who she was and what she did. "What about the baby crying?"

Miguel reached forward and squeezed her hand. "I believe that is your grief. You told yourself you did not deserve to grieve because you were not expecting to have a child. That is your brain stepping in and telling you to let yourself hurt and to recognize you suffered a loss."

At that, Hannah burst into tears. For the first time since losing the baby, she understood she was aching for what she lost. She still grieved the baby because it still had been part of her. She put her face in her hands and sobbed as George rubbed her back. After a few minutes, she looked up, tipping her head. "So, the baby has nothing to do with this?"

Miguel shook his head. "It does. Grief and loss are powerful tools for opening spiritual doors. Part of you is there, part of you is here. There is a doorway. Losing your child has created an opening, allowing the boy and the motorcyclist to pass through. Do you hear the baby cry anymore?"

Hannah didn't hear the baby anymore. Hadn't since she was back home. It made sense. Since losing the baby, Hannah wondered where it went, if it saw her, and if they were still linked. Her connection to the baby opened the door and she'd kept it open. She stared at Miguel. "Do you believe me?"

He chuckled and patted her hand. "My belief is no matter. *You* need to believe you. You must settle your brain from all the doubt, accept what you know and find your calm. Once you do, I think we can find a way to find out what the boy and the motorcyclist are trying to tell you. That is why you have this young man with you. He can be your guide here."

He gestured to George. George sat forward, slipping his arm around Hannah's waist. "I'm here. Miguel helped me to settle myself when I first came to him. I was in pain and mentally in chaos. He taught me how to go within and trust myself. I couldn't do the tea ceremony until then."

"Ayahuasca?" Hannah asked.

Miguel nodded. "It is powerful and too many people think drinking the tea is the whole part of it, then they end up in a very dark place. There are many steps to the ceremony. The first is settling yourself, addressing your demons. Finding your calm. Once you have done that, we'll go through the other steps. The tea is last. Then we will counsel."

Hannah didn't understand it all but trusted Miguel and George. She wasn't sure how Sebastián played into it, if at all. Miguel stood up and took his leave. George pulled Hannah back against him on the couch and rubbed her arm with his thumb in a soothing rhythm.

"Ayahuasca has become popular, but a lot of people are administering it who shouldn't be. Bad things have happened. Miguel's family has been doing the ceremony for many, many years. He never had children of his own, as he and Sebastián are a couple. Since neither had children to teach, he's afraid the ceremony will die with him. He'd like me to learn it. To apprentice under him."

Hannah peered up at him. "Will you?"

George met her eyes. "I don't know. I want to help you through this and see if I'm able to properly administer all the steps. Miguel normally does the pre-ceremony but I'll do that with you. If you are okay with that?"

"Of course. I trust you with my life. What about Sebastián, what does he do?"

"Ah, Sebastián. He'll teach you to be in the moment. To be outside of your thoughts and worries. The greatest tool ever. You'll see."

Hannah liked Sebastián. Everything he did was so present. She hadn't realized he and Miguel were a couple until she saw them kiss, and could see how George had become like a son to them. He called them uncle, maybe out of respect for his father. However, they were like fathers to him, doting on him and teaching him their ways. Hannah rested her hand on George's leg.

"You love Miguel and Sebastián?"

George chuckled. "They're my family. They helped save me. When I came here the first time, they took me in and reminded me I existed for a reason. I was broken, lost. I stayed with them for almost a month the first time and came back once a year for the first few years. After the first ceremony, they helped me to understand what I experienced."

"Can I ask? What was it like? The ceremony."

"I won't lie, it was hard, scary, and beautiful. I saw things that made me feel like my soul was up for grabs. Dark beings, light beings. I saw how I needed to stand up for the boy I was, how he forgot himself. I took a journey through my life. The first time was the hardest."

"Oh." Hannah was scared.

"Hannah, I promise I'll be there with you. You may not know it then but know it now. I won't leave your side. You don't have to do this if you aren't comfortable."

Hannah nodded. "I want to do it. I want to understand what is happening to me. I'm just scared."

"I was, and still am, scared every time I do the ceremony, but it has gotten better. As I understand myself and other realms, the experiences are better, more enlightening. Like lessons to bring back."

"You were told about me?"

George sighed. "Oh, mi corazón. Yes. It was about a year after I split with my ex. I was feeling like no one would understand me, or the things I'd seen and learned. I did the ceremony and this light-being assured me there was someone out there who would know me. I asked how I'd know this person and was told they'd call me by my given name."

"My George." Hannah placed her face against his neck and sighed. She didn't even think of him as Buzzy anymore. "When did you know?"

"That it was you? When you called me George the first time at the hospital."

Hannah sat up and stared at him. "You knew this whole time? Why didn't you say something?"

"Because you didn't," George whispered.

"I guess. I knew I wanted to stay in touch with you. The idea of never seeing you again made me sad. I think I've felt so discarded and guilty, I didn't think I deserved you."

"That's one of the first things we'll work on. In order to do the tea ceremony, you need to address what is in you that can come out as demons or dark thoughts. Because trust me, if you do the ceremony and you haven't, that's exactly what they'll come out as."

Hannah chewed her lip and met his eyes dead-on. "I trust you."

George blushed, his ears turning pink. "Trust is the most important part of love."

"I've loved you long before I knew what you were to me, George. It was almost immediate. Like we were destined for each other."

"Do you believe in destiny?"

Hannah considered that. Now she did. She bobbed her head. "I think so."

"Good, because destiny is an important part of all of this. You have to believe your path is set out and you just need to follow it. You can't resist. You need to be open and ready to accept what is shown to you. That's where the counsel after comes into it. Miguel will sit down with you and help you unravel anything you experience you may not comprehend."

"Could bad things like evil spirits come in? Like things that want to harm me?"

George tipped his head. "It can seem that way, but nothing can harm you. You will be right in front of me, with my arms around you. You'll be safe. I promise that. No matter what you experience, it's in another realm and can't hurt you here. Do you still have that stone you found?"

"Segura? Yes."

"Bring that with you as a talisman to hold on to. I'll make sure if you drop it, I'll put it back in your hand." George sat up. "Hey, you want to take a walk and look at the stars?"

"Sure, that would be nice."

They got up and headed outside. The sky was bright, the stars clearer than Hannah had ever seen. George held her hand and pointed out different constellations. Hannah peered up in awe. There were too many stars to count. She thought she saw a shift of movement through the stars and it was gone. She cocked her head.

"Do you think Earth is it?"

George laughed. "Absolutely not."

"Do you believe in aliens?"

"Aliens? Cosmic beings? Not sure what to call what I believe, but I know we aren't alone. I think people have confused what is out there for spirituality and religion."

"So, God is an alien?" Hannah said, half amused and half curious.

"Something like that. We have no comprehension of what's out there, standing on our spinning rock," George answered honestly.

Hannah glanced at him, then back at the sky. "I like the way you think, George."

He squeezed her hand. "See, there *was* someone out there who understands me. You may be the first, ever."

She chuckled. "You and me, in a cosmos of disbelief."

"I believe in you, Hannah."

"I believe in you, George."

George turned Hannah to him and kissed her deeply under the stars. Her knees felt weak and she met his eyes, more beautiful than the night sky. She ran her fingers over his eyebrows, then sighed.

"The reality that I met you when my world was falling apart... because my world was falling apart, only solidifies my understanding that nothing is random. You knew about me before I even knew you. Before my world came crashing down, sending me spiraling out into chaos, something out there told you I was coming to you."

George smiled down at her, his eyes understanding her on a level no one ever had. "Even if we don't know the way, the universe does."

# CHAPTER TWENTY-TWO

T his time when she woke up, Hannah was standing in front of a restaurant in Xcalak. It was closed, as it was the middle of the night, but she was facing the colorful local hangout named Toby's. *That* couldn't be a coincidence. She was barefoot, however, she must have not walked far because her feet were still soft and not raw. She bit her lip and peered around. She vaguely remembered passing this place on the way in. The town was tiny, so it shouldn't be hard to find her way back.

A rustling behind her caught her attention and she turned. Sebastián was standing off to the side watching her, his face set in a calm, patient expression. At first, she jolted, then settled and smiled.

"I sleepwalk," she explained.

He nodded and came closer, grasping her hand in his. His English wasn't as good as Miguel's but he was so expressive, Hannah understood. "I follow. I was awake."

Hannah sighed. "Thank you, Sebastián."

He led her as he turned to head back toward home. "Come. Talk to Abeja."

She walked with Sebastián the few streets back to their home. George was awake and standing on the front porch, his face twisted in stress. When he saw them approach, his shoulders dropped and he let out a deep breath. "Hannah, I woke up and you were gone. I guess we let our guard down. I thought it wouldn't happen here for some reason."

"Sebastián found me."

George embraced Sebastián. "Gracias, Tío."

Hannah sat on a swing on the porch. "At least I didn't get far. I ended up at a restaurant in town. Called Toby's. Like my imaginary friend. Weird, right?"

George frowned, sitting down next to her. Sebastián got his attention and began to explain something in Spanish. George listened intently, his eyebrows raised. When Sebastián finished, George leaned forward resting his elbows on his knees, then bobbed his head. He faced Hannah.

"Sebastián said he was up reading when you passed by him and went out the door. He called out to you, but you didn't respond. He could tell you were asleep, so he followed to make sure you were okay. He said it was like you knew where you were going. You were walking strangely, though. Not stumbling, but not how you normally walk."

Hannah bit her lip, she had no recollection. "Strangely how?"

George turned to Sebastián and asked him in Spanish. Sebastián gestured with his hands, raising them and lifting them slightly up and down. He then said something familiar to Hannah as he moved his body from side to side. He repeated the words "Toby" and "baba" over and over.

George listened carefully, then met Hannah's eyes. "He said you were walking like a small child. Toddling. You kept raising your arms and crying, 'Toby, baba.' He explained it was like watching a toddler wanting to be picked up by someone. When you got to the restaurant, you stopped and just stood still, staring blankly at the sign."

Hannah shook her head. *Toby, baba?* A brief image popped into her head of her looking up at the dark-haired boy. Toby. She knew for sure that was him and he wasn't imaginary. *Baba?* She didn't understand. George cleared his throat.

"When I was little and couldn't say things, I called my brother Teddy 'Tay'. Hannah, is it possible in your sleepwalking you were a child and you were calling out for Toby?" George asked.

"Maybe, but what is Baba?"

"Brother? Like, how a small child would say it?" George offered.

It clicked. Toby *was* indeed her brother. Her head started to spin. There'd been an accident and he died. She remembered snippets. Why had her parents never talked to her about this? Why did they hide his existence from her and allowed her to forget? It was cruel and unforgivable. Pain clenched her chest as she felt hot tears prick her eyes. She jumped up, enraged.

"Toby! My brother! He *is* the dark-haired boy, not my imaginary friend. The nightmare about the accident wasn't a nightmare, it was a memory. What the hell?" Hannah screamed and stomped off toward the garden.

George rose to follow her, but Sebastián put his hand on George's arm to stop him. "Un momento."

George watched as Hannah made her way into the garden and fell to her knees, sobbing. Sebastián was telling him to let her process this. Part of her getting ready for the ceremony was to come to grips with the ghosts of her past. Once her sobs stopped, her shoulders hunched and she leaned forward into the soil. George wanted to go to her, to make it better, but he needed to stop being a barrier between her and reality.

Hannah pressed her forehead to the dirt and let out a shaky breath. Once the realization set in, more memories came. Toby carrying her around. Him showing her bugs in the backyard. Them playing in the closet. Lying on a blanket, gazing at the clouds, giggling about some game they were playing. He was a few years older than her, her big brother. Her baba. She was furious at her parents for removing him from their lives. How could they be so heartless? She stood up and walked back to the porch.

Sebastián stood up and embraced her. "El viaje ha comenzado." He motioned to George, then to Hannah as he headed inside.

"Sebastián said the journey has begun. He will meet with you in the morning for his part of the ceremony."

Hannah plopped down next to George. "I don't think I'm ready for this."

"You are. This is just a shock."

"To say the least. So, all along in my childhood, my imaginary friend Toby was actually the memory of my brother? How seriously fucked up is that? I was grieving for him! For my big brother. How could my parents be so cold, so callous? They allowed him to die twice."

George sighed, shaking his head. "I can't speak for them, but there must have been some reason. Maybe they thought they were protecting you?"

"From what? From the one person who I adored?"

"Hannah, I don't know. I'm sorry. I know this hurts. You have every right to feel the way you do."

Hannah was ready to argue, however, hearing those words took the steam out of her. It did hurt. Her heart felt like it was breaking in two. She felt betrayed. Fresh tears slipped down her cheek. She had an answer, but not one she wanted. She didn't want to know Toby had been real and ripped away from her. Then erased like his life didn't matter. She didn't think she could ever speak to her parents again. They weren't the people she thought they were. They lost a child, then went on as if nothing happened. She turned to George.

"I can't think anymore tonight. Can we go back to bed? I'm tired."

George reached out and stroked her cheek. "Of course. I'll hold you as tight as I can."

They went back to the small room they'd been using in the house and climbed into the large bed. As promised, George wrapped his arms snugly around Hannah as another memory surfaced.

"I used to climb in Toby's bed and he'd hug me until I fell asleep. I remember that. You know you remind me of him?"

"I do? Why?"

"With you, I feel safe." Hannah remembered finding the rock where she'd seen the dark-haired boy... Toby, by the tree. Not a random moment, a message. "Segura."

"Oh, Hannah, I'm so sorry you lost him. That must have been terrible for you after."

"I don't remember. My parents made him invisible. Took all of the pictures of him down and never spoke about him. I hate them," Hannah replied bitterly.

"No, you don't. You're just hurting. This was a startling revelation. You need time to process all of it," George whispered.

Rage at her parents surged and she sat up, staring at George. "Don't tell me how I feel!"

"Hannah, I didn't mean it like that. I just meant to give this time-"

"Time? Are you kidding me? They took *decades* away from me. Decades of memories and emotions."

"I'm sorry, I didn't mean to hurt you more. I just think you need to speak to them and ask them why."

"George, stay out of it!" Hannah yelled, making him flinch.

George stared at her, clearly hurt. He nodded and set his mouth in a line. He rolled over with his back to her and sighed. Hannah was being unfair, but at the moment she didn't care. She pressed herself against the other edge of the bed and mashed her eyes together, seeing rage spots blinking behind her lids. She'd been betrayed and no one could fix that. She felt George turn back over. He placed his hand on her back and she jerked away. He let his hand drop.

The next morning, the bed was empty when she woke up and she lay, staring at the ceiling. She was still angry. Like years of angry. She'd never go back. Her parents could lose both of their children. It would serve them right for what they did.

She sat up and rubbed her face hard. She dressed and went to the kitchen. Sebastián was sipping coffee and smiled at her.

"Good morning, Hannah. Abeja and Miguel left."

Left? Hannah poured coffee. "Where did they go?"

Sebastián considered his English, then shrugged. "To find."

To find? To find what? Hannah took a sip of coffee and grimaced. Sebastián liked his coffee strong. Sebastián chuckled at her face and went to get cream. She poured enough in to make it palatable and thanked him.

They drank their coffee in silence when Sebastián placed his hand over hers. "We begin?"

Oh yeah, she was supposed to start her lessons with him. She had no idea what that meant but she bobbed her head. "Okay."

He led her out to the garden and showed her how to pick the vegetables off of the vine without damaging the plant. They did this for a while when Hannah wondered if he was going to start the lessons.

"Are you going to teach me?"

Sebastián grinned at her and pointed back at the plants in the basket. He wanted her to keep picking. She shrugged and worked down the row she was on. Maybe he'd teach her later. As she picked, her mind relaxed and she pressed a warm tomato against her cheek. It was smooth and her skin became one with the sensation. She placed it in the basket and did this with the other vegetables. By lunchtime, they'd picked all the ripe fruit, weeded the garden, and the sun was high in the sky. Hannah wiped beads of sweat off her neck and picked up the basket.

They headed in and made lunch. Because of Sebastián's limited English and her limited Spanish, they worked around each other mainly in silence. Hannah didn't mind, it was like meditating.

After lunch, they washed the dishes and Sebastián went to take a nap. Hannah wandered around the house, looking at the art and artifacts. She felt at home there. Like she belonged. Following Sebastián's lead, and a lack of sleep the night before, she went to lie in bed. George's face surfaced in her mind and she wondered where he and Miguel went.

To find.

After a nap, Hannah felt in much better spirits. Sebastián showed her how to plant new rows and tend to fragile plants. She liked this work. It had meaning. By nightfall, George and Miguel weren't back and she began to get worried. She noticed George left his phone behind and she doubted Miguel had one. She pressed Sebastián.

"When will George and Miguel come home?"

He shrugged. "No sé."

He didn't know. Hannah frowned. "Tonight?"

Sebastián shook his head. "No sé."

He wasn't any help. He didn't seem concerned, either. Maybe Miguel left like this a lot. They made dinner and ate, just like lunch. They washed the dishes in silence, then Sebastián read. Hannah didn't know what to do with herself. She fidgeted and watched the clock, listening for their return. The road stayed quiet. Sebastián turned in and Hannah went to the room. She shouldn't have been so unkind to George. Her last words were so cruel. He'd just been trying to offer her a gentle alternative to her rage. Instead, she'd twisted her anger onto him.

She sat on the bed and tried meditating, but she was agitated. Why didn't he take his phone? She tried lying down, tossing and turning. What if they were hurt? What if the gangs got them? What if George was out there injured and alone? She'd been unfair. What if they got in an accident and he died like Toby? Hannah cried into her pillow. Finally, she drifted off into a fitful sleep. What she would do to feel George next to her. To feel his arms around her.

The next morning they were still not back and Hannah found Sebastián on the front porch, rocking. He smiled at her. Hannah couldn't understand how he was so nonchalant.

"Sebastián, where did George and Miguel go?"

He watched her, his eyes unreadable. He pointed out to the horizon and turned his palm up toward the sky.

"To find."

# CHAPTER TWENTY-THREE

*A* week passed with no sign of Miguel or George. Hannah followed Sebastián's lead and tried not to worry. He clearly felt they were safe and stayed focused on tending the home and garden. Each morning, they'd wake up, have breakfast and coffee, work in the garden or forage, then have lunch and a nap. Every evening was filled with reading and music. Sebastián could play guitar and would bring it out some nights to play for Hannah. Instead of struggling around their language barriers, they learned to read each other and found silence to be rejuvenating. Sometimes Sebastián would take Hannah out to the beach to collect little rocks and shells. They'd place them in the garden and sit, enjoying the quiet. By the end of the week, Hannah felt like she was in a more peaceful place. No longer raging at her parents, but still not ready to speak to them. She hadn't sleepwalked or had any visions, either.

Hannah was working in the garden, pulling tiny weeds out from between the rows when they drove up. Miguel and George. George got out of the passenger side and watched her. She stood up and brushed the soil off of her knees. Sebastián went to Miguel and embraced him, patting him on the cheek. George and Hannah stared at one another, neither making the first move. Hannah knew it was hers to make. She wandered over to him and stood as close as she could without touching him.

"Did you find what you were looking for?" she asked.

He cocked his head, confused. "What I was looking for?"

"Sebastián said you left 'to find'. So did you find it?"

George glanced at Sebastián, his brows furrowed, then back at Hannah. "Oh. I went on a trip with Miguel to learn. What we were seeking was inside us."

"Why did you need to leave to do that?"

George shook his head. "We left for you to work with Sebastián. My journey was with Miguel to learn more about the ceremony, so we went to the ceremonial site and performed a ceremony on me to go within. Sebastián wanted you here alone. No one to distract or protect you."

"No one to protect me? That sounds ominous," Hannah said, attempting humor, but she was miffed. What if she *required* protection?

"You need to be able to protect yourself, Hannah. To understand the demons you think are after you, are *you*. If I was here, I'd want to shield you from hurt, from suffering. You wouldn't be able to connect to yourself and find your own strength. Toby was your protector, then your parents, maybe Parker, then me. I'd love nothing more than to keep you safe, but that has to come from inside you. At least in this instance."

Hannah took a step back. She *was* always looking for safety in others. This last week she had to push past that and depend on herself. Even Sebastián acted like nothing more than a companion. He didn't tell her what she needed to do or who she was. He had her pick vegetables and plant things, collect little rocks and shells, sit in silence. His presence a steady guide, while stepping away and allowing her to flourish.

Oh! Sebastián was teaching her all along. He was showing her how to be. Just *be*. Like meditating but all the time. She glanced at Sebastián and he winked at her. She smiled and winked back. He was showing her how to find her calm. No amount of words or instruction would've shown her what learning to be present did. She turned back to George.

"How was your journey within?"

"It was good. It was right. I needed to step away from you and stop trying to make everything okay. I was harming myself."

That stung a little. "I was harming you?"

"No, I was harming myself. My ego believing I could protect you from all of this. I started out wanting to guide you and ended up trying to be the wall between you and your path. Loving you and forgetting myself."

Hannah chewed her lip. So, was their revelation of how they felt about each other a mistake? Was he saying he should've stayed as just her friend? A pit formed in her stomach. Had she let him in and now he realized it was the wrong path? She met his eyes, trying to understand.

"Oh, I see."

He eyed her carefully. "Hannah-"

She turned and went back to the garden. Miguel and Sebastián disappeared inside the house. Hannah knelt and began to pull weeds again. She needed to let her mind breathe. George came and knelt beside her. He didn't speak but started pulling weeds with her. Once they were done, he touched her hand.

"Will you take a walk on the beach with me?"

Hannah stood up. She didn't want to, she wanted to be alone... but not really. What she wanted was to go back to when she could rely on George. He cleared his throat.

"Please?"

She nodded and they headed out toward the isolated coastline. Neither spoke for some time when George turned to Hannah.

"How did you feel this week with Sebastián?"

"Calm, I guess. Simple. My brain was clear."

"Good. I think I wanted so badly to help you, I was forcing something which might have needed to work itself out."

"Forcing us?" Hannah asked, her throat tight.

George looked at her, then sighed. "Hannah, Miguel wants me to stay here and continue learning what he has to teach. I'm going to. It was unfair of me to drag you into all of this, which seemed to make it worse for you."

"It didn't make it worse. These things were happening to me before we came. Being here has dredged up a lot of my past, but it needed to."

"Did it? Do you feel knowing about Toby has made anything better? You're angrier, you don't want to speak to your parents. You lashed out at me. Is this better?"

"Am I happier? No. But it *is* better for me to know the truth." Hannah surprised herself with the revelation.

"I agree, but the truth comes out in a lot of ways, more gentle. I feel like my presence has spun you more into chaos. I know I've felt more chaotic and unsure about everything since we started this journey."

"I have to do this, George. I need to find answers to why I keep seeing Logan Slip. I needed to know about my brother Toby. Otherwise, I would've probably ended up right back in the mental hospital. Don't you see, you've been my one constant in all this?"

"That's the problem, Hannah. I can't be your constant. *You* need to be your constant. Sebastián and Miguel can help you with the ceremony, but in order for you to be ready, I need to step away and let you do the work. What started out as a quest for knowledge became a vacation and our focus shifted to each other."

"Do you not love me anymore?"

George winced and put his head down. "I'll always love you, Hannah, but part of love is letting go."

"I can't do this ceremony alone, George. I need you with me."

"I will be there, that won't change. As part of my training, I'll be there as a support and guide for you. I love you, Hannah, please don't doubt that."

Hannah stared at him. "How can you say that when you are abandoning me in my time of need?"

"Time of need? Since I have known you, you've been in a time of need. I'm not trying to be mean, but you have to find the part of you willing to fight for yourself. Become a warrior. Stop wanting to be saved."

Hannah glared at him. "How dare you? I don't want to be saved, I *need* a friend! I thought you were that friend."

"I am, and that's why I need to take a step back. Keep working with Sebastián. Miguel will start meeting with you to prepare you for the tea ceremony. I'll be with him sometimes and sometimes not. I'm not abandoning you, Hannah. I'm setting you free."

Hannah had nothing else to say and turned her face away from him. They walked back to the house and had lunch with Miguel and Sebastián. After lunch, George headed to the RV to rest, while Miguel and Sebastián went to their room. Hannah was too conflicted to sleep, so she left to take a walk. She ended up on a long, low pier and made her way to the end. She slipped off her shoes and sat, dangling her feet in the water. George wasn't wrong. She gravitated toward safety nets. Even Parker had been one. He'd never challenged her or required anything from her. He was there when she needed him. As memories of Toby surfaced, she could see he was always looking out for her. He'd reminded her of George, who was always looking out for her. She wasn't looking out for herself.

She rested back against the pier and stared at the sky. Her life was a series of events of her bouncing from one safety net to another. She loved George. Not like Parker or her parents. She loved him so much, she wanted to protect *him*. If he needed to step away from her, she wouldn't fight him on it. Her week with Sebastián had helped her to see things more clearly. It would be hard being around George without being with him, however, she knew it was for the best. They hadn't been intimate beyond kissing and holding hands. Sleeping in the bed alone again would be a challenge. She needed to grow, to find her strength, and stop depending on him.

She sat up and gazed out over the water as a fishing boat trolled by. The old man at the helm raised his hand to her. He was the man from her dream about the cave. No warning this time. There didn't need to be, because he'd been warning her about herself. About the twisted path she was losing herself on.

Hannah stood up and wandered around the town for a bit, then headed back to the house. She passed by Toby's restaurant and paused. At least now she knew. She could find a way to connect Toby back into her life and stop running from his memory. George was talking with Sebastián on the porch when she came up. He met her eyes and she smiled, letting him know they were alright. She leaned in, kissing him on the cheek.

"I understand now," she whispered and went inside.

He watched her depart and turned back to Sebastián, his eyes sad. He'd done the right thing for Hannah, but his heart was broken. He'd given a piece of himself in the process. Sebastián took his hand.

"Un corazón roto todavía late." A broken heart still beats.

George wiped a tear away from his eye and nodded back at Sebastián, touching his heart. "That it does."

The next few days were awkward, but they eventually learned to be around each other without pain. Miguel began the process of explaining the ceremony to Hannah. What to expect, how it would feel. George was often present at these discussions, and Hannah could see he was watching closely to learn Miguel's ways. Miguel had George do daily meditations with Hannah, though this time they didn't hold hands. Sebastián continued having her work with him in the garden; this was her favorite part of the day. Hannah stopped sleepwalking and had neither visions nor nightmares. Her sleep became more regular and she woke up feeling peaceful.

After a couple of weeks, Miguel told her she was ready. Even though she was nervous, she was no longer scared. She trusted Miguel, George, and Sebastián. She trusted herself. The night before the ceremony, George sought her out and asked her to go for a walk. Outside of meditating, they'd not been alone since their last walk on the beach. They meandered the streets in the town and went out to the pier Hannah sat at earlier. Neither spoke but enjoyed their quiet time together. Their chemistry was different, secure. They sat at the end, staring out over the ocean. George was the first to speak, his voice soft.

"I'm proud of you, Hannah. I can see you've been working hard to get to this place and you seem like a different person. Calm, sure."

Hannah smiled. "Thanks, George. I feel it. I think for the first time in my life, I realized I don't need anyone."

George glanced away, a quick frown crossing his brow. She hadn't meant it that way. He'd been her rock for a while. Without him, she wouldn't have made it this far, but now she needed to depend on herself. She reached out and took his hand.

"You taught me that. It doesn't mean I don't want people around, but you were right. I needed to learn to stand on my own two feet, to believe in myself. To find myself within. You are my closest friend and I'm grateful for you. You forced me to see my own strength."

George met her eyes, tipping his head. "I'm glad to hear that, Hannah. We started this trip with an image of a mask and a few details. Now, you're about to embark on a journey like no other. I'll be there with you. As a friend. As someone who cares very deeply for you."

Hannah nodded, understanding. "I know, George. I care very deeply for you, as well, and wouldn't have traded these experiences for anything. I'm happy you're here with me, and I'm glad I got to know you through all this."

George squeezed her hand, then let go and stood up. He peered out as the sun dipped in the sky, creating an array of colors around them. "No matter what, we're forever connected. You are my best friend, Hannah. Let's go back and try to get some rest before tomorrow. If we can."

He reached down and helped Hannah up. They walked back hand in hand, this time as equals, ready to jump into the unknown together. Where they started from the moment they first met.

As friends.

# CHAPTER TWENTY-FOUR

T he next morning, Hannah woke with the sun and stared at the ceiling. A sense of anticipation engulfed her and she was ready to take the leap. Miguel explained they'd leave early and spend the day doing cleansing rituals prior to the ceremony. She wouldn't do the Ayahuasca ceremony until the night. She slipped on a pair of drawstring pants and a tank top, heading out to the kitchen.

Miguel was in the kitchen and peered up at her from something he was working on at the counter. She noticed there was no sight of Sebastián or George. Miguel finished what he was doing and motioned for her wrist. She put her hand out and he tied a woven bracelet on her wrist.

"I made this for you. You are our family, now. You are always welcome here and if you ever choose to stay, you have a roof over your head with us."

Hannah was touched by his kindness and ran her fingers across the bracelet. It was a series of tiny knots, creating a strand of purple, yellow, and blue stripes. She sat down across from Miguel at the counter and smiled.

"Thank you, Miguel. You and Sebastián have been like uncles to me. I'm sorry if I caused any issues."

"Issues? No, no. You and Abeja are still on a journey. Paths can come together and diverge, yet go in the same direction."

"How did you end up calling him Abeja for Buzzy?"

Miguel chuckled. "When he first called, he told me his name was Buzzy, but I did not understand. He kept saying 'buzzy, buzz like a bee'. I started calling him Abeja and it stuck."

"He really loves you," Hannah replied.

"He is love, that boy. He is like a son to us. We are glad he is staying to learn our traditions. Maybe one day you will, too."

Hannah shifted uncomfortably, wanting to change the subject. "Where are George and Sebastián?"

"They went to return the camper. There is a drop-off an hour from here and someone wanted to book it."

Hannah was surprised. The original plan was for them to drive it back to the United States and catch a plane to Virginia. However, they'd had it longer than they were supposed to and George wasn't going back. She wasn't sure how she'd get back now, either.

"There is an airport a few hours from here. We will take you when it is time to fly back to your home," Miguel said, reading her mind.

Home. Her lease was up and she'd decided not to renew. She'd resigned from her job and hadn't spoken to her parents since letting them know she was staying in Mexico longer. She wasn't sure there was a home to go back to. She'd even sold her car for the money. She smiled at Miguel and nodded, then stood up to look out the window. She'd know more in time. Miguel excused himself and left the kitchen. They were leaving as soon as George got back. Sebastián had completed his part and would stay back to watch the house. Hannah mentally brushed off any thoughts of the future, embracing her path for the day. She needed a clear mind, not to create spirals that might hinder her. For now, she was here.

By the time Sebastián and George drove in, Hannah was pacing the floor, ready to get started. George came in and handed her something. She looked at it, then grinned. It was her stone.

"It was still in the RV. I scoured the space, searching for anything we may have left behind, and found this tucked in the window by the couch," he explained.

Hannah slipped it into her pocket. "Thank you, George! I would've been sad if I'd lost it. So, the RV is done and gone?"

"Yeah, they were starting to tack on extra fees, so we took it back. I don't figure we still need it. I can drive you to the airport when you're ready."

Hannah met his eyes. "Okay. I don't want to think about that right now. Just focus on today."

George watched her as if he was going to say something, then tipped his head in agreement. "Just focus on today."

They loaded up in Sebastián's vehicle and headed out. George explained the site was about forty minutes inland, in the woods. Hannah pictured grass huts and having to hack their way in, so was pleasantly surprised when they came to a beautifully crafted circular building off a long winding road, surrounded by six small cabins. A few people were milling around the area and

Hannah was surprised to see a white couple coming out of one of the cabins.

"Miguel does these ceremonies about once a month. They are very in demand, however, he insists people come to stay, do the cleansing rituals, and prepare for the ceremony. People book the cabins for a week prior, do other healing rituals, then complete the Ayahuasca ceremony. After the main ceremony, they spend a couple of days in counsel before heading home. All in all, Miguel sets aside two weeks per ceremony. Ayahuasca is just one small part of the overall process."

Hannah peered around, fascinated. She wouldn't be the only one taking the ceremony that night. They climbed out and George showed her to her one-room cabin. She set her bag down, taking a deep breath.

"Now, what?"

"Now, spend some time meditating. Someone will come to get you shortly for your preparation rituals. You brought a few changes of clothes?"

Hannah nodded, motioning to her bag. George smiled and went to head out the door. Hannah had one more thing to say. "George?"

He paused, cocking his head. "Yeah?"

"Thank you. For bringing me here to Mexico, to Miguel and Sebastián. For standing with me. I know... I know what we have has been different, but I need you to know I love you. I think through all this, I've come to understand love differently. Not the stuff of romance books and movies. It's more than that. It's knowing another person as who they are, not who you want them to be. I love you for who you are, Abeja."

George grinned, hearing her call him Miguel and Sebastián's nickname for him. "I love you, too, mi corazón."

He ducked through the door and went out. Mi corazón. He hadn't called her that since before he and Miguel had gone "to find". Hannah tucked that in her heart and rolled out a mat to meditate on. After about an hour, she heard a soft knock at the door and glanced up to see a small, weathered woman standing at the door. The woman waited for her to get up and put her mat away, then motioned for her to follow. She led Hannah to a shower and instructed her to wash herself to get ready for the cleansing rituals. She took Hannah's clothes and replaced them with a fresh set.

After the shower, Hannah was given a smoke cleansing ritual and another where she sat on a bench under a covering, while steam from native plants washed over her. Even though she'd yet to do the Ayahuasca ceremony, she already was feeling her mind and soul were opening. After those rituals, she joined the other participants for a special lunch, consisting of foods meant to help the process. It was explained Ayahuasca often caused nausea and vomiting, purging the system of any impurities. Hannah, not relishing throwing up, picked at the food, only eating what she needed to silence her stomach.

The group was quiet as they ate and Hannah glanced around. There was the couple from the cabin earlier, maybe in their late twenties. A young, long-haired guy, who smiled shyly at her. An older man, who if dressed differently, looked like he could be the CEO of a company. Two middle-aged women, who by how they were with each other, appeared to be a couple. Finally, at the end of the table was a very old man, who seemed to be a local. There were eight of them taking part in the ceremony that night.

Once they ate, they were instructed to go back to their cabins to meditate and center. Hannah wandered past the large building where the ceremony was to be held. She could see Miguel working with George and a few other facilitators in training. She paused and watched as Miguel blew smoke over each of them. This was their ceremony as much as it was the participants. Everyone was preparing. Hannah felt honored. She dropped her head and went to her cabin.

She lay on the bed and thought about what George told her about the ceremony. Miguel's family had been performing them for generations. His family was originally from Peru and had migrated to Mexico a few generations ago. They brought their knowledge with them and performed not just Ayahuasca ceremonies, but many plant-healing ceremonies. Miguel met Sebastián as a young man and knew he was in love. Due to cultural restrictions, they lived as roommates for years and eventually decided they were comfortable letting the world know of their love. Since neither had children, Miguel decided to train George as his apprentice and wanted to hand off the center to George after he passed on. George would stay in Mexico, at least the majority of the time. He'd still have time to travel the world as he wished.

Hannah meditated for a while and considered what she was there to do. At first, it was answers to why she was seeing Logan Slip and Toby. Now, it was more. Hannah thought back over her life and came to understand she'd never really known herself. Her purpose or intent. When she'd done hallucinogens with Parker, it was to escape. Not to connect. Every time they did it was to heighten whatever experience they were having. It was fun, but she'd never come out of it with any enlightenment.

Her mind drifted to Parker. How when they first met, she was immediately drawn to him. He laughed easily and made everyone feel welcome. She'd been a shy child and being around him she felt alive. When he looked at her with those eyes, she felt special. Once they were together, the excitement never stopped. They saw music almost every weekend and when there wasn't a show, they'd invite their friends over to party. Really, his friends. They came along when he did and left when he and Hannah split. When Hannah found out she was pregnant, the collective advice from the group was to get rid of it. When she lost the baby, none of them reached out to her. She'd always been alone with them.

Not with Parker, though. He meant something to her. He'd been the one to draw her out of her shell. He made her laugh and showed her so many things in the world. Music, art, how to experience life. Now, he was getting married to someone else and settling down.

Hannah felt a pang of jealousy but realized it wasn't that she wanted Parker. She wanted to be loved like that. Where she was more than a companion or someone to party with. Where she was loved for who she was. Including the dark parts of her. She didn't want to have to conform to someone else's beliefs. She wished Parker well. Everyone deserved that kind of love.

Hannah thought of the baby they lost and her hand instinctively drifted over her womb. She'd cried when she first found out she was pregnant, but as time went on, she'd thought more about the baby as a being. As part of her. When she'd lost it, she was relieved but felt a hole inside of her. As if the baby had taken part of her soul with it when it left.

Lying in the cabin, she drew the baby to the surface and brought it back into her mind. It may have never become a human being but it still *was*. Its soul and being still existed. She imagined cradling it in her arms and singing it to sleep. She thanked it for picking her and apologized for not being ready to be a mother. As she worked through the process, she closed her eyes and imagined letting the baby go, it turning into a butterfly and flitting away. She wanted to be at peace with their connection on the spirit realm.

Lastly, she thought of George. How from the moment they met, her soul knew. She remembered when she was prostrate on the hospital floor, crying, refusing to let anyone touch her, he came to her. He knelt beside her and met her eyes. She'd yelled at him to get away from her, hoping he wouldn't. And he didn't. He sat on the floor cross-legged and introduced himself. She'd eyed him and moved away, her back against the wall.

They'd sat like this for some time before she let her guard down and said, "I'm Hannah."

After that, he was the only one she'd let in to know her. A little. She talked to Dr. Bob but knew what to say to him. Buzzy was her friend. She'd loosened up and joked with him, eventually showing him part of her soul. When the time came to leave the hospital, she didn't want to leave him behind, however, they were warned of forming any relationships there. Even friendships. It could be codependent.

They were right, of course. She'd become co-dependent on him. It wasn't fair to him, or her. But she loved George. Not because he could save her, but because he *knew* her. Because she *knew* him. Their relationship evolved and she could let him go. She could be free. Like a butterfly. Still part of one another's souls, but free to fly.

Hannah dozed off and was woken up after dark. A warm hand was on her cheek and she peered up into George's hazel eyes. He was smiling at her, then nodded.

It was time.

# CHAPTER TWENTY-FIVE

*H*annah took a deep breath and slipped on her shoes. She wasn't scared like she expected, but her skin felt like it was vibrating. George took her hand and they walked to the maloka. They moved slowly, not feeling any kind of urgency. Hannah paused and stared at the night sky. The stars twinkled as if they were communicating with her. George squeezed her hand as he turned to face her.

"I'm here for you, Hannah. I want you to know that."

Hannah smiled at him. She knew. She tipped her head, then squeezed his hand back. "You're my best friend, George. I couldn't have taken this journey without you. I wouldn't have even known where to begin. I'm eternally grateful to you. Miguel and Sebastián, too. I don't know what to expect, however, I do trust the process."

George grinned. "That's exactly right. Trust the process. No matter what you experience, it is important. Do you have any questions before we go in?"

Hannah thought, however, nothing came to mind. They'd gone through so many classes and rituals, she felt she understood. She shook her head, frowning. "No, I think I'm okay. I feel something, but it isn't like nerves. Something else?"

"Expectation? Like waiting on guests you are excited to see arrive?"

"Yes! That. I want to fling the door open and let them come in."

George chuckled. He wrapped Hannah in a hug and she let her head rest against him. No matter what she was shown from what came out of this, she was ready. Miguel explained it wasn't always positive, that sometimes Ayahuasca revealed things people have buried and makes them face it. The first experience could be very soul-wrenching. Hannah knew whatever she was shown, she needed to see it. To allow her brain to face the dark corners within her. She stepped back, meeting George's eyes. He kissed her forehead and bobbed his head. She stood with him for a moment, then stepped into the maloka.

The other ceremony participants were in there and each had taken their place on mats on the floor. George led Hannah to an empty mat and they knelt on it. Miguel and a couple of other facilitators sat behind a table on one end. Miguel began to speak in a mixture of Spanish and English, explaining the ceremony. He then invited each participant to the front to drink the Ayahuasca mixture. Hannah watched each person go forward and drink the mixture, speaking quietly to Miguel.

When it was her turn, Hannah walked up and kneeled before the low table. Miguel smiled at her, meeting her eyes. He gave her a blessing and motioned to the mixture which looked like murky tea. Hannah drank it, swallowing the bitter, earthy thickness. She set the cup down and thanked Miguel. He reached out and touched her hand, which he hadn't done with the other participants. He was her uncle, too.

She made her way back to where George was sitting and sat down. At first, she felt nothing and wondered if she was going to be the one person who was completely unaffected by Ayahuasca. Once everyone was back in their areas, Miguel and the two others at the table began to chant and wave some sort of plant fronds. One of the women near Hannah started to shake and vomit, followed almost in sequence by others around the room. Hannah still felt nothing and glanced at George in question. He placed his hand gently over her heart, then on her forehead, and leaned in to whisper in her ear.

"Let go."

As if those words were the turning of a doorknob, Hannah felt something open inside of her. She bent over and threw up. It wasn't like a hangover puke which felt toxic. It felt like she was ridding her body of blocks in her soul. No shame came over her as she let it take over. She vomited until she felt there was nothing left to come out and a sense of cool water flowing through her veins washed over her.

All of a sudden, she felt like she was falling internally and panic came over her. She threw out her hands to grasp onto something as she fell endlessly. In the distance, she could hear George talking to her as he held her hands. As he did, she jerked to a stop and found herself standing at the bottom of a stairwell. The stairwell from her dream. Afraid, she began to ascend the stairs and came to the door from before. She hesitated before pushing it open. The boy was sitting there with the baby. The boy... her *brother*. Toby.

He smiled and waved her over but she froze at the door. What he needed to show her, she didn't want to see. She spun and walked back to the stairs when something stopped her. A woman. No, not a woman. A feminine angel or spirit. The entity wrapped itself around Hannah and drew her close, allowing the fear to wash away. She didn't speak but still communicated with Hannah to let her know she was Ayahuasca. Or what Ayahuasca carries. Hannah began to cry and fell into the spirit, asking for help. The spirit let her know the only way forward was to go back. Back to Toby and the baby. Hannah didn't want to leave, so the spirit told her to stay as long as she needed. After some time, Hannah couldn't tell how long, she knew she needed to go back and face what Toby needed to show her.

He was still sitting in the chair, holding the baby when she came into the room. He opened his arms and Hannah ran to them. The baby was gone and she was in the boy's arms. She was small, just a child of two. He rocked her and whispered in her ear, soothing her wounds. He gathered her close and sang her a song. Then he put her down and stood up, taking her hand.

"I have something to show you," he said, walking her to the door. Hannah grasped his hand and toddled beside him.

They were back in the hallway, but it was different this time. Instead of doors, there were screens like on a tv. Each screen was playing a scene, a memory, and Toby took her to each one. Her birth, then him standing over her cradle, stroking her cheek. Them playing hide and seek. Hannah climbing into his bed when she was scared. Them running around outside in the sprinkler, laughing. His fifth birthday party when he had her help blow out the candles. From there the scenes got darker.

The one of them riding in a car and Hannah dropping her doll, crying for it. Toby, unbuckling his seatbelt, reaching down to retrieve the doll, telling her it would be okay. The accident and him being thrown from the car, dying on impact. Her mother wailing, holding his lifeless body. Hannah crying for him night after night. After that, the scenes ended. Hannah felt tears streaming down her cheeks and fell to the floor. She felt the pain of being that little girl, weeping for her brother. She suffered his loss all over again. Toby wrapped his arms around Hannah, helping her up. Then, she was no longer little. There was more. He opened a door to show their parents, her mother unable to leave the bed. Her father throwing himself into work. She'd lost everyone from the accident, not just Toby.

Hannah called out to her mother but her mother couldn't hear her. She lay in bed, her eyes vacant and red from crying. Hannah wanted to go to her but couldn't move. Toby led her to another door and opened it. Hannah saw her toddler self in a tiny bed, clutching a teddy bear to her chest, sobbing. It was the middle of the day. She remembered the bear was Toby's. The Hannah she was watching fell asleep, hiccuping with tears. She watched as Hannah climbed out of the bed, still asleep, wandered down the stairs, and out the front door. They followed the sleepwalking child outside. She toddled across the lawn, calling Toby's name. Hannah tried to wake her but she wasn't there. Sleeping Hannah made it to the highway and paused. Hannah called out for her to turn around but Toby shook his head.

"She can't hear you, she is you," he explained.

Terror came over Hannah as she watched herself go into the middle of the road and lie down. She could hear it before she saw it. The music, repetitive circus music over and over. He didn't see the child lying in the middle of the road.

The man driving the ice cream truck.

A scream pierced the air behind them, causing a jolt to run through Hannah. "Hannah!"

Hannah turned and saw her mother running in a panic to the child in the road, screaming her name. Hannah watched as her mother rushed past her toward the highway. She turned back and saw herself in the road sit up, still clutching the teddy bear. Confused and alone. Just as she sat up, the ice cream truck driver saw her and slammed on his brakes, veering off the road seconds before he hit the small, unaware child in the road. Hannah's mother darted into the highway and scooped the child up, sobbing into her golden hair. The ice cream truck driver bolted from the vehicle toward them, fear marking his face. He checked on Hannah and her mother, then burst into tears as he realized what almost occurred, hugging them both.

The scene evaporated before them and they were back in the room. Hannah stood staring at Toby in disbelief. She'd almost died as a child. Her mother's grief had been so large, she hadn't paid attention to Hannah's. It had almost cost her both her children. Toby took Hannah's hand and they went out of the door, down the stairs, then back outside. It was different this time. It wasn't her parents' yard. They were in the most beautiful place Hannah ever saw. They walked along a flower-lined path to a creek and wandered along the bank. Toby held her hand tightly. Hannah turned to him and was shocked when she saw him at the age he'd be now. She could see now why she was so drawn to Parker. They were similar. Dark hair, mischievous smile, deep twinkling eyes. Toby was different, though. Softer, his eyes holding a sadness Parker's never did, more like George's. He didn't look like Parker exactly, but there was enough there that Hannah must have remembered Toby when she first saw Parker. She reached out and placed her hand on his face. Oh, how she wished he was still alive and there for her. He placed his hand over hers.

"You are not alone, Hannah."

She shook her head. "I am."

He pointed to the water and she glanced in. She saw her parents around the table, talking about her, worried about her. She saw George holding her in the maloka, keeping her safe. She saw Miguel and Sebastián, how they now felt she was their own, like George. Lastly, she saw Toby with her, always by her side. She could feel all their love and their protection of her. She wasn't alone, she'd only convinced herself of that. They kept walking and came to a meadow. In the middle, was the spirit Hannah met before. She was emanating such love, Hannah felt any doubt within her crumble. Toby let go of her hand and motioned for her to go to the entity. Hannah watched him and knew he was always there, she didn't need to search for him anymore. She embraced him and moved toward the glowing form in front of her.

The form encased her and she let go, to allow herself to go where she needed to. She saw her earthly self and could feel the heaviness she'd been carrying. The heaviness she'd inadvertently passed on to those around her. She saw Parker and felt his sorrow over the lost baby, about their ended relationship, and her distance. She sensed her parents' stress and worry for her safety over her like a cloak. Her ankles felt like she was dragging boulders behind her. She experienced George's love for her and his realization that if he didn't let her go, he'd allow her to drag them both down.

The spirit opened her heart, and Hannah felt the immeasurable grief of not only losing Toby but also of losing her own child. She buckled and felt like she'd become a rushing river, casting her body against sharp rocks. She didn't even try to cling on this time. She let it carry her down, tearing at her skin and knocking her asunder. She came to a waterfall and tumbled over, falling for what seemed like years before she hit the pool below, broken and battered. She crawled out and lay on a flat rock, letting her body recover from the fall. The sun warmed her and she felt her wounds begin to heal.

When she sat up, the spirit was hovering above the water, holding her baby. Hannah's baby. Parker's baby. The spirit came closer and stretched her arms out toward Hannah, urging her to take the baby. Hannah gingerly took the tiny child and held it close to her, peering down at its perfect face. It blinked at her, its tiny, pink lips forming a bow. Hannah felt such an overwhelming love for this child, she clutched it to her. She never wanted to let it go.

The spirit guided her on what to do. Hannah knew and sensed her body opening. She placed the infant inside of her and saw her body close around it. The spirit spoke in a gentle whisper.

"Forever your child. She will come back when it's time. You didn't lose her, she just wasn't ready to be here yet. You weren't ready for her to walk with you on your journey."

Hannah understood. Her baby's soul would always be a part of her and one day when they were ready, she'd come back to Hannah. Hannah stood up on the rock and knew there was still something left for her to do. A final piece. The spirit welcomed her in and she was transported to another time and place.

Hannah was standing on the edge of a soccer field, watching some teenage boys play. They were laughing as they kicked the ball back and forth. Hannah frowned and tried to understand why she was there. She turned and saw people in the stands, cheering the boys on. She saw an older couple jump to their feet and yell as one of the boys made a goal. Hannah faced the field and stared at the boy who made the goal.

It was him. She watched the couple beaming at him with pride. His parents. A girl about his age was shaking a sign and grinning as he met her eyes and waved at her. She waved back and bit her lip. His girlfriend. The girl raised the sign in the air and yelled at the top of her lungs.

"I love you, Logan!"

# CHAPTER TWENTY-SIX

*H*annah wanted out. She searched for a path to run away, but her feet were stuck in place. Logan was laughing, his head tipped back with the freedom of being a teenager. The whole world in front of him. He kicked the soccer ball as hard as he could, sending it veering off in Hannah's direction. It rolled to a stop at her feet. Panic overtook her and she stared at it helplessly as he ran toward her. She saw his shadow fall over her feet and peered up, terrified at what she might see.

"Sorry about that. I didn't think it would go that way," Logan said, catching his breath. "Are you alright? It didn't hit you did it?"

Hannah met his eyes and felt like she was melting into a puddle of lava. She shook her head. He scooped the ball up, tucking it under his arm. Hannah blurted out the first thing that came to her mind. "I hit you."

Logan tipped his head, his blue eyes twinkling as he knitted his brow. "How's that?"

Hannah stared at him. He was so alive, so beautiful. In an instant, the skies around them darkened and the stands disappeared. They were left standing on the highway where their paths collided. She could see her car coming over the hill toward her road, the music blaring out the windows. Her hair was flying in the air around her like a halo. She came to a stop, oblivious to what was coming. They both watched frozen as Logan and his friends came up the road. Hannah clutched her arms around her as she watched Logan nod his head to his companion and pass her car on the left, just as she saw the opening and gunned the engine. As his life was taken, Hannah caught a sob in her throat. Logan was silent beside her, shocked by the scene before him.

After the accident ended, Logan glanced at her, then stepped toward his body lying in pieces on the highway. Hannah wanted to stop him but couldn't make herself move. He stood over his own chest and head, staring down in horror. He crouched beside himself, resting his hand on his helmet. His pain was palpable and Hannah summoned the courage to move toward him. She came up behind him.

"I'm so sorry. I didn't see you. It all happened so fast, it was an accident. I... I-"

Logan put his hand up to stop her. "There are no accidents, Hannah."

Hannah froze. He knew who she was. He cocked his head, meeting her eyes. In them, she saw all the pain she'd caused. The life she'd destroyed. He put his hand out and she took it. He pulled her down next to him and they sat in the center of the horrible scene. Hannah wanted to avert her eyes but couldn't. It was her penance. Logan was still holding her hand and squeezed it as if to comfort her.

"I wasn't ready to go, you know?" His voice was faint.

Hannah nodded. "I'm so sorry."

"I know you are. I want to show you something. But first I need to do this." Logan laid down next to his mangled body and Hannah gasped as the two bodies became one, his pieces being drawn together from across the pavement. The mangled Logan sat up, his face torn open, his right eye sunken deep into his face. He attempted to smile at her but half his teeth were missing and his jaw hung weirdly off his face. When he spoke, his voice was garbled. "To begin, we must start at the finish line."

He stood up and reached out for Hannah. She took his hand to stand up and pushed down the bile in her throat. His hand was in a glove but was no longer a hand. What Hannah was gripping felt like a bag of coins or rocks. Just bits and pieces. She resisted the urge to yank her hand away and rose next to him. He waved his free arm and the highway disappeared. They were standing in a home. Hannah glanced around and saw a photo of Logan on the wall.

His parents' home. She could hear sobbing from another room and left Logan's side to see where it was coming from. A woman was lying on her side on the couch, weeping as she clutched a bottle of pills in her hands. She swallowed a handful and threw the bottle across the room. As she slipped into an unwakeable sleep, Logan's father rushed into the house to her side. He grabbed her and shook her as hard as he could. Her head rolled back and he yelled her name as he pressed buttons on the phone. He kept talking to her, trying to wake her until the sirens drew closer. The paramedics rushed in and shoved a tube down her throat, forcing her to vomit up the pills. They injected her with something and she began to come around. When she realized she was still alive, she started to scream.

His mother wanted to die, even tried to kill herself after Logan's death. Hannah experienced her pain and fell to her knees. Losing Logan for his mother was the worst pain imaginable. Hannah couldn't escape it and wanted to die. She felt Logan place his hand on her shoulder and she shook her head. She couldn't. He dragged her to her feet, forcing her to face him. As she turned to see his torn face, they moved again. They were in a park, behind a girl staring out over a pond. Guilt poured off the girl like steam. Logan's girlfriend.

They moved closer and Hannah could read inside the girl's thoughts. The girl and Logan were supposed to go to the movies that day. She'd canceled at the last minute to run errands with her sister. Logan understood, he'd meet up with some friends to take a motorcycle ride. She'd told him she loved him and they could go in the evening. He joked she better not bail on him again. He was dead by the evening. It was all her fault.

Hannah wanted to tell the girl it wasn't her fault but her mouth wouldn't move. She hovered close to the girl, attempting to reach her when she saw the girl take a small knife and draw it down her arm like she had done so many times before. Blood welled up and the girl clasped her hand over the wound, sobbing. She pulled her sleeve down over the wound and gazed over the water, allowing the physical pain to numb her emotional pain for a moment.

Hannah spun to face Logan but his face was blank. There was nothing he could do for them anymore. He was an observer trapped on this horror show ride. Hannah turned back but the girl was gone. They were alone in darkness. Hannah closed her eyes and tried to let the darkness absorb her, but Logan grabbed her and shook her. She dropped her shoulders. This was part of the ride. He guided her through scenes of all that transpired since, then they were sitting on a low brick wall. Hannah looked around. It was her old elementary school. Probably Logan's, too. Back when they were told everything was possible. Images of them in their own timelines there flashed through her mind and she smiled. The age of innocence.

"Why are we here?" she asked, watching Logan adjust his broken body on the wall.

"A breather. It wasn't all bad, you know? Life had good things, as well. I thought we could both use the chance to remember that," he explained.

Hannah nodded. They sat in silence in a timeless suspension. Hannah felt her mind begin to settle and turned to face Logan. "Why do I keep seeing you?"

Logan cocked his head. "You tell me."

Hannah frowned. "Is it real? Am I losing my mind?"

Logan smiled, this time almost like his whole self. "Yes and yes. On some plane, it is real. You're losing your mind because in order to grow, we need to break the shell. You can't go back to before, so you have to lose yourself to find yourself. I'm part of the equation."

"Have you been trying to reach me?"

"Of course. We are connected. But you called me to you, not the other way around."

"Oh." Hannah considered this. All the times she saw Logan, her soul was beckoning him. "Why?"

Logan shrugged. "Only you truly know, but I guess you needed me."

Hannah felt tears slip down her cheeks at this. She did need him. For absolution. That was unfair. He shouldn't be setting her free from her guilt. She did this to him. "I'm sorry. Did I trap you? Like in some sort of limbo?"

Logan met her eyes, shaking his head. "You don't have that power, Hannah. I chose to stay close for my own reasons. I came when you called, but I chose to. I didn't have to."

"Why did you then? I don't understand." Hannah wiped her nose, staring at him.

"You didn't *do* this. It happened. Do you understand? You didn't murder me. No one did. An event happened we were both a part of. Things came together which made this happen. That's all. I wanted you to understand that. I want everyone to see that. My girlfriend, Cassie, didn't do this. My parents didn't. You didn't. Even I didn't. An unfortunate series of circumstances came together, and here we are. Do you see?"

Hannah did. She'd been blaming herself and could see so many involved were, as well. That's all life was... a series of circumstances. Their idea of control and decision was less than what they believed. Hannah let the wall fall away and wrapped her arms around Logan, as much as to hold herself together as him. His time wasn't done. He would cycle back. She let go and faced him, without fear. He was whole again and grinned at her.

"It will be okay. This is just one round," he promised. "Me... and Toby, will have another chance. We just need you to accept and live your life."

"You know Toby?" Hannah asked, her brain reeling.

"As I said, we are connected. Are you ready?"

"For what?"

Logan motioned in front of them and Hannah peered over to see the spirit waiting for her. She looked at Logan. "Will I see you again?"

"Only if you want to," he answered gently.

Hannah tilted her head and placed her hand against his cheek. She rose and went to the spirit, letting it envelop her. As it carried her, Hannah felt layers fall away from her, like skin peeling off an onion. She closed her eyes and allowed herself to be vulnerable. She was herself before the accident, before Parker, in school, as a young girl, a toddler, a baby, a soul. As she transitioned through all of the phases of her life she became nothing.

She became everything.

Hannah wasn't sure where she went next, but she had the sensation of floating through every cell and timeline that ever was. She let go and let herself pass through eternity. As she came back to earth, she could feel the heaviness of her limbs return to her. She reconnected with her physical self and listened to the world around her re-form. She was in the maloka. Her eyes came into focus slowly as she glanced around, attempting to understand this existence and her place in it. Everything seemed to carry a vibration to it. Even inert objects contained energy around her. Her hand felt warm like an umbilical cord back was connected to it, pulsing. She stared at her hand and the umbilical cord took form. A hand. An arm. She followed it up. Eyes. A reason. No, *the* reason.

George.

He watched her silently, letting her complete her journey back. His hand clasped hers to remind her she wasn't alone. Hannah felt so tired. She just wanted to sleep. George nodded and laid down next to her, curling her in against him. Hannah rested against him like a baby new in the world. George wrapped his arms around her and whispered in her ear.

"Welcome back."

When Hannah woke up it was daylight, she didn't know how much time had passed. George was sleeping next to her and she rolled over to watch him. He'd been her guide, her gift. Her best friend. She sat up and pulled a sheet over him. He needed the rest. The Ayahuasca was working its way out of her body, however, her experience wasn't over. She needed to do her part now for it. She kissed George on the forehead and left to take a walk. Her limbs felt weird, but she felt more in her body than she ever had. She wandered down a path to the stream and crouched down by it, letting her fingers float in the coolness.

She was part of it. The water, the earth, the air. She was a part of everything and needed to step up to do what she was called to life for. She made her way to the maloka and saw George talking to Miguel. He caught a glimpse of her and headed in her direction.

George.

Hannah moved toward him, wrapping her arms tightly around his waist. He wound his arms around her and they stood in silence for some time. She could feel their blood coursing through their veins, sensing their heartbeats synchronizing rhythmically. Georgie drew back meeting her eyes.

He knew.

Hannah ran her fingers across his lips and murmured, "George, you are everything to me."

He smiled but didn't speak. Hannah knew she needed to take the next step on her journey. There were too many doors left open. She didn't know what would happen with her, or George, however, the pull was too strong. She sighed, then nodded.

"I need to go home. I have things I left unfinished," she whispered, her voice not hiding the sadness.

George didn't seem surprised. "I know."

# CHAPTER TWENTY-SEVEN

*B*y evening, Hannah was packed and had a flight booked out of the Chetumal International Airport for the following morning. She'd spent the day in groups and one on ones with Miguel and George to talk about her experience. Ayahuasca didn't make everything better, however, it showed her where she needed to work. She couldn't run anymore. The only way to come to grips with all that happened was to face the people and places which held the pieces. By early evening, she was exhausted and went to rest in her space. She was awakened later by a knock on the door.

Sitting up, she saw George through the screen and it reminded her of the day she'd left the hospital. He'd been at the door then, too. Always making sure she knew she wasn't alone. She waved him in and rubbed the sleep from her eyes. He slipped in, holding a basket.

"You missed dinner but I packed us some food. Do you want to take a walk?" he asked and sat down next to her.

Hannah watched him, a catch forming in her heart. How could she leave without him? Face what was next? No, this was her journey and she needed to own it. She peered in the basket at the food.

"Oooh, it looks good. I'm famished. Where to?"

"There's a cave not far from here. It's not deep, more just an opening. I thought we could hike over there and eat, spend some time together. If you aren't too tired?"

Hannah felt nervous energy, shaking her head. "Not at all. I feel like I have electricity running through me."

George laughed and stood up. "I thought you might. We can go hang out as long as you'd like. What time is your flight tomorrow?"

"Um, I think around ten. Let me check." Hannah pulled up the reservation, scanning for the time. "Ten-thirty-five. How close are we to the airport?"

"Not far. We can have an early breakfast, then head over there. We'll take Miguel's truck."

"I appreciate you taking me. I was worried about being in an unfamiliar airport on my own. I might end up in Sweden," Hannah joked.

"I'd never leave you to figure that out. You've come a long way, Hannah, but I don't want you to end up on the other side of the world. Besides, it gives us a little more time together."

Hannah eyed George. Theirs had been a very strange trajectory. He was her guardian in the hospital, friend out, more in Mexico, then back to friend and guardian. He was staying in Mexico, she was going back to Virginia. The next leg of her trip would be completely on her own. She had no doubt they'd stay in contact, but it would be weird to not have him at arm's reach anymore. She shook the thought away and smiled.

"I'm ready when you are."

George led the way out of the door, handing her a flashlight. The sun was setting as they hiked, so by the time they reached the mouth of the cave, Hannah needed to click on the light to see the path. The cave was large with a wide opening and boulders outside they set the food on. George pulled out a blanket to sit on as he unpacked the food. He handed her a Mexican Coke, then reached forward to pop the top. He cracked one for himself.

"A treat before you go. I had these chilling all afternoon. A toast." He held his bottle up and she did the same. George met her eyes and grinned, showing his pointy teeth. "To finding the way."

Hannah clinked her bottle against his. "And each other."

George cocked his head. "We were never lost from that. Just a series of events needed to happen to bring us together."

That reminded Hannah of what Logan said to her. A series of circumstances. "Logan told me it wasn't my fault, or his. Or really anyone's. The accident, I mean. He said it was just how things happened. How circumstances came together."

George listened and took a sip of his soda. "How do you feel about that?"

Hannah considered. "Better than blaming myself, but he still died. My car still hit him."

"True. Say you had me over for dinner one night, and the stove malfunctioned to no fault of your own and blew up, killing me. Would you blame yourself or the stove?"

"I guess the stove... but if I hadn't invited you over, you wouldn't have been killed."

"Right, but I came on my own. No one forced me to come over. You didn't make Logan pass you on the left. He did, not knowing it would cost him his life. He still did it, knowing it wasn't right. You aren't to blame. Neither is he. He made a choice that led to circumstances, as he said. A series of events which happened. You can forgive yourself and him. As humans, we tend to want someone to blame, someone to be at fault. Sometimes things happen. Blame doesn't make them unhappen or make it okay."

Hannah stared at the mouth of the cave. She could forgive herself, but she needed to face the fallout first. As the last bits of light began the trek into dark, bats emerged from the cave in droves. Unlike the first time at the campground, she found it comforting. She watched as they dove and darted in the sky above them. She recalled what George had said about them being tasked to carry the souls of the dead to the other side. They were there to ease death. She needed to do the same. She needed to carry the dead.

George fell silent and watched the bats with her. They ate the food he packed and retreated into their own thoughts. Hannah glanced over and could see George's outline in the rising moonlight. He was so beautiful. So at peace. She reached out, taking his hand in hers. He gazed at her and tipped his head, understanding. This journey had been theirs, now it was hers. Hannah cleared her throat.

"Buzzy... George, I want you to know no matter where our paths take us, this time with you has changed my life. Saved my life. I'm ready to go back and be the person I should've been all along. The person who saw everything wasn't about them. Be there for my parents. Be there for anyone I impacted, whether it was my fault or not. Be me. I couldn't have come to this without you. I was thinking about the guy in the ice cream truck with the mask. The duality mask. I've come to realize that was partly you all along. Buzzy. George. But me, too. Two sides of completeness I needed to understand. I was only facing one side of me. It's time I donned the mask and brought myself together."

George pulled his hand away. Hannah tried to make out his face in the dark, to see if she'd said something wrong. He lifted his hand and wiped his cheeks. He was crying. Hannah felt heat rise in her face and reached to touch his face.

"Did I say something wrong? Did I hurt you?" she asked, afraid she'd crossed a line.

George took her hand, his damp from the tears. "No. Not at all. I'm just humbled and awed to have been part of this experience with you. Most people live their lives with half a soul. To observe someone discover their other half is the most beautiful and vulnerable experience to be a part of. Thank you, Hannah. For trusting me. For trusting yourself. You've made my heart grow in a million ways."

Hannah grasped his hand. He was thanking her? Yes, he was thanking her. No person was an island, right? By her coming to herself, he grew as well. She laid back on the blanket to watch the stars. George joined her and they remained in silence, not needing words to understand. By midnight, they gathered up their things and headed back to the camp. Hannah wanted to hold the moment walking on the trail with George. It was the most at peace she'd ever been in her life. He accompanied her to the door and paused. Hannah took his hand.

"Please come in. As my friend, my other half. We only have a few hours left together," she whispered, drawing him inside.

George followed and they climbed into the small bed, facing each other. George placed his hand on her cheek and met her eyes. Hannah rested her hand on his chest and did the same. They stayed, staring into one another until sleep took them away. They would always have that moment.

The next morning was a flurry of activity and Hannah was glad to see Sebastián came to see her off. Miguel and Sebastián invited George and her to join them for breakfast. They sat in Miguel's hut around a low table. Miguel reached out and took her hand.

"You know you always have a place with us here. Sebastián and I are going to miss you so very much. You are our mariposa sobrina."

Butterfly niece.

Hannah choked back tears. She looked at George. Their abeja sobrino. Bee nephew. George winked at her. Sebastián nodded with tears in his eyes.

"You are our family," he concurred.

Hannah had her family back in Virginia but this was also her family. She held each of Miguel and Sebastián's hands and smiled. "You are my family, too. I need to go and finish this, but I'll stay in touch with you."

After breakfast, Hannah hugged them each as tightly as she could, while George loaded the truck. It wasn't much, but he was giving them space to say goodbye. Hannah gazed at Miguel and Sebastián, feeling deep love for them. They, too, helped her find the other part of her soul. A rebirth. She wiped away tears as she headed to the truck. Her heart hurt in a good way.

George climbed in next to her, checking the map. Hannah watched him peering at the directions and smiled. He caught her looking and grinned. He raised his brows.

"Don't want to get us lost."

"You won't. You're the best guide."

George laughed. "You're the best companion."

Hannah looked out the window and took a deep breath. "Okay, I'm ready."

The drive to the airport felt short. Too short. Hannah began to feel panic about leaving George. She could see he was feeling stressed, as well. After they parked, he grabbed her bag with one hand and grasped her hand with the other as they made their way into the terminal. Once they got to the gate, he set down her bag and turned her to face him, his eyes pained.

"Someone once told me death was like saying goodbye to a loved one at the airport, never knowing if you'd ever see them again. Watching them disappear down the hallway to board a flight you can't be on, to a destination unknown. It feels like this. A kind of death. I want to see you again, Hannah."

Hannah stared at him, her mouth hanging open. "We will. Somehow. We're connected, right? Besides, George, I don't think you should be talking about death and airplanes when I'm about to board a plane alone."

Her attempt at humor fell flat and the pain that passed between them was crackling. George glanced away, fighting back tears. Hannah wound her arms around him. He rested his hand on her back and let his chin set on her head. They both knew

Hannah needed to go on the next part of the path on her own, but it didn't make saying goodbye any easier. Hannah drew in a shuddering breath, George's scent filling her nostrils. She'd miss that. The intercom announced her flight was boarding and they drew apart, meeting each other's eyes. This was it. George picked up her bag and walked her to the door. They both glanced down the long hallway, leading her away from him.

In a way, it was like death. Hannah was going alone. George was staying. Neither knew when, or if, they'd see each other again. Their paths had diverged. George leaned in and kissed her cheek, his breath warm. Hannah rubbed his lips.

"I'll let you know when I land. When I get home."

"I'll be waiting to hear from you."

"Okay, I'd better go. George... Buzzy... I love you."

George peered down the hall, then sighed. "Hannah, mi corazón, I love you."

With that, Hannah took her bag and headed through the door. She kept her head down until she got to the bend in the hall, leading to the plane. She stopped and glanced back. George was watching her, tears streaming down his face. She raised her hand, realizing tears were streaming down hers as well. George lifted his hand, then placed it over his heart. Hannah wiped her tears and blew him a kiss.

Once on the plane, she questioned everything. Leaving Mexico. Going home. However, she knew there was no life forward without going back. One question still gave her doubts.

Was there life without George?

# CHAPTER TWENTY-EIGHT

*H*annah's parents met her at the airport. She deboarded the plane and saw them standing off to the side, whispering to each other. They hadn't seen her yet, so she took the moment to observe them. She was still upset they never talked to her about Toby, however, at least now she had some small understanding of why. Instead of being angry, she felt sad. Sad, that in order to protect her, they thought they needed to hide Toby's existence. Well, that was all going to end now. It was time to carry Toby back into their lives. For them all to face losing him and honor his memory again.

Hannah shifted her bag on her shoulder and set her chin. It was time. She headed toward her parents, smiling as she approached. Her father embraced her and her mother watched her closely. She could see the difference in Hannah. Hannah hugged her, feeling her mother stiffen with a primal knowledge. Whether or not she knew Hannah was aware of what happened to Toby, she knew Hannah had changed on some level. Her mother drew back, placing her hand on Hannah's cheek as she searched her eyes for clarity.

"How was your flight?" she asked, the real question lying underneath.

"Long."

"And George? He didn't come home?" her father inquired.

Hannah shook her head, not ready to think about George. "He took a job there."

Sensing her need to move on from the subject, her mother wrapped her arm around Hannah's waist and guided her through the crowd. "Do you want to come home with us?"

Hannah nodded. "I gave up my lease while I was in Mexico."

"What about all your belongings?" her mother asked, surprised by the news.

"Well, the little I had that was personal, I had moved to storage and the rest I asked the movers to donate. I need a fresh start."

"You're always welcome home," her father assured her.

"Thanks, Dad," Hannah replied, meaning it.

They drove home and chatted about her trip. Hannah sat in the back seat, gazing out the window. All the places she knew. Where previous events in her life happened. Yet, she felt nothing. No nostalgia, no connection. Just a place that was familiar. She watched her parents interact and smiled. They were still home to her. She glanced at the seat beside her, Toby flashing in her mind. Once it was the four of them. Then it was the three of them and an unmentioned ghost. She placed her hand on the empty seat beside her and willed Toby to be there. Even if it was all in her head, she felt something. A presence.

"So, in this quaint little town we stayed in, there was an adorable restaurant by the pier called Toby's. It was perfect," Hannah said, knowing she was creating a trigger.

At the name Toby, she saw her mother's neck become stiff and straight. Her father glanced at her mother, then back at Hannah as he drove. "That right? What kind of food did they serve?"

"Mostly local fare and their version of American food. It seemed so familiar. The name seemed to ring a bell," Hannah said, hoping they'd break down and confess so she didn't have to call them out. They didn't.

As they pulled into the driveway, Hannah knew this wasn't going to be easy. She glanced up at the upstairs windows. Her bedroom and her mother's craft room on that side. Her mother's craft room. Hannah remembered the night she saw the curtains move in there. Toby's room. It had been Toby's room. It was *still* Toby's room. She pushed the car door open and stepped out. Maybe she could let it ride today. Just have a nice dinner with them and get some rest.

Once inside, she felt heavy and tired. "Hey, I'm going to lie down for a bit. Can I take my old room?"

"Of course, honey. I put on fresh sheets this morning." Her mother waved toward the stairs. "We'll wake you up for dinner."

Hannah shuffled up the stairs and stopped to look back. Her parents let a look pass between them and she knew bringing up Toby's name caused them pain. Pain was not always a bad thing. Sometimes it cleared things out. She headed upstairs and set her bag in her room. She wandered to her mother's craft room, easing the door open. There was a table with assorted ribbons and beads on it. A few drawers filled with randomly started projects. Her mother liked the idea of crafting more than actually doing it. Hannah chuckled and ran her finger in the light dust along the front of the table.

The partially open closet door caught her eye and she walked over, pausing before opening it. Her hand reached out and drew the door open. Stacked inside were boxes of supplies and extra blankets. She dragged them out and sat down on the floor of the closet, trying to summon a memory.

That's when she saw it.

She shoved some fabric rolls aside and about two feet from the floor, she saw two little figures drawn in crayon. A stick-figure boy and a sitting baby stick-figure with a bow. Toby and Hannah. The stick-figure boy had a big smile. Bigger than his face. The baby was staring at the stick-figure boy with large, round eyes. Even in the crude child drawing, Hannah could see how much he meant to her. Below the drawing was an artist's signature. Toby, but with the 'b' backward. Tody. Hannah laughed and felt warm tears roll down her cheek. No matter what, Toby had existed and still was there on some level. She was ready to bring him back into the light.

She climbed out of the closet, gently shutting the door. She went to her childhood bedroom, the one where she'd cried for Toby when she was little. As she lay in her own cool bed, she fought off the heaviness of her eyes. George. She needed to let him know she'd made it home. She dug in her bag for her phone.

"Home safe and sound," she texted as she laid back down. Her eyes closed almost immediately.

A soft knock at the door let her know hours had passed since she'd dozed off. She sat up and saw her father standing at the door. "Hey Han. Dinner's ready."

"Thanks, Dad. I'll be down in a minute."

He closed the door and she heard him padding back down the stairs. Shaking off sleep, she picked up her phone and clicked it on. George had texted her back.

"Thank you for letting me know, I was distracted all day until I heard. Tell your parents I say hello."

Hannah wanted to say so much. To tell him she missed him already. That she wanted him in her life and wished she didn't have to go. She started to type that out but erased the words. Instead, she replied, "I will."

Dinner was easy and Hannah felt almost as if she'd never left for Mexico. Yet something was still off. She knew the secret now and everything else was pretend. She pushed her plate away, leaning back in her chair. She was ready to bring Toby up when her mother placed her hand on her father's arm as if to steady herself. They stared at each other and her father nodded, then faced Hannah.

"Hannah, we're glad you're home. While you were gone we had a lot of time to miss you. We also had a lot of time to think. Your mother and I want you to know that you mean everything to us, and we never wanted to hurt you."

"Hurt me?"

Her mother shifted uncomfortably in her seat. "Honey, there is something you need to know."

"Is it about Toby?" Hannah asked, surprised by the words that flowed from her mouth.

Her parents sat back in their seats, shocked. Her father rubbed his forehead and rested his elbows on the table as he processed what she said. "Yes. Yes, it is. Hannah, I don't understand. What do you know about Toby?"

Hannah watched them, then sighed. "I know he was my brother and he died in a car accident when I was little."

"How?" her mother asked, clearly not expecting the conversation to go this way.

"Um... wow, I don't even know where to start. Dreams, visions, drawings. Let's just say I learned about Toby recently. Why didn't you tell me?" Hannah responded, attempting to not sound accusatory.

"Hannah. It was terrible when we lost Toby. Everything fell apart. I fell apart," her mother explained. "I was no good to anyone. I failed you."

Hannah recalled seeing the vision of her mother sobbing in bed. She chewed her lip, waiting for them to go on. Her father wiped his eyes, clearing his throat softly before meeting Hannah's eyes.

"It was no one's fault, but it happened. We never thought we'd have to bury a child. No one should have to. There is no excuse for our failing you, but we were so consumed by our own grief. You were so sad and kept asking for Toby. You called him Baba. You began to wander and one day..."

He stopped speaking but Hannah knew. One day she toddled out of the house, down the street, and into the highway where she was almost crushed by an ice cream truck. She didn't need them to explain. She reached out and took each of their hands, her heart melting at how much they must have suffered.

"I understand. What you went through was horrific. You were doing your best. I'm alright. I'm here. I know I must've missed Toby terribly and it made me search for him. You wanted to keep me safe. I get that. I'm not mad at you. I was when I first remembered... not anymore." Hannah choked back a sob and shook her head. "But I want to talk about Toby. I want to see pictures of him. I want him to be included in holidays and our life. I want to hear his name."

Her parents visibly relaxed, allowing their tears to flow freely. Her mother squeezed her hand. "I'd like that, too."

"Can you tell me about him? What he was like? Do you have pictures?" Hannah asked, hoping Toby hadn't been completely erased.

Her father stood up and went to the hall closet. He pushed a piece of board up at the top and climbed on the baseboard as he fished around inside. He pulled out a box and came back. "There's more, but we can start here."

He plopped the box down on the table, sliding it toward Hannah. She peered up at him, then pried the lid off the wooden box, blowing away the dust. Inside were drawings and pictures. Pictures of Toby. Pictures of her with Toby. Pictures of all of them. A happy family. Hannah drew each one out, letting her mind trace the images. With them came snapshot memories. Toby laughing, swinging her around. Seeing these made her feel complete. The part of her she didn't know she'd been missing was restored.

As she sorted through the box, her parents added in memories, stories behind the pictures and drawings. Hannah felt a joy bubble up inside her she'd never felt. She wasn't an only child and she hadn't been abandoned by the one person who was her world. The tightness and fear she'd unknowingly carried in her soul let loose.

Her father put on coffee and they stayed up late into the night until none of them could keep their eyes open anymore. They packed away the photos into the box and promised they'd keep Toby a part of their lives from that point forward. Hannah ascended the stairs to her room, feeling lighter than she ever had. As she climbed under her covers, she was back to being the small child who lost her brother. Except this time she didn't need to search for him. He was no longer ripped from her life, leaving her broken and lost. Now he was tucked safely in her heart and part of her forever.

She could hear her parents talking low in their room, their voices free from stress and secrets. To protect her, they'd needed to erase a part of themselves. While she'd been angry, thinking they were withholding Toby from her, they were withholding him from themselves. This was tearing them apart every single day. She'd been too selfish to see. They couldn't bear the thought of losing her, too, so they took their love and feelings and shoved them deep down. She hoped they'd be able to move forward now, and bring Toby into the present while remembering the past.

The next morning, she shuffled down the stairs and paused as she came to the bottom. Her heart filled with joy and the years of not knowing came to an end. As she faced the wall adjacent to the last step, she knew she could release the pain.

A photo of their complete family, smiling and hopeful, had been hung for all to see.

# CHAPTER TWENTY-NINE

F or the next few weeks, Hannah did nothing more than hang out with her parents. She'd always felt like the years of her childhood, which although loving and supportive, had been missing something. Now, she found those unknown cracks were being filled in. Her father no longer passed through rooms, rather he sat down and initiated conversation. Her mother let go of the reins, encouraging Hannah to take time to discover what it was she wanted out of life. Toby's name flowed off their tongues and before long it was as if decades hadn't passed since he'd been part of their home. Hannah wanted to think she was done on her journey.

She knew better.

As the month anniversary crept up of her return home, the pull to take the next step was never far from her mind. Bringing Toby to light was just the beginning. The harder steps were to come. One morning, when she heard her parents leave for the store, Hannah used the computer to search for any information she could find on Logan Slip's family and girlfriend. The parents she found immediately but had no luck in narrowing down his girlfriend. She jotted down the parents' address and slipped it into her bag. She was scared they'd slam the door in her face, however, it was a risk she needed to take.

Once her parents came home, she helped unload the groceries and ate lunch with them. She watched them and tried to understand the pain of losing a child, so she could approach Logan's parents with delicacy. She twisted her napkin into a knot and tapped her foot repeatedly under the table, quelling her nerves. She drew in a deep breath.

"Can I ask you both something? Something kind of sensitive?" she asked, hoping they wouldn't balk.

"Of course, honey. What's up?" her father replied.

"Okay. This is hard, so please forgive me if it doesn't come out right." Hannah paused and considered her words. "When Toby died. Well, after. Can you explain how it made you feel? How you learned to cope. To move on?"

Hannah's mother stared, her mouth partially open. Then she shook her head. "You don't move on after losing a child. Whether they died as a baby or at fifty years old, you live the rest of your life imagining what it would be like if they were still alive. Who they'd be. What they'd look like. You spend moments creating conversations and events which will never happen. I miss Toby as much today as I did the day he died."

She stopped there and glanced at Hannah's father. It was like they were working off the same thought pattern. He nodded and took her hand. "How it felt? It feels like your soul is being wrenched from your body and torn into pieces. Every second is work to get through. Every day feels like a marathon. Then as time goes on, the seconds pass quicker, the days come to end without utter exhaustion. However, Hannah, the pain is always there. There isn't a day that goes by we don't think about Toby. He'll always be a part of us and there will always be a hole here," he said, tapping his chest. "I don't know if that answers your question, but why do you ask?"

Hannah felt shame rise in her cheeks and gripped her fingers together on the table. "I'm going to go see Logan Slip's parents. I need to apologize."

Her parents sat stone still. It became so quiet, Hannah could hear the hum of the refrigerator. She didn't know if she needed to explain more or let her parents process what she said. Not being able to take the silence anymore, she blurted out. "Did I say something wrong?"

Her father leaned forward and took her hand. "No, that's very thoughtful of you, but you don't know how they're going to react."

"I don't, but I need to do this. I can't put this behind me until I do," Hannah replied, her voice cracking.

"See, Han. That's sort of the issue. You're going to try and put something behind you. This is something they can never put behind them. If you are going to clear your conscience, don't. It's unfair and hurtful." Her father's words were harsh and firm, but heartfelt.

Hannah stared at them, unsure what to say. He wasn't wrong. She *was* going to absolve her guilt. She wanted them to offer their assurance they didn't blame her, that they were going to be alright. What if they weren't? What if they screamed at her and accused her of murder? What if she made everything worse? She closed her eyes and considered what she hadn't before. The goal was not to make her feel better. It was to make her accountable. She met her parents' eyes.

"You're right. I need to think more about this. I owe them my humble compassion. Thank you for talking to me about this. You gave me a different point of view. If it's alright with you, I'm going to take a drive to clear my head."

"Sure, take my car," her mother offered.

Hannah got up and grabbed the keys off the hook. She could feel her parents' eyes boring into the back of her head. She turned to face them. "I'm really sorry. About Toby, about everything you went through. I know I wasn't always the best daughter and was downright shitty at times. I love you both so much."

"We know you do, Hannah. You've always been such a gift to us. Raising children is tough. They get to be selfish and petulant at times. It's our job as parents to guide and tolerate. You weren't all that bad," her father responded with a wink.

Hannah smiled, then headed for the door. She passed by the family photo and stopped, placing her fingers on Toby's face. What would it have been like if he never died? Sorrow twisted her gut and she understood what her parents were saying. There would always be the what ifs. She dropped her hand and went out into the daylight. She drove around town for about an hour, not feeling like she was getting any clarity. As she passed the coffee house, she slowed down and a bell went off in her head. She found a parking lot and pulled in, turning off the car. Her fingers shook slightly as she dialed. It rang a few times and she was afraid she'd get voicemail when he picked up.

"Hannah, long time no talk!" George exclaimed.

It had been too long. They hadn't spoken since she'd come home and only randomly sent each other a text message. "Hey, yeah, I suck at phone calls. How are you, George?"

"Keeping busy. I've been building a house on the ceremony land for myself. Figured Miguel and Sebastián might want their house back."

"Ha, they love having you around," Hannah said with a snicker.

"True, true, but this way I can be on-site at all times here, as well. What brings this call?"

"I need a sounding board. I also talked to my parents about it, but now I'm more conflicted. I was going to go see Logan's parents and tell them I'm sorry for what happened." Hannah paused to think of how to explain.

George was quiet for a moment. "Are you? Sorry for what happened?"

"George! Of course, I am." Hannah felt defensive. How could he even ask that?

"Could you still be sorry without talking to them?"

Hannah considered it. She could, but then how could she move on? Oh. There it was. She was sorry but was still wanting to see them for her own benefit. How could she let them know she was sorry, without trying to clear her guilt? "How do I do this, George? I do want to let them know I didn't just put this behind me. That I *am* sad about Logan. He deserved to live. They shouldn't be living without him."

"See, now you're getting it. Saying sorry is just a way to absolve guilt if there isn't motivation for change behind it. Are you motivated for change, Hannah?"

Hannah's head hurt. Change? She couldn't change anything. What was done was done. There was no way to change the outcome. "I'm lost. I can't bring him back."

"No, but you can dig deep inside and see what it is about you that needs changing," George offered.

Hannah pressed her head against the steering wheel. What about her in regard to Logan's death did she need to change? It wasn't technically her fault. Technically. He still died. She still hit him. Her life still ended his. She'd been in her own thoughts that day. About the baby. About Parker. She wasn't at fault, nor was she completely clear. She was so wrapped up in what she'd gone through, her suffering, she'd neglected to pay attention to the world around her. She sighed.

"Thanks, George. I think it's beginning to come together. Logan said it was just a series of events which happened, and that's true. But I was still in my own bubble, convinced what I was going through was all that mattered in the world. My suffering created a ripple of suffering and I threw the pebble into the pond. I need to go back and clean up my mess before I see them. Make sure my intent is pure."

"You can do this, Hannah. I know it's tough but you have come so far. Do you know the next step?" George asked.

Hannah did. It had been in front of her face the whole time. "I need to go see Parker."

"Okay. You know where I am if you need to talk."

"Always. You're the best sounding board, George."

He fell silent and Hannah knew there were still unspoken words between them. She tried to think of a way to bridge the gap when he spoke. "You can't build a house without laying the foundation. No matter how badly you want to have dinner at the table, you need to do the hard work of constructing a safe space first. You got this. The rest will come when, or if, it's supposed to. Focus on the task at hand."

"See? You always seem to have the right words to say," Hannah replied. She wanted to tell him she loved him and missed him, but the words dried up in her throat. "Bye, George."

He paused and she listened to hear him say something to bring her back. He sighed. "Bye, Hannah."

With that, the line went dead and she fought back tears. The gap was too big. She typed in Parker's number which she still had memorized and was surprised when he answered. She assumed he'd screen her call. When he said hello, she almost hung up but caught herself. It was now or never.

"Hey, Parker. It's Hannah. Can we meet to talk?"

They agreed to meet at a nearby park and Hannah fought back butterflies as she drove in. Parker was sitting at a picnic table, smoking a cigarette. She climbed out of the car and walked slowly toward him. He caught a glimpse of her and turned, smiling. His dark hair fell over one eye, giving him a boyish charm. She could see it again. Toby. He raised his hand and stubbed out his cigarette as she approached.

"Hey, Hannah! I was surprised to hear from you today. Everything alright?"

He stood up and all of a sudden Hannah felt faint. This was almost the father of her child. They almost had a life together. The memories of their time together came rushing back, filling her senses. She began to shake and sob uncontrollably, relieved when he wrapped his arms tightly around her. Him holding her was so familiar, so safe. She buried her face in his chest and wept for everything they'd lost. They met as wide-eyed kids and left each other as broken adults. Only Parker knew the loss she'd experienced with the baby. He was the one person who'd lost their baby, too. He'd lost everything when she did.

As Hannah came to this realization, she understood she needed Parker in her life.

# CHAPTER THIRTY

*T*hey sat at the table in the park for some time. First, just talking about what they'd each been doing over the last few months. Parker talked about his fiancé and planning their wedding. He seemed unsure of it all but spoke about his girlfriend with deep love. Hannah expected to feel pangs of jealousy but none came. The bond she had with Parker was different.

Finally, after they'd exhausted the conversation that didn't really matter, they sat in awkward silence, facing each other. Hannah knew this was her burden to bear. To carry their baby back from the dead and give her the proper consideration of their love. She watched Parker, now wondering what their baby would've looked like. His eyes were sharp and dark, always with a hint of mischief. She could see a little girl with those eyes... and long brown hair. She was surprised when tears stung her eyes.

"Parker, I want to talk about her."

"Her?"

"Our baby," Hannah answered.

"Oh. Hannah, are you sure? I mean, what's left to say?" Parker was frustrated but not unkind.

"I want you to know I have a lot of regrets. About what happened. I know we couldn't prevent the pregnancy from ending, but it's not just that. I wasn't fair to you."

Parker ran his hand through his dark hair, letting it fall back over his eyes. He shook his head. "No, don't do that. We were going through a lot and we took it out on each other. We weren't fair to each other."

"Do you ever think what it would be like now if she'd been born? I mean, do you ever wonder if we would've worked it out?" Hannah asked, her words fading near the end.

Parker met her eyes. "Every damn day."

Neither spoke for a minute when Hannah stood up and paced beside the bench. "I'm sorry. I didn't mean for this conversation to go this way. I'm not trying to rake us over the coals or try to destroy what you have now in your life. I came to apologize. Mostly, I came to tell you that I think our baby was a beautiful gift and I want to honor that. To tell you I'm grateful I met you. I'm grateful we started her life, even if she-" Hannah paused and pinched her nose to stop the tears. "I don't want you to ever think I.... ugh, sorry. I want you to know I'm glad for our time together and will always look back on those memories with love and appreciation. Our baby was beautiful and I'm ashamed I ever questioned her life."

Parker watched for a moment, then stood. "It's okay to question, Han. We were, we *are* young and didn't have our shit together, you know? I grieved, too, after you... after *we* lost the baby. I wasn't ready to be a father, I don't think, but it doesn't mean I wasn't also hopeful. I admit part of me was relieved, and I was ashamed of that. Really ashamed. We were just fighting all the time and I felt like I could see you disappearing in the distance."

It was true. She had been. Every time he reached out, she'd found a way to pick a fight and widen the gap. Hannah rubbed her nose and stared off at the trees. "I'm sorry, Parker. I was so disconnected from myself and I blamed you for life not being perfect. It was childish. I don't have an excuse. I don't know what it was I was looking for... I still don't, but I do know you matter to me. Our baby matters to me. I want to honor the time we had together and her life. I need you to still be part of my life."

Parker hung his head, letting out a deep breath. "I was hurt. Maybe I didn't say it enough, but you meant so much to me. We both lacked the maturity for what we were facing, but the worst part is that we turned on each other. So many nights I wanted to reach out and hold you, but I could tell by the way you held your body you didn't want me to touch you. I allowed my fear to lash out at you. No one is at fault. It was just how everything played out. However, I promise you, Hannah, I loved you. I love you. Everything we went through hasn't been erased."

They watched each other, the pain of the past surfacing and leveling out. The love was still there, but time had moved on. It wasn't the love of a couple, rather the love of those who went through a tragedy together. Love of two people who shared a secret that scarred their souls. No matter where they went or who they ended up with, that connection was always there. Hannah walked over and hugged Parker, as he crumpled against her. To him, her protecting herself by building walls was another way he'd been shut out of their life together. She pulled back and placed her hand on his cheek.

"I will always love you, Parker. You made me so happy. With you, I discovered parts of myself I didn't know existed. Had our baby been born, I believe we would've learned at least to be good parents. Regardless, I want you in my life. Even if it's only sending each other a holiday card every year. We are connected."

Parker smiled and kissed her fingers. "I'd like that, Hannah. It's been so hard trying to resolve the last couple of years. I knew it wasn't a waste, but it felt so fractured."

"Do you love her?" Hannah asked, referring to his fiancé. She knew he did, and she wasn't wanting to go back in time. She just needed him to hear himself say it in front of her.

He wiped a tear away and bobbed his head. "I really do. She makes me feel whole."

"I love that for you. I mean it, Parker. You mean so much to me, I want you to find a life that brings you joy. You deserve a love like that."

"What about you?"

Hannah dropped her hand and closed her eyes. There was someone who meant more than the stars to her, however, she didn't know to what end. George was the best friend she'd ever had. He was her confidant and guide. She loved him, but not like she'd loved Parker. With Parker, it'd been self-serving... how it made her feel, what she got out of it. With George, she wanted to protect their bond, to weave it like a fine thread through the needle of her heart. She nodded, meeting Parker's eyes.

"I'm working on my journey. Learning to not be so damn selfish. Attempting to come to situations and other people with their needs at the forefront of my mind. I knew I needed to talk to you because you matter. The first time I saw you, something in me clicked and your presence was such a light to me. I never said it then, so I am now. You, our baby, were gifts to me. I grew because of you. I need you to know that."

Parker stepped back and brushed the hair off his brow. "I needed to hear that. Thank you, Hannah. Our timing wasn't right and life handed us more than we could handle. But we were something special and for that I'm glad."

Once those words were out, it was like a weight lifted off both of them. They let go of any emotional burden they were carrying. Hannah understood this is why she needed to talk to Parker. He was a reminder that while she was only thinking of herself when they were together, she still brought value to his life. The same as he did to hers. Their connection was now beyond earthly. She tipped her head with a smile.

"I'm glad I met you, Parker."

"I'm glad I met you, Hannah."

With that, they headed back toward their cars. They paused before turning their own directions and locked eyes. Parker bit his lip and raised his hand in a wave. Hannah raised her hand back and climbed into her car. She watched as Parker went to his car and drove out. Their meeting had released her and she knew she could take the next step. She now understood what it meant to go to someone without the intent to absolve her guilt or emotions. To go with the intent to relieve theirs. George had helped her reach Parker.

Hannah took the long way on her drive home, taking the time to trace her mind over the moment with Parker. She was genuinely happy for him and his life moving forward. In truly loving someone, she was able to put their happiness in equal importance to her own. She turned into the driveway of her parents' home and let the car idle. She still wanted to reach out to Logan's parents but now understood the reason why. It wasn't to make things right or try and make them feel better. It was to let them know Logan's life mattered, that their pain mattered. That would take time to prepare herself for. She didn't know what the future held, but for now, she needed to stay in place.

As she was about to climb out of the car, Hannah paused and pulled her phone out. She sent a quick text. "George, I hope you know that every moment of every day, you've made my life better. I love you."

She closed the phone, not needing to see his response, and headed in. Her parents were in the living room, laughing about some shared joke when she came in. Even they seemed lighter since they'd talked about Toby. She went to the kitchen and made herself a sandwich, eyeing them in the other room. She couldn't take their pain away, but she could acknowledge it and let them know she was there to help carry the burden. They would always grieve for Toby, but now they were free to remember the joys as well. She wanted to give that to Logan's parents somehow.

Tired from the day, Hannah crept up to her room and rested in the dark on the covers of her bed. At one point as she started to doze off, she felt a heaviness like someone was standing beside the bed, hovering over her. She opened her eyes and could see a shadow close to her. She tried to move but was paralyzed. She tried to scream, however, no words came out. The shadow moved closer, extending a long appendage toward her. She tried to jerk away but lay motionless on the bed. Its face was covered by a cloak-like fabric and it bent into her.

Not near her, *into* her.

She could feel the weight of its internal misery embedded under her skin. As it became one with her, the cloak fell away and she found she was staring into her own face through a mirror in her brain. Her reflection was hollow, dead.

Just as she was sure she would disappear in the layers of gauzy darkness, her father called up the stairs to her, breaking the trance. Hannah gasped and jerked upright in the bed. Why now? After all she'd done. After the progress she'd made. Why was she coming back to haunt herself? She rubbed her arms with vigor, releasing the cold which had come over her. She thought of all that was behind her with taking Ayahuasca. She was taking the right steps, doing the work. What was she missing?

She climbed out of the bed, her body shaking, and opened the door. "Dad, I'm up here."

"Come on down and join us. We were going to play a card game."

Hannah thought to say no but was afraid to stay in the room alone. She glanced back at the empty room and stepped out into the hallway. She took the stairs one at a time, thinking about the visitor in her room. Its body was like the grim reaper. The face was hers. Was she the grim reaper? Toby died trying to get her doll, her baby died, Logan died. Was she the harbinger of death? She shook off the thought and came around into the living room. Her mother made popcorn and her father was shuffling the cards. He glanced up at Hannah, then frowned.

"You okay, Han? You look like you saw a ghost."

Hannah gritted her teeth and sat down across from them. What she'd seen was worse than that.

She'd seen inside herself and it was scarier than any ghost she'd encountered yet.

# CHAPTER THIRTY-ONE

*W*e are all just skinned-covered ghosts, Hannah told herself as she buried herself under the covers. That world and this one were only separated by breath. So, why was she so afraid? What exactly was she afraid of? She knew, or at least thought, she couldn't be physically harmed. They were visions there to teach her. But teach her what? She wanted to call George, however, she needed to stop using him every time she sought answers. She sat up and clicked on the light. She sifted through the nightstand and found an old journal from her high school days with a pencil tucked in the spiral binding. She flipped through and cringed at how dramatic she'd been about everything back then. Every situation was the end of the world.

She flipped to the back and found empty pages. She wrote down a list of visions she'd seen.

> Toby-brother, deceased
> Logan-motorcyclist, deceased
> Baby (crying)- my child, deceased
> Myself-me, alive (?)

She stared at the page and chewed the pencil. Every vision was someone she'd lost in some way. Even Logan had taken a piece of her with him, even when she hadn't known him personally. So, why herself? She was alive and as far as she knew, wasn't someone she needed to resolve anything with. She thought about Toby, Logan, and the baby. What it was she owed them, what her eventual intent in their lives was. She needed to honor their lives, to carry the dead. She circled her name and drew an arrow off it.

*Am I dead?*

Clearly not in the physical sense, as she was here and people were talking to her. Did she want to be dead? She flopped back on the bed and stared at the ceiling. No, she didn't want to be dead... but she *was* denying life. She was existing just to breathe. Breathe in, breathe out. Second after second. Required steps to the end. She'd managed to always care about people just enough, but not so much it was essential to invest herself fully. Even the baby had scared into that reality. A being that needed all of her, not just what she was willing to give. She rolled over and turned to a new page and wrote letters to everyone she loved. A living suicide note of sorts. Ones she never intended to send, but to express how much she struggled and hurt in the relationships she'd had with them. Parker's was the easiest because they'd opened that door a little. Her parents next, same because they'd been talking.

Logan's made her sob, even if she wanted to give it to him, she couldn't. Part of her felt he was reading it over her shoulder anyway. The baby's was gentle and her tears eased but flowed in a different way. She ended, promising for them to find a way to be together again. Toby's was short but she drew a picture of him holding her hand and walking along a creek. That made her smile. Her constant companion. Her first best friend.

That brought her to George. Her last best friend. As she wrote about what he meant to her, shame washed over her as she realized how much he'd given her, she hadn't reciprocated. He'd never left her side, never doubted her, never made her feel like she was losing her mind. She'd pushed him away and then been hurt when he held up the mirror. She closed the book and let out a deep breath. She'd been incredibly self-serving. In all of these relationships, she'd been the one needing and not seeing the other person for what she could bring to them. She wasn't a ghost, she was a monster.

She fell into a fitful sleep and woke up in the morning to begin setting things right. She made breakfast for her parents and joined them around the table. They were clearly surprised by the gesture. Hannah poured syrup on her pancakes and smiled at them.

"It's a little thing, making you breakfast. I wanted you to know how much you mean to me. You're the best parents ever."

Her parents glanced at each other, then back at her. Her father tipped his head. "What brought this on?"

"I know you have been through a lot. The worst. But you always made me feel supported and special. I've always known I had a home to come back to, arms to hold me. I may never have told you, but I'm so happy you're my parents."

Her mother smiled. "We're glad you're our daughter. You have brought us so much joy. Even after Toby died, you were the first thing to make me laugh again."

"Aw... but let me gush on you two for a moment. You don't owe me anything. You have made sure all of my needs and wants were met. You put my grief above your own. Thank you from the bottom of my heart. Toby and I were so lucky to have parents like you."

They nodded and her father cleared his throat. "The people we walk this earth with, and beyond, are all that matters."

They finished breakfast and Hannah excused herself. She'd asked her parents where Toby was buried as she wanted to visit his grave before her next task. She headed out and followed the map to the cemetery. It was quiet and she eyed the markers until she got to the row his grave was on. She drove slowly down the gravel path until she saw his name carved on a headstone. She parked and pulled out a teddy bear she'd bought.

If she'd ever been there, she didn't remember. He had a heart-shaped headstone with his picture on it. On the back were etchings of a toy dump truck and a yo-yo. There were fairly fresh flowers in a concrete vase next to the stone. Her parents were still coming to visit all the time. She set the bear next to the vase and knelt, running her fingers across the smooth stone. She stared at the photo of Toby. He was just so little. In her mind, he was her older brother, so she forgot how young he truly was when he died. She found words bubbling up and let them out.

"You were my best friend, Toby. You put the stars in the sky. Your last act in life was to make me happy and I'm honored you loved me so much. I wish we'd grown up together, so I could have pestered you. I imagine you being over-protective and annoyed by me. Judging my boyfriends and watching out for me. I didn't get that, but I did get you to be my big brother. I will never, ever let you go. You can become part of me if you want. You can join my body and we can live this life together."

A gentle breeze stirred and Hannah let tears roll down her cheeks. She sat for a bit longer, then knew it was alright to go. She kissed her fingers and placed them on Toby's picture. Part of her felt like his essence was in her and she held that close to her heart. She glanced back once she got to the door of the car and for a moment she thought she saw her outline still kneeling at his grave, Maybe they *had* traded pieces of themselves.

She questioned her next stop, however, knew she needed to do it. She drove up to a small office in a strip mall. The sign on the door confirmed she was in the right place. The Logan Slip Foundation. She wiped her hands on her pants and took a deep breath. Now or never. She pushed the door open and went into the building. A woman was on the phone with her back to the door when Hannah came in. Hannah stood awkwardly, waiting for her to finish. The woman hung the phone up and turned to greet Hannah with a smile. Her face shifted, the smile becoming a grimace. Logan's mother.

Hannah moved closer. "Hi. I'm Hannah Moore."

"I know who you are," Logan's mother replied. "What do you want?"

Hannah bit her lip and words caught in her throat. This wasn't about her. She was there for them. She motioned to a chair. "May I take a seat?"

The woman stared, her lips pressed together. She probably wondered what dare brought Hannah around. She stiffly motioned to the chair. She turned her head toward a back office. "Hal, I need you to come here, right this instant."

A man came to the door frowning, then he spied Hannah. He moved behind his wife and nodded, his face tense. "Hannah Moore. You aren't someone we thought would ever darken our doorway."

Hannah fiddled with the tie on her shirt. "I needed to come to see you, to apologize."

When she said that, it looked as if both of them deflated a bit. Logan's mother rested her head on her hand. His father pulled a chair up next to her, placing his hand on his wife's back. He met Hannah's eyes hard.

"I understand you feel you need to do that but it doesn't help. It doesn't bring Logan back. Mind, we don't blame you. Our son made bad choices that day which cost him his life. But seeing you only reminds us of what we've lost. I hope you understand but we need you to leave and never come back."

Hannah sat shocked, speechless. She expected them to be surprised by her visit but not to rebuff her apology. She was probably delusional to think they'd offer any sort of solace, however, they couldn't even stand to see her. Her mere existence was a dagger in their hearts. She stood up, her words jumbled.

"I just wanted you to know that Logan's life matters to me. I'm sorry about what happened, but I *will* carry his memory for the rest of my life. If you need anything or I can help in any way, please let me know."

Logan's mother stared at her through red-rimmed eyes. Her voice cracked in a hoarse whisper. "Please, just get out."

Hannah stood up and backed toward the doors, jumping when she bumped into them. She muttered an apology and bolted outside. That didn't go how she was expecting. It wasn't how it played out in books and tv. They *hated* her. They didn't blame her, but still, they hated her. She got in the car, shaking. She didn't remember driving but ended up at the pond. She found a place to park and ran to a secluded spot, screaming at the top of her lungs. She pounded her fists on her leg. Angry tears poured out of her and she felt like she'd swallowed pepper.

Once she was spent, she stared out over the water. That was it. She tried to reach out but they didn't want it. She couldn't blame them, however, it still hurt. A motion across the water caught her eye and she saw Logan standing there. Not dead motorcyclist Logan. Logan whole, like from when she took Ayahuasca and saw him playing soccer. She wandered around the lake, expecting him to disappear. He didn't but motioned for her to come. She saw him slip into the woods and she followed. She came to a small clearing surrounded by trees but he wasn't there. She paused and knew what to do.

Sitting in the clearing, Hannah closed her eyes and meditated. After a few minutes, she opened her eyes and he was sitting in front of her. He smiled, his blue eyes catching the light. "Hey, Hannah."

"Logan. You're here."

"For the moment."

"I tried to go see your parents and apologize. It didn't work, they told me to leave," Hannah confessed.

"I know. It's okay."

"How is it okay? How can I help them and continue my journey if I'm being shut down? If they won't hear me out?"

Logan met her eyes, then motioned around them. "We don't control the universe, we only control our actions. You did what you needed to do. You went to them, you can't determine how they'll feel about it. That's their journey. Do you see?"

Hannah didn't. If they didn't talk to her, did anything actually happen? "I don't get it."

"See, your path was to step outside your own experience and see another person's reality. To understand my parents' suffering. You just saw it firsthand. They lashed out at you because they are suffering and you recognized it. You didn't demand their forgiveness or expect them to be alright with it. You extended yourself and respected when they didn't want it."

It made sense. Hannah thought she was going there to try and make them feel better. She didn't have that power. She was going there to see their pain, to humble her experience. To offer what she had to give. They didn't owe her to take what she was offering. That was the lesson. To give, with no expectation of anything in return. Hannah chewed her lip and tilted her head. "I see."

"My parents are on their own path and they need to own it. Only they can ease their suffering. However, Hannah, you didn't do *nothing*. What you did still mattered."

"How?"

"Everything we do is planting seeds. You put yourself out there to them. They may have sent you away but the seed was still planted, ready for the next journey. They saw a young woman rise above her own ego and suffering to come to them and reach out. It may not be today or tomorrow, but that action has put into place a movement. It may stay dormant for months, or even years, but one day it will grow. Maybe it will take their hearts to soften. However, your kindness, your effort will stir something in them eventually, and they'll use it as a catalyst for other good. You did what you were called to do. You may never see it, but know it will happen. Believe in the greater purpose and what is meant to be will be."

Hannah shook her head. "How can you know that?"

Logan grinned at her and passed his hand through his body to remind her he saw things she couldn't. He reached out and placed his hand on her chest, creating a warm glow within her soul.

"Because this is why you came."

# CHAPTER THIRTY-TWO

*H*annah closed her eyes and practiced the movements George taught her those days on the beach in Mexico. Half a dance, half a fight. Months passed since she'd had any visions. Since last seeing Logan. She knew it was time to start thinking about planning for the future. Her parents had been more than gracious to let her stay and she'd even begun seeing a therapist. She sought out one who believed in other realms, so what she needed to say didn't come across as half-crazed. Through a metaphysical shop in town, she was given a referral to Tania who not only was a grief counselor but also worked as a spiritual guide. Through sessions with Tania, Hannah came to accept her experiences as part of her path and spoke openly about her loss.

Tania suggested she take up a physical activity to help her connect with herself on a whole. Hannah wasn't ready to take a class or anything which might put her on edge. She started practicing what George taught her and asked him for further instruction. Once a week they met online and he showed her other movements. Hannah looked forward to this every week.

Every morning she practiced and found a deeper connection within herself.

George was taking a more active role in the Ayahuasca ceremonies, allowing Miguel to step back and spend more time with Sebastián. They were getting older and they wanted to spend their days together. Hannah felt her heart ache every time she thought about her second family down in Mexico. However, she knew her place was in Virginia for now, and she needed to work on the parts of herself she'd buried over the years. Every day brought a lightness from the day before. She focused on breathing and journaling.

To not be a financial burden, she'd taken a job at a small herb shop downtown and was fascinated with how much she'd learned about using them for healing and ceremonies. She'd read almost every book on the shelves and went on to purchase her own, using different concoctions on herself to learn the right balance. She wanted to learn more and knew eventually she'd need to seek a teacher outside of books. This made her think about Sebastián and how patient he'd been with her during their time together. His gentle teaching made absorbing the information easy.

On her drive home from work, she glanced around the little shops and smiled. She'd been born and raised there and while some shops came and went, many were still the same. She was staring at a small toy store she remembered going in as a child when she saw her. Logan's girlfriend. She was coming out of a shop next to the toy store, fishing in her purse for her keys. Her face was lined with worry and Hannah pulled her car over. She didn't want to accost the poor girl, however, something in her told her it was time. She jumped out and walked at a fast pace toward the girl.

"Hey, do you have a moment?"

The girl stared at her with discomfort. She darted her eyes to the side to look for an escape in case Hannah was trying to sell her something or was off her rocker. Hannah caught up to her, smiling kindly.

"Sorry. Didn't mean to startle you. My name is Hannah. Hannah Moore."

The girl's eyes widened as recognition came to them. Hannah prepared herself for what happened with Logan's parents. The girl dropped her shoulders, then nodded.

"I recognize you. You were in the accident with Logan."

In the accident with Logan? Hannah didn't expect that take. She could see the girl was carrying something emotional she couldn't release. "Yes, my car hit and killed Logan. I'm so sorry. What's your name?"

"Cassie."

"Hi, Cassie. I saw you out here and felt like I needed to talk to you."

"How'd you know it was me?"

Hannah considered this. She only knew because of Ayahuasca but that was probably more than the girl needed to know. "Are you spiritual or religious?"

Cassie shook her head, eyes narrowed. "Not anymore. No god would allow what happened to Logan. It's all my fault."

"It's not, but let me go back. You may think I'm crazy and that's fine, however, I've seen Logan since the accident. We have spoken to each other."

279

Cassie took a step back, horrified by what Hannah said. "Don't say stuff like that!"

"It's true. I won't get into all of it, but he showed me you. He showed me a vision of you, sitting on the bench at the pond staring out. He showed me your arms, that you've been cutting yourself." Hannah gestured to Cassie's arms, covered by a long shirt.

Cassie stared at Hannah, then glanced at her arms and protectively wrapped them around her chest. She shook her head but didn't speak. Hannah reached out gently and touched Cassie's arm.

"I'm here if you need to talk."

With this, Cassie burst into tears, turning to run. She darted between two buildings. Hannah followed and found Cassie crouched against a wall. Cassie stared up at her, her jade eyes glistening.

"I have seen him, too. I didn't tell anyone because I thought they'd lock me up."

Hannah could relate. "I believe you, Cassie. Where did you see Logan?"

Cassie sighed. "I was falling asleep and saw him at the end of my bed. He looked so sad and was reaching out for me. I was terrified, so I buried my head under my covers until the morning."

"Have you seen him any other times?"

"In the distance. Like he is watching me but afraid to come too close. I sense him near me all the time. I wish I hadn't hidden from him that first time. Maybe he'd come to see me again." Cassie sounded defeated.

Hannah squatted next to her and placed her arm over Cassie's shoulders. "He wants you to know it wasn't your fault. It was just an unfortunate series of events no one could have prevented. He loves you very much and doesn't want you to hurt."

Cassie stared at the brick wall in front of her. "I love him. Sometimes I wonder if he'd loved me, if we would've eventually grown apart and broken up. We were young, that's what usually happens. Now, I'll love him forever. We will always be together, no matter what happens in my life. If I ever fall in love again, that person would need to understand Logan was, and will always be my first love."

"The right person will. You should never have to choose. Love is not jealous or possessive. You have room in your heart to love many people in many different ways. Logan wants you to be happy, Cassie. To let go of any guilt or regret. He will always love you."

Cassie stood up and Hannah followed. Cassie turned to face Hannah. "I never blamed you, I hope you know that. Logan was young and reckless at times. I read the articles. He shouldn't have done that. He took himself away from all of us. I don't blame him, either. It was a moment that changed everything. That changed all of us. We have all suffered because of it. I'm glad you reached out to me. I needed someone to know."

Hannah reached forward and wrapped Cassie in her arms. "I know. I'm going to give you my number and email address if you ever need to talk."

Cassie rested her head against Hannah's shoulder. "Thank you. I probably will. Thank you, Hannah."

They exchanged contact information and parted ways. Hannah watched Cassie walking away, her gait less heavy. She sensed Logan walking beside Cassie and bit her lip. What they had was real, whether they were young or not. Hannah wandered back to her car and climbed in. As she eased out and headed on, she felt her own baggage to be lighter. She'd carried Logan to Cassie and released them both.

She parked in front of a small shop with a blinking neon sign which flashed "TATTOO" over and over. She slid out of her seat and headed in. An older man with his feet propped up was reading a magazine and gave her a wave.

"What can I do you for?"

Hannah expected to feel nervous but wasn't. She took out a drawing she'd paid to have created for this purpose. "Can you tattoo this on me? On my inner wrists?"

The man took the paper and peered at it. "Both wrists? That's a sensitive area, so you know."

"I know. I'm okay with it. Emotional pain is harder to take than physical pain, and I've had my fair share," Hannah explained.

The man eyed her, then tipped his head back, laughing. "Ain't that the truth? Sure, come on over and sit down. Let me get these ready for you."

Two hours later Hannah walked out of the shop, both her wrists bandaged. She sat in her car and felt happier than she had in a long time. She peeled back the bandages and stared at the two bats, one on each wrist. Carrying the dead. She stopped to pick up a newspaper on her way home. While she loved her parents, she needed to find a place of her own again. Figure out a way to jumpstart her future. She knew she wanted to learn more about herbalism and would start there.

At a late dinner, her parents grilled her about the tattoos, finally accepting them once Hannah explained their significance and permanence for growth in her life. They didn't seem thrilled, but she was an adult and it was her body. Afterward, she sat on the back porch and scoured the classifieds for an apartment. Everything felt flat to her and she shoved the paper aside. She didn't want to just exist anymore, she wanted to live. Maybe she should look elsewhere to live, someplace which might support her interest in herbalism. She opened her laptop and started searching for herbalist schools and teachers, not sure exactly what was required. She was scrolling down the page when a black-and-white picture caught her eye. She held her breath and clicked on it. It couldn't be. He was younger, but it was him.

Sebastián.

It was in an article about international herbalism experts. Hannah devoured the article and was shocked to find out Sebastián was world-renowned as an herbalist and came from generations of herbalists. Little, tomato-growing Sebastián. He never said anything, even though he was always showing her things about plants. She rested back in the chair and closed her eyes.

Could this be a coincidence?

There all along, what she was wanting to study was right under her nose. She considered maybe the seed had been planted in her head, spending days with Sebastián. Then working in the shop took it to the next level. She read the article again and picked up her phone to ask George if he knew. There was no answer, so she set her phone down and went to take a walk. She wandered down the streets she'd grown up around and paused to let memories cascade over her. It had been a good life. Stable, loving. Her parents laid a foundation she could safely leap from. It was time to take that leap.

The house was dark when Hannah got back and she slipped into the kitchen. Her parents had gone to watch television in their room. She peeled off the bandages and applied ointment to the small bats, feeling like they were more than just ink under her skin. She covered them and went out to grab her laptop and phone off the back porch. She tucked them under her arm and headed up the stairs, clicking off lights as she went. Something told her to stop by her mother's craft room, Toby's bedroom. She gently eased the door open and gasped.

Standing at the window with his back to her was Toby.

She stepped into the room and waited. He motioned her over to the window. She moved slowly, afraid of what she might see. She peered out to see the sky full of bats and a sense of dread washed over her. They were on a mission. They came with a message. At that moment, her phone began vibrating and she saw it was George calling her back. Mesmerized by the bats and Toby she didn't answer. She'd call him back later. The bats were moving in a large circle and swooping toward the window. She could almost reach out and touch them. She glanced at Toby for confirmation but he was gone. Her phone lit up and she saw there was a text from George. She opened the phone and stared at the message, her heart dropping to the floor.

"Sebastián has been taken to the hospital. It doesn't look good. He's asking for you."

# CHAPTER THIRTY-THREE

*B*y the next morning, Hannah had a flight booked to Mexico and her bags packed. There was no way she wasn't going to be there for Sebastián, after all he'd done for her. She'd called and George put the phone to Sebastián's ear. He was too weak to speak, but Hannah was comforted she could hear him breathing. She promised him she was on her way and to hold on. George told her Sebastián had a stroke and a heart attack. He was awake but not very responsive. His eyes followed Miguel wherever he was, though.

Her parents didn't question and drove her to the airport when the time came. She'd spoken often about Miguel and Sebastián, how much they meant to her. Her father handed her an envelope of money for her trip and her mother hugged Hannah close to her.

"Be safe, Hannah," she whispered. "Call us when you land."

"I will, Mom. Thank you for being so understanding," Hannah replied, fighting back tears. She hoped Sebastián could pull through. On the flight, she journaled all of her memories of

Sebastián and jotted down little prayers for him. She'd wanted to make a trip back to Mexico, however, not like this.

George met her at the airport and she practically tackled him with relief. He smiled, wrapping his arms around her.

"How I have missed you, Hannah!"

Hannah let her tears fall and met George's eyes. "How is he?"

George shook his head. "Hanging in there but not any better. The doctors said his heart is weak and another attack will stop it."

Hannah gulped past the lump in her throat. "Can we go straight there?"

"Of course. Do you have luggage to pick up at baggage?"

"Yeah, I didn't know how long I'd be here this time. I only got a one-way ticket for now. My parents said they'd pay my way home when I'm ready to go back."

"Alright, let's go and see if they have the bags out yet. Have you eaten?" George asked gently.

Hannah watched him from the side. His hair was braided down his back. He seemed older, yet more full of life. He glanced at her, his eyes full of concern. Hannah reached out and brushed his cheek.

"I have missed you too, George," she whispered, aware his checking on her eating was his way of caring for her.

They gathered her bags and headed for the truck. The ride to the hospital was quiet, Hannah not sure what she was walking into. Last she'd seen Sebastián, he was smiling as he said goodbye to her. The memory warmed her with hope. He was strong. George said when they first brought him in, he'd asked where Hannah was. He hadn't said much since, but he watched the door often as if he was waiting on someone to arrive.

When they got to his room, Hannah calmed herself outside the door. He didn't need to see her stress. He had enough of his own. George led the way in and Hannah followed. Miguel was sitting beside Sebastián and jumped up when he saw Hannah rushing to Sebastián's side. He embraced her, murmuring something in Spanish. Hannah looked at Sebastián, who seemed tiny and frail in the hospital bed. She stepped over and took his hand in hers, feeling him lightly grip hers as his eyes locked on her face.

"I'm here, Sebastián. Now, you need to get better, so we can all go home and catch up."

She swore she saw a small smile play at the corners of his mouth and squeezed his hand. Miguel looked like he was running on fumes and went to lie on a fold-out cot in the room. George pulled a chair over for Hannah to sit on. He kissed the top of her head.

"I'm going to grab us some food. The bathroom is right over there and this is the nurse call button," he explained. He put a blanket over the now-sleeping Miguel and paused at the door. "Will you be okay?"

Hannah nodded. "Yes, now that I'm here, I'll make Sebastián get better."

George smiled, his eyes sad. He put his finger to his lips and pointed at the sky. Hannah understood. Hopefully, someone out there was listening to them. Hannah turned her focus on Sebastián. His face was tired but he watched her. Hannah leaned in close to him.

287

"Get some rest, Tío. I have some things I want to talk to you about. You sleep and when you wake up, we'll talk."

Sebastián closed his eyes and Hannah was relieved when his chest rose and fell into a peaceful slumber. George came back with sandwiches and they ate as a Spanish program played on the small television mounted on the wall.

"I'm glad you came, Hannah," George said, his voice low and soothing.

"Of course! Sebastián and Miguel are family to me. I'd never have forgiven myself if I hadn't. They needed me here. I needed to be here."

George eyed her, then glanced away. "I needed you here, too. I was so scared when it happened. We were in the kitchen, joking around. All of a sudden, Sebastián looked far away. I teased him about daydreaming and then he just dropped to the floor. He didn't clutch his chest or do anything to let us know what happened. He fell to the ground and was unconscious. It happened so fast, I thought he was dead. We began doing CPR on him until the ambulance came. The doctors said he had a stroke and heart attack within a short span of each other. They didn't know what happened first."

"Does he have family?"

"None that came. His parents have passed, no children, and a couple of siblings he rarely speaks to."

"Oh."

"We are his family," George stated.

"Yes, we are. That night you called, earlier that evening, I was looking up schools and teachers to study herbalism, and I couldn't believe it. As I was searching, I found an article saying

Sebastián is a world-renowned master herbalist. Did you know that?"

George raised his brows. "I knew he knew all of that stuff but not to that level. That's wild."

"I want him to teach me."

George glanced at Sebastián, then furrowed his forehead. "Hannah-"

"No, George, don't say anything bad. I want him to teach me. I'm going to tell him when he wakes up. You don't have to believe, but I do," Hannah said with determination. Sebastián had to live to hand on his knowledge to her.

George bit his lip and smiled. "This is why you are here. You bring the fight with you. By the way, I like the tattoos."

Hannah glanced at her bats. This time she wasn't carrying the dead. She was carrying the living. It hit her like a brick. She was meant to be a healer. Like Sebastián. In learning to be a transport for souls, she'd found her calling in healing. She stood up and went to Sebastián's side. His eyes flickered open and met hers. She placed her hand on his cheek.

"You aren't done here yet. I come to you as a daughter and ask you to teach me. I want to be your apprentice, to learn how to be one with the earth to heal. Will you accept me as your daughter and your apprentice?" Hannah never blinked.

Sebastián raised his hand and placed it over hers as he barely nodded. "Mi hija," he whispered. My daughter.

Miguel raised his head and watched, tears streaming down his cheeks. Hannah's own words to Cassie resonated in her mind. She didn't have to choose. She could have all the family she wanted. Her parents, Toby, George, Miguel, Sebastián, her baby,

289

Parker, even Logan. All of them had their place in her heart. The more she gave it to others, the more it grew.

Miguel came to Sebastián's side and kissed his forehead. Sebastián smiled, more this time. Hannah knew deep down that Sebastián's time on the earth was coming to a close, but that she'd propped the door open a while longer. They both had a destiny to fulfill.

Three days later, Sebastián was sitting up and able to eat small amounts of food. He had left-sided weakness from the stroke but could manage to move very slowly with a cane. A week later, they were able to bring him home. While Miguel waited at the hospital with Sebastián, George and Hannah ran back to their home to prepare things for Sebastián's arrival. They cleared out any clutter, hung up art, and rearranged the furniture so Sebastián could move throughout the home on his own. George built a small ramp off the porch and made sure the pathways in the garden were wide and open.

After Sebastián was home and settled in, George asked Hannah if she'd like to take a walk with him. Unsure about leaving Sebastián, Miguel waved her off. "It is fine. He is sleeping soundly in his bed. Go, go. All is well."

Hannah chuckled at Miguel practically pushing her out the door and joined George on the porch. They meandered through the streets and ended up at the long pier. It was almost as if she'd never left. Or maybe part of her was always there. They made it to the end and stared out. Hannah glanced at George, a small excitement building in her gut. George cleared his throat.

"I'm glad Sebastián is doing better and is going to be your guide, he has so much to teach you."

"I'm excited. I can't ask for a better mentor," Hannah agreed.

"Once you are done learning, or if... well, if Sebastián can't teach you anymore. What then?"

Hannah glanced at him, understanding what he was getting at. "Well, hopefully, Sebastián will be around for years to teach me, because I don't think I'll ever know everything. He has generations of stored knowledge. However, say I did learn it all miraculously and he had no more to teach, that doesn't change where I want to be."

"Where do you want to be?" George asked, his eyes flitting over to her and back to the water.

"Where I always wanted to be, George. I love my parents, and Virginia will always be partly my home, but it's not where I'm called to," Hannah answered.

"What is calling you?"

Hannah laughed, not sure if it was her, or George, who was dragging this out. She turned and grabbed him to face her. "Do you honestly not know, or are you messing with me?"

"I need you to say it," George said, baring his wounds.

She'd put him through hell. He'd given everything to help her find herself. He'd laid himself on the line and she'd only been thinking about her own realities. She watched his face and could see the vulnerability there. Never once had he asked anything of her over the time they'd known each other. He'd recognized she couldn't truly love anyone until she faced her demons. So, he pushed her away to force her to stop cowering and fight. Fight, she did. Now, she knew she needed to fight for what mattered the most in her life. The living.

"George, from the first moment we met, you were making sure I had a safety net until you knew I didn't need it. I know that must've taken a lot from you. Not being able to lean on me. I *want* you to lean on me. Let me tend your wounds. I need you to trust me with your heart. I'm here to fight for you, to fight for us. To fight *with* you, side by side. I always knew you were something amazing to me. Now, I know you are eternity to me. If you will open your heart and let me in, I promise my body and soul will honor your body and soul."

George stared at her, his face a blank slate. Hannah could see he was neatly concealed by a wall of thought. She reached up and ran her fingers over his lips. As if that was the key, his face relaxed and he grinned at her. Hannah leaned forward and placed her lips on his as she wound her fingers through his own.

Tension released from his body and he drew her close. "Forever?"

Hannah gripped his hand, nodding.

"I'm not going anywhere."

# EPILOGUE

$S$ebastián lived three more years. He passed peacefully in his sleep and a heartbroken Miguel followed two days later. In the three years Sebastián stayed on the dirt and rock earth, he taught Hannah about everything he could. She transcribed his lessons as he taught, so there would be a record to pass on. After his death, she had it made into a limited edition book to add to herbalist libraries around the world. She wanted his knowledge to help others. With her learned knowledge, she helped with the Ayahuasca ceremonies and traveled to help others in areas where medical care was limited.

Her parents split their time between Virginia and Mexico, not wanting to be away from their only surviving child. Hannah and George also traveled back to Virginia at least once a year, however, with each visit Hannah felt more and more disconnected from the world she was raised in. All she wanted was to live in a tiny home with a big garden, a couple of cats, a few chickens, and George.

George. The moment their lips touched on the pier, their hearts combined forever. They did a small handfasting ceremony before Miguel and Sebastián passed and swore themselves to each other, their family, and their mission. Their mission being helping others on their spiritual and health journeys. There was never a time when Hannah would see George coming and her heart wouldn't flutter just a bit. Not even when they were old and gray. They still traveled when they could around the world and brought back knowledge from other cultures to weave into the ceremonies.

George continued to perform Ayahuasca ceremonies and eventually brought in his own apprentice to pass on Miguel's family knowledge. Hannah did the same with what Sebastián taught her, finding an unlikely first apprentice. She and Cassie stayed in touch over the years and one day Cassie showed up for a ceremony. Hannah was pleased and welcomed her in. After the ceremony, Cassie asked to stay and learn from Hannah. Hannah was honored and Cassie fast became one of the family. A few years later, she met a nice young Mexican man, and they married. Cassie had two adorable children who were often seen chasing each other around the campsite.

Hannah and Parker stayed in touch. They sent holiday cards, as promised, and Hannah was delighted to see Parker become the father to his small brood, he was not ready to be when they were together. He had two sons and a daughter. The boys resembled him and the daughter.... well, suffice it to say Hannah took a secret joy in watching her grow up from afar. She looked like Hannah had imagined their own daughter to look. Parker's children were her baby's siblings in some realm. This brought her deep comfort and a connection she couldn't help but honor.

When a young father showed up late one night, holding a tiny baby, Hannah and George knew life was about to change. The man was thin and poor, explaining his wife had died. He couldn't take care of the baby by himself. Hannah and George offered the man a place to stay, so he could keep his baby but through tears, he said he was dying from a broken heart. He left sometime in the night, leaving the baby behind. He'd signed a paper saying he was giving his parental rights to them, with his sincerest apologies. A follow-up meeting with a lawyer confirmed it was legal. They never saw or heard from the young man again. Maybe he did, in fact, die from a broken heart.

As for the baby.

Hannah and George took her in and loved her with all their heart. They'd never felt driven to have children of their own, but this little ball of light filled a spot in them they didn't know was empty. Through a lawyer, they legally adopted her and named her Tobie Mariposa. Hannah's parents were thrilled. George's parents were polite. Tobie was a curious and quiet child. Often as she grew, they'd find her sitting beside the creek, her nose in a book. It was as if this wasn't her first go-around in the world. She caught onto Sebastián's teachings easily and by the time she was ten years old, she'd be right there beside her mother, Hannah, creating medicines.

George was the father every little girl dreams of. Thoughtful, attentive, patient, and most of all respectful. Their bond was delicate, yet unbreakable. Hannah felt insurmountable joy at watching her daughter and husband connect on levels beyond the physical realm. The love George had given Hannah also encompassed his daughter without boundaries.

Cassie was Tobie's favorite aunt and Cassie's children were all the cousins or siblings she ever needed. Miguel and Sebastián were present physically for her first year of life and carried on after their bodies set their souls free.

What struck Hannah the most was sometimes she'd peer over at her studious, dark-haired daughter and she'd see the passed-on generations in Tobie's eyes. Miguel, Sebastián, Toby... The thing Hannah couldn't deny was that when she first held the tiny baby in Mexico, she'd known in her heart. She wasn't aware she was ready then to be a mother, however, that bow-lipped baby did.

That baby, Tobie Mariposa, knew when it was time to fly back into Hannah's waiting arms.

# ACKNOWLEDGMENTS

Thank you to my ever-adventurous mother who took my brother Scott and me across the country and into Mexico in an RV she managed to commandeer. At the time, that experience wasn't one I understood, but I am glad now for the experiences.

To the children in Mexico, who never treated me like I didn't belong. On my 10th birthday at a campground in Cancun, they made sure to make me feel special by throwing me a party including a piñata, cake, and songs. In a cantina by the ocean.

Thank you to Lizzy, Justin, Bee, and Jack for allowing me to constantly bounce ideas and chapters off them.

Thank you to Alyssa Aldana for reading and giving feedback on Mexican culture and language!

Thank you Justin Sexton for the use of your original art piece for the cover.

# AUTHOR INFO

## Books currently available:

Do Over

We Don't Matter

Prick of the Needle

Through the Surface

Trigger Point

Carrying the Dead

Catch the Earth

In Dreams, We Fly

## Check out upcoming books, news, and events:

*authorjulietrose.com*

Made in the USA
Columbia, SC
10 October 2023

23997656R00181